Dear
Barbara,
a gift for you.
Love Batilda

Hidden In Plain Sight

Hidden In Plain Sight

Karen Batshaw

ISBN: 1530782481
ISBN 13: 9781530782482
Library of Congress Control Number: 2016905387
CreateSpace Independent Publishing Platform
North Charleston, South Carolina

Dedication

THIS IS BOOK is dedicated to the people of Greece, who suffered so greatly during the Nazi occupation. And specifically I dedicate this book to the Greek Jews who were almost totally annihilated and the Greek Orthodox Christians who tried to help them.

Acknowledgments

T0 MY HUSBAND, Mark, who encouraged me to return to my writing.

To Nadene Geyer, who introduced me to Jacques Frances. It was the incredible story of his family's survival in Volos, Greece, that intrigued me. And so began my research into the unknown history of Greece and its Christians and Jews during World War II.

To Susan Talley, who listened as I told my Greek stories about the Nazi occupation, over and over again. One day she said, "Why don't we go to Thessaloniki?"

To our wonderful guide Athina Trigoni. In Thessaloniki, although we were told the Jewish tombstones were not littered around the city, she humored me and let me take her to the Saint George Church courtyard where indeed the tombstones can still be found.

To Margarita Lazarou, who assisted me in my immersion into her Greek culture. She also helped me with the Greek language and Greek Orthodox customs.

To Margarita's father, Alexander Lazarou, who was a young teen in Athens during the war. He helped confirm many details of the occupation.

To Aphrodite Matsakis, who encouraged me with my exploration of Greece during World War II.

To Debby Lazar, my sounding board and preliminary editor.

To Andrew Gipe, for his wonderful evocative cover and for connecting me to Kehila Kedosha Janina in New York City, the only Greek Jewish Synagogue outside of Greece.

And to Marcia Haddad Ikonomopoulos at Kehila Kedosha Janina, who encouraged me in my pursuit of this little-known part of Greek history and the Holocaust.

To Aviva Tuchman, who helped me with Ladino.

To my readers who gave me so much encouragement in my venture to write a historical novel which was such a departure from my earlier novels: Marty Hamed, Judy Palmer, Ellen Shaw, Katherine Marsh, Evelyn Clair, Debby Lazar, and Susan Talley.

And lastly, to all the people who listened to my nonstop retelling of the story of the Jews and Christians in Greece during the war.

CHAPTER 1

1963: Thessaloniki (Salonika), Greece
Ippokratio General Public Hospital

THE TALL MIDDLE-AGED doctor, a stethoscope slung casually around his neck, inhaled on his cigarette and inwardly sighed as a young colleague approached him. This would be the second request this week for him to extend his hours so that young Masokis could leave early for his rendezvous with the pretty new nurse on their ward. Alexander could say no, but he wouldn't. There was no one waiting for him in his apartment, only memories of happier times, memories of those days when he was not alone. Perhaps this weekend he would call Alathea, the attractive widow with whom he had a special arrangement. She had been left with a surplus of funds upon the death of her rich husband. Fortunately, she had no desire to remarry.

"Thanks, Alexander. I won't forget this." The younger man started to remove his white coat. "It's room three, a young girl, American tourist. You and I are the only ones fluent in English, or I'd have asked someone else. I'm sure it won't take you very long."

"Tell me it's not another one of those free-thinking American girls who need an abortion or some birth-control pills. I can't imagine who would ever marry a girl who gives herself to any passing stranger."

"Alexander, you're so old fashioned. It's a new world out there, and those American girls are a blessing from God that has been bestowed on us Greek men. You must take advantage of what's come to our doorstep. I'm sure there are some girls who like old men. But take heart, this

1

American girl actually took a spill on one of the ruins. She has a possible concussion and an injured ankle."

Alexander stubbed out his cigarette in the ashtray and walked down the linoleum-tiled floor. He opened the door to find an attractive young girl with long, straight brown hair perched on the examining table. She was looking very annoyed at the nurse, who was speaking loudly and slowly in Greek in an attempt to make herself understood.

"I am Dr. G," he introduced himself. His Greek name was usually too hard for non-Greeks to master. And he didn't appreciate having it mutilated on the tongues of foreigners.

"Finally, someone who speaks English!" The girl's large brown eyes flashed with impatience.

"Yes, I speak English." He found himself smiling at her in spite of her impertinent manner.

"At last!" She smiled back at him. "Really, I shouldn't be in a hospital. My friends dropped me off here, just to make sure it wasn't anything serious. My foot is getting better all the time. I feel great. Please, just let me go. I need to go back to my hotel, or my mother is going to worry about me."

"I need to do a brief exam to check you over. If you're okay, I promise not to keep you." There was something about her face, her eyes, her mouth that reminded him of someone. He sat down in a chair and looked at her chart for the first time.

"Miss Caplan, Suzanne Caplan from New York in America."

"Yes."

"How did you injure yourself? I presume you were sightseeing, although we don't see many tourists here. It's hard to compete with Athens and the beaches on the islands."

"I was backpacking my way through Europe with two friends, and my mom wanted to meet me here in Greece. My friends and I were going to Athens and some islands, but my mom said she wanted us to meet her in Salonika. Never heard of it before, but it's nice enough. Well, my mom and I and my friends were sightseeing. This is quite an interesting city, you know," she rambled on. "Anyway, we noticed these paving stones on some walkways, and can you believe it, there were large stars of David and Hebrew script everywhere. They were tombstones from a Jewish cemetery. How gross! What kind of people use tombstones to pave a walkway?" She paused, waiting for him to answer, and when he remained silent, she continued, "Don't Greek people have any respect for the dead? Or perhaps the tombstones needed to be Greek Orthodox to demand respect."

He put down her chart and started to tenderly probe her ankle with his large sun-darkened hands.

"You are of the Jewish faith?" he inquired.

"A person doesn't have to be Jewish to be outraged by using tombstones as building materials."

"No, a person does not."

"And you? What religion are you?" She held up her head defiantly. "I suppose you're Greek Orthodox?"

"Yes, I am, as are most people in my country." He smiled at her and thought, this young girl wants to argue with me, just for the sake of arguing. The young can be so self-righteous. He remembered when he believed he had all the answers to life's mysteries. But he was younger then, and that was before the war turned everything upside down and almost destroyed his country. "Miss Caplan, are you trying to engage me in an argument?"

"Well, anyway, as I was saying," she ignored his question. "I know I talk a lot, but that's just me. So, we were sightseeing. Greece is quite a beautiful country. I'm an American history major in college and I must confess I don't know a thing about modern-day Greece. In all the other European countries I've visited, they keep talking about World War II as if it were recent history. They even show you the bullet holes still in the walls. But it was twenty years ago, not yesterday. Was Greece involved in the war? What side did the Greeks fight on? Were they with the Germans or the Americans?"

"Greece had a very brave army, but it was small. We did not fight on the side of the Germans." Well, he thought, at least this young American showed some curiosity. Most of the Americans with whom he'd come in contact knew only about classical Greece and had no interest in anything else.

"So as I was saying.... we were out sightseeing. My mom is a doctor, so she's seen just about everything bad there is to see. She takes one look at the marble tombstones in the walkways and she almost passes out. She tells me she needs to go back to the hotel and I went on with my friends. We were climbing near this ruin when I slipped and fell."

Alexander took his small flashlight and peered into her eyes, checking for uneven dilation of her pupils in order to rule out a concussion. As he drew close, he was momentarily taken aback. Those large dark eyes, the beautiful smile...It was as if he was seeing his own mother as she had been as a young girl, as she appeared in the photograph he kept at his bedside. He kept it there to remind himself of the woman who had died giving birth to him.

"Do you know there were over fifty thousand Jews in Salonika before the war and only two thousand survived? I just learned that today," the girl informed him, obviously proud of the information she was imparting to him.

"Yes, I know that," he said softly and turned his back to her in order to retrieve her chart from his desk, this time reading it in its entirety. Suzanne Caplan, aged nineteen, date of birth July 14, 1944. "You were born in America?" He turned back to her.

"What? Can't I just go? See, I'm fine. I need to get back to the hotel before my mother shows up at the hospital. She's kind of overprotective, and when my friends tell her they dropped me off here, she'll waste no time in coming here."

"Where were you born?" he asked again.

"Well, actually I was born in Greece, but I came with my mom to America when I was very young, so I don't remember it. You aren't going to scold me for not speaking Greek, are you? My friends think I should speak Greek, because I was born here. But my mother only speaks English."

"Your father, Mr. Caplan is also from Greece?"

"Oh no, he was born in New York. He's a doctor like Mom. He's my stepdad. My dad was a Greek Jew, just like my mom. He died when I was little, before we came to America."

"And your mother's name?"

"Really." She sighed in exasperation. "Why do you need to know my mother's name?"

"Your mother's name is Anna," he stated in a voice suddenly gone hoarse.

"Yeah, it is. How did you know that? Well, anyway, Dr. G, I am fine, aren't I? Just let me out of here."

Alexander sank down in his chair, his face paling beneath his tan.

"Dr. Giannopolous," said the nurse. "Are you not well?"

He sat still for several moments, seeming to study the girl's chart. When he looked up and got to his feet, his eyes were filling with tears. "Suzanne." He walked over to the girl and reached out to her small hand. "You are my daughter."

"Are you nuts! My father is dead, and he most certainly was Jewish."

"I am Greek Orthodox, and I am your father."

C H A P T E R   2

December 1940: Greece
Train between Salonika and Athens

DECEPTION, SHE THOUGHT, I've never been good at it. The train had stopped again and another soldier was arrogantly walking down the aisle, his face pinched with distain. This one seemed very coarse and determined. He was shouting at an old man, grabbing his papers in his beefy hand, and then pulling him up by his collar. "A Jew with false papers!" He shoved the old man to the other end of the car. The man's face contorted with fear.

The old man disappeared from view, and the soldier returned. "Any other vermin with false papers? Any other Jews!" he yelled. "So many low lives with false papers, trying to flee our country before the Germans arrive. What stupid fools! Where are they going to run to?"

Anna kept her eyes down on the book she was pretending to read. Don't be nervous, she reminded herself. Your papers were crafted by calligraphers who are masters of forgery. You've done as your parents asked, dressing this morning in your drabbest garments. "Don't draw attention to yourself," her mother cautioned her. "No makeup, no high heels. I found you some oxfords to wear for this trip. When you arrive in Athens, you'll be safe. Your father knows best. You must do as he says." Her mother gave her a big hug, as she wiped away her tears.

"I'm safe here in Salonika," Anna had started to protest, although she doubted her own words. She had heard the ugly rumors herself. Bad times were coming for the Jews of Salonika.

"My daughter," her father spoke softly, as was his way, "if the Italians occupy our city it perhaps may not be so difficult for the Jews. But the Germans…" His voice trailed away. "So many think the Italians are base people and the Germans are so cultured, but our people are deluding themselves. The Germans are persecuting Jews wherever they go. But our family belongs here in our home in Salonika. Your sisters and brothers are married with children. We have a large family. You're unmarried. You can travel by yourself. I feel in my heart you should seek sanctuary in Athens. Salonika is in the north, and it will be the first big city the Germans would occupy. If I am wrong, you will only be in Athens for a short period of time, and then you'll come home, and we all will be together again."

She didn't argue. Maybe she should have protested more strongly. How could she leave her family, even if what Papa said was true? She had just returned home a few short months ago after receiving her medical education in America. She was so happy to be with Nona - her grandmother, her parents, and her sisters and brothers. But she understood what was going on in the world and how precarious it might be to be a Jewess even in Salonika, home to fifty-five thousand Jews. The Germans had quickly taken over so many countries, which fell like a deck of cards under their onslaught…. Holland, France, Denmark, Poland and now the bombing of England. All those countries where the Nazis had taken charge, imposed harsh restrictions upon Jewish life.

"Papers!" the fat soldier barked at her.

Anna opened her purse. "Here, sir," she said respectfully.

He looked over her papers. "Despinis Kalodosis, you are from Athens?"

"Yes."

"Going home?"

"Of course."

"You should take care, traveling alone in such perilous times."

He nodded and moved on to the row of seats in front of her. She was no longer Despinis Anna Carraso. Despinis Michaelitsa Kalodosis was her new Greek name. She must always respond to it. She kept repeating it over and over in her mind. She could breathe normally now, until another soldier entered the train checking papers.

She had arrived so late that it was almost dark. Because of the blackout restrictions, nightfall meant total darkness. There was no moon to illuminate the streets on the way to the Giannopolous house. From the Larissa train station, she took a taxi to Kolonaki, an exclusive, wealthy suburb of Athens. She had memorized the address. "You will be safe there," her father told her. "Kìrios Antonios Giannopolous, a Greek Orthodox man, is a dear old friend from my business dealings in Athens. He's a good man. He heard from a business connection that the Germans will surely be coming to Salonika. The Greeks have repelled the advance of the Italians, but Germany will not stand idly by while their allies suffer defeat. Giannopolous is offering his protection for our family. If the Germans also come to Athens, it will be safer to be a Jew in such a big city of many Greek Orthodox, to blend in, to disappear. Our family is too large. But you, my special child, with your spirit and education… you must be the one to go forth to certain safety. When the war is over, you will tell us all about your time in Athens. Alexander, his son, is a doctor, so he will be able to find you a position. But one last thing you must promise me."

"Of course, Papa."

"As I said, Kìrios Giannopolous is a good and honorable man. You must do as he says at all times, without argument. You have always thought for yourself, my daughter. So this may not be an easy task for you." He paused and smiled fondly at her, as she narrowed her eyes with annoyance. "Perhaps it will be easier for you to find a Jewish husband in Athens who would be able to overlook a woman who speaks her mind and does not understand the concept of female subservience."

"Oh, Papa," Anna sighed with exasperation.

"Now Anna, forgive me. I shall miss teasing my youngest daughter. You will listen to Kìrios Antonios Giannopolous, and he will keep you safe. He's a man to be completely trusted."

Placing her suitcase down on the pavement, she stood in front of the large house and knocked on the heavy door with the brass knocker as snowflakes began to swirl around her. It had not been easy to identify the house in the dark, but the taxi driver assured her it was the correct address.

Within a few minutes, a middle-aged woman answered the door. "Yes?" she inquired with a frown on her face.

"I'm here to see my cousins, Kirìa and Kìrios Giannopolous," Anna said, delivering the words she had rehearsed so many times. "Please tell them their cousin Michaelitsa has arrived."

"Yes, of course. May I have your coat and your suitcase?" the servant said as she bent to retrieve her valise. Anna took off her coat and followed the woman down the wide hallway lined with exquisite statuary, until they stopped before a room with a closed door.

The woman knocked on the door, and when she was told to enter, she walked inside, motioning for Anna to follow her.

A middle-aged couple rose to their feet and extended their arms in welcome to her. "Our little Litsa. How you have grown into a beautiful young woman since we last saw you in Kos. Ariadne, please bring some refreshment for our guest, and close the door when you leave," the man instructed.

Anna walked over to them, exchanging kisses on their cheeks. Anna swallowed hard. These people were strangers to her. Was her father sure they would help her? What if he was wrong? What if they would inform the authorities she had false identity papers?

"We are so glad to have you visit us, cousin," the tall gray haired woman said with a quiver in her voice.

Anna could sense her hesitation. She's nervous as well. Maybe her husband offered their help to her father, but Kirìa Giannopolous didn't agree.

"Tell us about your journey on the train." Kìrios Giannopolous indicated a chair for Anna.

"Well, it took a very long time, because the train kept stopping and the soldiers came on board to check identification papers over and over again," Anna said as she sat down.

"And your papers, of course, were beyond reproach."

"Yes."

"Well, one never knows if the soldiers will try to find an irregularity, even if one doesn't exist. Ah." He smiled as the servant brought in some refreshment, sweets and glasses of ouzo.

Once the servant left and closed the door, Kìrios Giannopolous lowered his voice. The amicable smile vanishing from his face was replaced by an earnest expression. "I am Kìrios Antonios, and this is my wife, Kirìa Maria. We are glad your journey was uneventful. Now show me your false identity papers."

Anna reached inside her purse and handed him the papers with her photo and her new name.

He retrieved his reading glasses from his breast pocket. "Your father's people did well." He nodded and returned the papers to her.

"Thank you for offering to help me. I have my medical degree, and Papa feared if the Germans came to Salonika that I might be prevented from practicing at the hospital. I'm sure that won't happen, but Papa thought it was a precaution that I should take." Anna tried to explain why she had come to Athens.

"My dear." He smiled at her again as his wife offered pieces of pastry and glasses of ouzo. "Your father was wise to send you. He and the rest of your family should have come to Athens with you. I'm sure he told you that I've been informed by a member of the government that if the Germans come to your city, it will not be good for the Jews."

"Yes, he told me. But you know that my family aren't observant Jews. We are more Greek than Jewish." She looked at him, waiting for him to acknowledge her wisdom, but he said not a word.

Anna took a swallow of the clear ouzo to bolster her courage. "My father gave me a large amount of gold coins to repay you for your kindness to me."

"Please, Michaelitsa. Would your father insult me to pay for your welfare? I shall take the coins for safekeeping. But when you return to your family in Salonika, you must use this wealth for your dowry."

A dowry, she thought. In America, women didn't need such archaic things. "I have my diploma from medical school with me. My father told me that your son Alexander is a physician and could perhaps help me find a position."

"You will speak with him tomorrow and show him your credentials then."

"Well, again I thank you. Is my lodging very far from here? I'm rather tired."

"No, no lodgings for you. You shall stay here with our family. Hiding in plain sight, we say."

"Here? How kind of you," was all she managed to say. She had envisioned a small room somewhere inconspicuous, where she would be alone.

"Tomorrow is Sunday," said Kiría Giannopolous. "We leave for church early in the morning. Please join us for breakfast at seven, and then we shall walk to St Dionysius together."

"Church?" Anna's eyes widened.

"My dear," Kìrios Giannopolous patted her hand, "remember you are now Michaelitsa Kalodosis, and your nickname shall be Litsa. You are a good Greek Orthodox girl. And you're very much looking forward to seeing the beauty of our church, meeting our friends and neighbors and our priest. I know you have been trained as a medical doctor, but you must embrace your role as an actress. Remember you must trust no one outside of our family. If you see a person you recognize from Salonika, you must walk by as if he is a stranger. That is very important. There are collaborators and fifth columnists everywhere, and we don't know who they are. I believe our servants are honorable, but one cannot be sure."

"But," she began and then silenced herself. "Yes, of course. I will be delighted to go to church with you tomorrow."

"Here." He withdrew a crucifix from his desk drawer. "This is a *stavro* for you."

For a brief moment, her hand which should have been reaching out, felt paralyzed. A cross. It was forbidden for a Jew to wear a crucifix, the

11

symbol of Christianity. "Thank you," she managed to say politely, as she took the necklace with the cross and placed it in her pocket.

"Our son, Alexander is out carousing with his friends tonight. Alexander agreed with me that I must help my Jewish friends. He said the Germans will show no mercy to the Jews if the Nazis come to Salonika and Athens. He'll join us tomorrow morning at breakfast and then go to church with us for worship."

Worship, she thought, as she finished her glass of ouzo. I'm Jewish. I'm a Jewish woman. My family is descended from the Jews who were expelled from Spain during the Spanish Inquisition in 1492. We have remained Jewish for the past five hundred years, never forsaking our faith. And now I must go to church as a Christian? It had never occurred to her that if she had the name and papers of a Christian woman, that she'd also be required to go to church. She remembered what her father said about following what Kìrios Giannopolous advised. She had heard that because of fear of the approaching Germans, some Jews pretended to be Christians. But surely there were other ways to blend in here in such a large city. Yes, there must be another way for her to stay safe. Well, she'd go to church tomorrow. Maybe this family would realize that she couldn't pass herself off as a Greek Orthodox woman, and then they would find another way for her to live safely in Athens.

"Michaelitsa, in a few minutes you may join us while we listen to the radio broadcasts on the BBC. We are plotting on our wall map all that is reported about the war. We hope for good news, but it never comes," Kìrios Giannopolous told her, and Anna sensed his sadness. It was the same sadness that had taken hold of her own father and never seemed to let go after Nazi Germany started gobbling up one country after another.

"Well," Anna hesitated. She so much just wanted to lay her head down on a pillow and close the door, shielding herself from this play-acting that had unexpectedly been thrust upon her. She didn't want to listen to the reports of new Nazi brutalities that most certainly would be announced on the radio broadcast.

"You can listen with us tomorrow evening," he said in soothing tones. "I think you must be tired. My wife, Maria, will also retire. She finds news of the war to be too upsetting."

Anna awoke to the smell of freshly baked bread. At first her mind clouded as she looked around the handsomely furnished room in which she found herself. Yes, she remembered. She was in Athens, in the home of the Giannopolous family. She would be going to church this morning. She would pretend to be an Orthodox Christian woman. A role in a play, she thought, yes, that is how I must think of this. When she was a child she had enjoyed taking part in theatrical productions, before the sciences had captivated her.

She unfastened the window shutters. There on a distant hill, she could see the Acropolis, with the Parthenon's gleaming white pillars under the rays of the winter sun. She'd seen that wonderful structure once before, when the family had visited Athens many years ago. What magnificence! It truly took one's breath away. She could stand here forever, just looking at it in the morning light. But delaying the inevitable was an exercise in futility.

Anna dressed in what she thought would be appropriate clothing for her morning in church. She didn't have to dress so drably today. Her spirits were lifted as she looked at her reflection in the mirror. Today she could dress fashionably with a navy floral frock, silk stockings, a small hat in the latest style, and her midheight heels. She applied a beautiful shade of scarlet lipstick, and brushing the dark brown hair away from her face, she fastened barrettes against her soft curls. She looked down at the crucifix on the dresser table. How can I do this? she thought. It was against everything and anything she believed in as a Jewish woman. But she reminded herself, she'd had the courage to leave her family and attend a medical school in a foreign country. She was in a class of few women and people who only spoke English. Surely placing a cross around her neck wasn't an impossible thing for her to do.

She opened the door, ready for her role as Michaelitsa Kalodosis. The light was streaming in through the tall windows, dappling across the tiled floor, as her heels clicked loud in her ears. She heard the sound of voices and followed it to where the family was having breakfast. Kirios Giannopolous and his son were engaged in a heated argument, which abruptly ceased when Anna entered the room.

"Put away the newspaper for now. We will discuss this later," the older man tersely instructed his son.

Alexander put down the newspaper and looked up at Anna. She knew he intended to politely look up, for only a brief moment. But he stared at her.

"Ah, cousin Michaelitsa," Kirios Giannopolous welcomed her. "Breakfast is awaiting you. Alexander, surely you remember Michaelitsa, though you haven't seen her since she was a child."

He politely rose to his feet. Anna locked eyes with the handsome, tall black-haired man, a dark mustache above his mouth. "Hello, Dr. Giannopolous," said Anna.

"Please not so formal. Don't address me as doctor. I am Alexander. Michaelitsa, we are pleased to have you with us." He offered her a chair.

Anna suddenly felt self-conscious. Yes, he was an attractive man. Her fiancé, Daniel had been attractive. But she couldn't take her eyes off this man, and he boldly matched her gaze.

"Some coffee?" Kiría Maria asked her.

"Yes, *epharisto*. Thank you all so much for offering your help to me."

"So let us speak frankly." Kirios Antonios walked to the door and closed it. "You are Michaelitsa Kalodosis, or, as we shall call you, Litsa. You are related to us, through my wife, Maria's brother, Artemis. You are from the island of Kos, where many people have olive skin."

"Patéra, while we are instructing her as to her new history, there is the problem of her accent." Alexander spread quince jam over his rusk and took a bite.

"My accent? What are you talking about?"

"You see, Patéra. Listen to her Greek. My Jewish friend Isaac, who was a colleague at the Sorbonne, also came from Salonika, and his

Greek has a particular accent that a collaborator could easily identify. If she speaks Greek, it might give her away. You speak other languages, Michaelitsa?"

"Yes." Anna set her mouth in a firm line. What an arrogant man! Did the Greek Jews of Salonika really have an accent? He obviously was waiting for her to mention the languages in which she was fluent. But she was annoyed with him. He was the doctor who would help her find a medical position, but why did he have to be such a know-it-all?

"French? German?" he offered, and in his voice she heard compassion, and it disarmed her feelings of annoyance.

"And Italian as well. I pursued my medical education in America, so of course I am fluent in English."

"Very good. I think it best if we speak mostly French, and if you do speak Greek, we will mention you spent much time in France and America and therefore acquired your strange accent."

"Strange accent," she muttered under her breath.

He frowned at her.

She needed to be polite, she told herself. These people were offering her their guidance. She was a guest in their home. Where were her manners? "I know you're trying to help, and I thank you. I'm well aware of what is happening in the rest of Europe. But Greece is so remote from Germany, Poland, and France. Do you really think the Germans will come to Greece? I've heard the British are coming to defend us, and they would defeat the Germans, wouldn't they?"

"Mamà," Alexander got to his feet, "it would be better if Litsa and I talk in private of those things that you might find upsetting. Litsa, please take your coffee and plate with you. I will speak with you in the library. We'll return in time to go to church, Mamà."

"Alexander, remember after church we have invited the Nomikos family to our house for luncheon," his mother reminded him.

"Yes, yes, I remember. How could I forget?"

Anna noted the mild irritation in his voice.

"Alexander, please. Their daughter is quite charming and good-natured. They are a good family, and it's time for you to think about marriage and children."

"I'm too young," her son laughed.

"You are not too young," his mother protested. "Your brother Marko is younger, and he already has a family in America. Three sons!"

"Father wasn't married at my age. I can wait."

"This war changes everything. You must think of your future."

"Of course, Mamà." He kissed her on the cheek and walked out of the room.

Anna retrieved her breakfast and followed him to the library. It was a beautiful room with dark mahogany furniture and glass-enclosed bookshelves lining the walls. Anna found herself drawn to the books, noting the titles on the gold-embossed leather spines.

"Feel free to borrow any of our books. But please, sit down; there's much for us to discuss," he told her politely.

"I have my medical diploma with me," she began, once she was seated, "and…"

"Litsa, I'm afraid that would be too dangerous in these uncertain times."

"What would be too dangerous?" She put down a piece of cheese, suddenly losing her appetite. He couldn't be saying she would have to put aside her career? No, surely she had misunderstood.

"I admire a woman who has pursued a medical degree. Especially for a Greek woman, it is most commendable. And so, of course, a woman doctor in Greece is very unusual." He paused and gave her a weak smile. "And you must not do anything to arouse suspicion and focus attention on yourself."

"How do you think my father persuaded me to come here?" Her temper flashed hot. "He said if the Germans came to Salonika that I wouldn't be permitted to work in a hospital. But Athens is so much farther south, and the Germans will never get this far. The British will defend us and keep Athens safe. I am a doctor. I need to use my skills to help people."

"Litsa," he spoke softly and with compassion, "I understand; truly I do. You'll see that the hospital is filled to the brim with the soldiers from the Albanian front. As a doctor or a nurse, you will be looked upon as an angel of mercy, I assure you. Let me try to explain further." He placed his hand over hers and then quickly withdrew it. Anna was about to offer him a quick retort for his patronizing manner, but the compassion she saw in his dark eyes took her aback, and she was silent.

Don't be an idiot, he told himself, as he tried to deny this instant feeling of connection between himself and this woman with the olive complexion. She was attractive of course, but he'd had many, many experiences with attractive women.

"I can easily find you a position as a nurse in my hospital. I know that isn't what you planned, but it wouldn't compromise your safety."

"My safety? I am one lone Greek Jewish woman. I'm sure even the Germans would not find me a threat."

Alexander leaned back in his chair as he sipped his dark coffee. She didn't understand at all. She was so naïve, but she was not the only one. He could so easily read the disappointment on her face, and beneath the disappointment, the simmering anger she was trying to control.

"Litsa, you will listen to what I have to say?"

"Well, it seems I don't have a choice, do I? I came here expecting to practice medicine as a doctor and now you've made the decision that I must be a nurse. But I do have a choice. I will buy a train ticket and return to my family in Salonika. If the Germans come, at least we will all be together, and I won't have to pretend to not be a doctor and not be a Jew. And that's really sounding more and more appealing to me."

Little fool, he thought. But he instinctively knew not to say such a thing to this educated woman.

"Why did we have to leave the breakfast room?" she raised her voice to him. "What could you possibly say that would be upsetting to your mother? Surely she doesn't care if I am a doctor or a nurse."

"My stepmother has a very nervous temperament. The impending occupation upsets her and talk of the approaching Germans has badly frightened her. If at all possible, my father and I try to shield her from news of the war. I didn't want to cause her any more distress, so I brought you to the library, where we can discuss your situation here in Athens. Litsa, your disappointment and anger are written all over your face." He tried to speak in a moderate tone.

"So I am not to be disappointed that my education as a doctor will not enable me to help the sick. And how do I dare show anger to the man who is making this stupid pronouncement to me!" She raised her voice in defiance.

"I am not stupid, Litsa, and neither are you. Have some patience, which I guess is not one of your virtues, and listen to all I have to tell you. Eat some of your breakfast, as lunch is many hours from now."

Anna's eyes narrowed with annoyance, as she took a bite of cheese and a sip of her coffee. Alexander watched her try to control her emotions.

"Yes, it's perfectly understandable that you are both disappointed and angry. But we are living in perilous times. We must mask our feelings before the occupiers of our country. And when the Germans come, I will smile and be so agreeable. I think my father told you that you must be an actress playing the role of a good Greek Orthodox woman so that you don't arouse suspicion. Realize that my family puts itself at grave peril to hide you in our midst, once the Germans come, and they will come. It is inevitable."

"I'm sorry," she said contritely. "I didn't think.... I was being selfish and thoughtless. It won't happen again, I promise you."

"You are new to this game that we play. I understand you have only just returned from America, and so you have much to understand about what is happening in Europe. May I ask why you didn't stay in America, where there are more opportunities for women?"

"I wanted to return to my family and to my country. I was homesick," she said, her gaze wandering away, seemingly deep in thought.

He sensed she was not telling the truth, but that was of no consequence. "Let us discuss what is happening in our country. I know you must be a very intelligent woman if you were able to obtain a medical degree. It's hard for a woman to compete in a medical school; for I have seen firsthand how difficult the professors make life for women. You didn't apply for medical school in Germany?"

"No, it would have been impossible for me to be admitted as a Jew. Jews were no longer able to attend higher institutions of learning there since the thirties. I was upset at first, because it's well known that the best medical education is in Germany. But we have cousins in America, so that's where I went to medical school, and my parents knew I would be well taken care of by family."

"I received my medical education in Germany, and you are correct," Alexander told her. "It was superb training. In particular I loved surgery, but here in Athens I do whatever is necessary to help our people. My skills are very much needed in our country. I also have a professorship at the University where I give lectures once each week. But enough about me.

"Now allow me to explain why I am so certain the Germans will soon be in Greece and your Jewish people will be at risk."

C H A P T E R   3

─────────────── ⧉ ───────────────

"I WAS IN Germany on November ninth, 1938," he sighed deeply. "I was there the evening of *Kristallnacht*, the night of broken glass. You know about this, of course."

"Yes, I know." Was he trying to scare her, insinuating that such things could happen in Greece?

"I was out strolling with my friends when the Nazi brownshirts filled the streets. They smashed the windows of the Jewish storekeepers and pulled many out into the street. Litsa, it is a sight I can never forget. They pummeled old men, beating them with nightsticks; there was blood everywhere. I, being a foolish man, tried to intervene while they were stomping on a poor soul. For my efforts, I was beaten as well. My friends pulled me away before I was severely injured. I still have a remembrance of that terrible night on my forehead." He touched a white scar over his left eyebrow. "It haunts me, Litsa. How can men behave like beasts to their fellow man? Such hatred, such terrible hatred.… My God, years before that night, the Germans even burned the books of authors they believed to be subversive. Can you imagine burning books?"

Anna had heard about what transpired that night in Germany. But she knew something like that couldn't happen here. She was certain of this.

"Litsa, the Nazis hate the Jewish people and when they come here to Greece, no Jew will be safe."

"But how can you be so sure they will come to Greece? They are far away, and why would they be interested in our country?" Anna countered.

"Over there." He pointed to a large map on the wall. "Come."

She walked over to the map of Europe and Greece, with pins decorated with flags of various colors.

"We fought the Italians in Albania." He pointed to the country north of Greece. "We won one important battle. Our soldiers continue to fight the Italians, but it is just a matter of time. Their partners, the Germans, will never allow the Italians to be routed. It's true that the Italians might not be so hard to live under. They don't understand the Nazis' obsession with persecuting Jews. But the Germans are coming, mark my words, and there will be nowhere safe for Jews, nowhere. They will come down through the mountains of Albania." He pointed to the area on the map, north of Greece. "There will be no way to stop them. Greece is not a rich country, but we have ports on the Mediterranean, and the Germans need our ports. As the war spreads to North Africa, they will need those ports for supply lines."

"But the British are coming, and surely they will help to defend us."

"Not many Brits are coming, and from what I have heard, the RAF will be outnumbered sixteen to one by the Luftwaffe. I have it on good authority they will flee the country once the Germans come."

"Good authority?" Anna questioned him, her stomach sinking. Her family in Salonika, would they be safe if what Alexander said was true?

"My father and I have many sources that I may not divulge. The less you know about such things, the safer you will be."

Anna turned away from him. The mask of nothingness, she told herself. Perhaps he was just testing her so that she could learn to show no emotions on her face. But, she told herself, she wasn't a fool. He was not testing her. He's convinced what he is saying is true, she thought.

He placed his hand on her shoulder. "I am sorry, Litsa. I didn't mean to sound so harsh, but you must know the truth."

"My parents," she turned back to him, "they must leave."

"Yes, Litsa. You must write to them and tell them my father will find safety for your entire family here in Athens. They shouldn't remain in Salonika."

"I-I will write to them. They won't believe what you are saying. My family has lived in Salonika for hundreds of years. Our ancestors are buried in the cemetery. My father says our family is too large for everyone to even think of leaving. My grandmother is too frail for such a journey.

Salonika is our home and they won't leave. Our Christian neighbors will help protect us."

"If only that were true," said Alexander. "I know that Salonika used to be a city with a Jewish majority. In the twenties, after the Balkan Wars and the Treaty of Lausanne, there was a population exchange between the Turks and the Greeks. The Turks left Salonika, and the Greeks of Asia Minor flooded Salonika, hundreds and thousands of refugees."

"Yes, I remember that time. I was a young child. My parents found a Christian orphan girl wandering the streets. She was my age, and our family took her in. We shared the same bed and talked long into the night. She was so sad. She told me terrible stories that I found so hard to believe about marching for days, for weeks, with hardly a crust of bread to eat or water to drink. She witnessed the death of her parents by savage Turkish soldiers. When I asked my father if that could be true, he told me it was true. After living with us for many months, people from the refugee community came to our door and took her away. I cried to lose her, but my father said it was for the best, that she was Greek Orthodox and should be with her own people."

"So many refugees came back to Greece, and so many came to Salonika that the Jews were no longer in the majority," Alexander continued. "The refugees were poor and desperate. They looked at the Jewish merchants who had done so well, and they were jealous and envious of your community. I am reminding you of this because I think it's foolish to believe your community will be helped by the refugees, and so many of the residents of Salonika are refugees from Asia Minor."

"Alexander," she said and took a deep breath, "what you are saying is frightening. I can't stop thinking of my family. Why should I be the one here and not the others, my brothers, sisters, nieces, nephews?"

"Your father made the choice for you, Litsa."

"Maybe it won't happen. Maybe the Allies will stop the Germans before they come to Greece."

"We can pray for that when we are in church this morning. Have you ever been inside a Greek Orthodox church?"

"Once, to a wedding."

"Well, you were not a participant," he observed.

"Of course, I was not the bride." She couldn't stop herself from snapping at him.

"Litsa, you speak too quickly without thinking. I know you were not the bride. But you were not a member of the Orthodox Church during the ceremony. Do you know how to make the sign of the cross?

"I'll take your silence as a no. Now the Catholics cross themselves in this fashion." He demonstrated a cross from left to right. "Greeks cross themselves in the opposite direction."

With a hand that she willed to stop shaking, she did as he demonstrated.

"Very good, Litsa. You will stand next to my mother and just do as she does. It won't be difficult for you to mimic our actions. The service is merely an hour. We will introduce you to everyone as our cousin from Kos. Also this is a very special service, as we are having a visit from the Archbishop Chrysanthus. It's an honor to have him with us today."

The Archbishop, she thought. Surely he will know I am not who I am pretending to be. "I won't disappoint you and your family," Anna told him.

"Litsa, do not think I don't realize how hard it will be for you to pretend to be a Christian. Not that it will make it any easier for you, but know there are other Jews hiding out in the open. If the Germans take over, these Jews are trying to do what they can to remain safe, pretending to be Christians."

"Thank you again, Alexander. I know full well that your family is taking a risk by helping me."

"Come. We will be late for church, and Mamà will not be pleased."

"Alexander, just one more thing," she paused, "are you sure it isn't possible for me to practice as a doctor?"

"I'm sorry. You will be a fine nurse; of that I have no doubt." He took her elbow and guided her out of the library.

Anna looked up at the beautiful painted icons on the dome of the church. Yes, one could appreciate their beauty, if one wasn't in this church pretending to be a Christian. She stole a glance across the aisle at Alexander, who was standing next to his father. Men on the right. Women on the left. The separation was somewhat similar to the synagogue, where women were seated in a balcony, away from the men. But in this church, it was only elderly women who were seated. Everyone else stood. She thought of how she and her family did not attend the synagogue very frequently. When she was in America, she had gone with Daniel and his parents that one time. That was when she had met his family, the family of her fiancé, and it was shortly thereafter that Daniel told her he was forced to break their engagement because his family didn't consider her a "real Jew." She was Sephardic, not Ashkenazi.

*A real Jew...*She remembered feeling as if she had been slapped in the face, her very identity denied. And today and from this day forward and for the foreseeable future, she would pretend to be a Greek Orthodox Christian, an identity not her own.

Anna crossed herself in imitation of Kiría Giannopolous. Anna followed the older woman up to the priest to receive communion, bread and wine, and then she took a piece of *Antidoro* bread from the basket as her heart beat furiously in her chest. Everyone will know, she thought. Everyone will know I am just pretending. But the priest nodded at her, and she sensed the kindness in this man in the priest's robes. The smell of incense and the gilded painted icons swirled around her. The other women who stood beside her on the women's side of the aisle smiled warmly at her. Anna tried to relax as she began calculating how much longer it was before the service would end. She clutched the prayer book in her hands. And then everyone knelt down, and as Anna followed suit, the words "Thou shall not bow down to graven images" echoed loudly in her mind. She closed her eyes for a brief moment. She could do this; she would do this. Everyone rose to their feet. She was relieved when there was no more kneeling. It was finished. Did this family with whom she dwelled, go to church every Sunday?

"Litsa, you have done very well today," Kiría Giannopolous, bent down and murmured softly in her ear, before she began to introduce her as the niece of her brother's wife. Anna said little, just smiling and nodding, hoping they would soon walk out of the church.

Anna followed everyone up to the Archbishop with the flowing beard, who sat in an ornate chair beside the priest. Anna took another piece of *Antidoro* and kissed the hand of the Archbishop in imitation of the Giannopolous family. "How glad we are to have you with us," he said to her.

"Thank you. It's a pleasure to be here," she responded, not daring to look up into his face. And quite suddenly it came to her that he knew. He knew who she was and who she wasn't, but he was playing this game along with the Giannopolous family and with her.

The family walked together on the cobblestone streets on the way back to their villa. Kìrios Antonios nodded at her. "Very nice, Litsa, very nice. You did well today."

"The Archbishop seemed a kind man." She knew not to say that she thought he knew her true identity, especially on a public street.

"He is a good man with a compassionate heart." Alexander spoke up.

"Alexander," his mother addressed him as they walked down the broad boulevard, "today at luncheon, please remember to be on your best behavior with the Nomikos family."

"Of course. I shall be a proper gentleman. Otherwise this poor girl will feel like she is a lamb going to slaughter when her parents attempt to arrange this marriage. Mamà, before they arrive, I'd like Litsa to go over some medical charts with me. I could use another opinion on some difficult cases." Alexander smiled down at Anna.

"Just be sure that the Nomikos family is not sitting at the table waiting for you. First impressions are very important. You aren't going to be difficult about this, are you?"

"Of course not. I shall be my charming self."

"There is nothing wrong with an arranged marriage," his father said to Alexander. "It worked for me with your mother, my first wife, may she rest in peace, and with my good wife, Maria, who bore me a son and a daughter. Your brother and sister both had arranged marriages before they left Athens. And as for you, Alexander, all those years abroad, and you have forgotten how it should be between a man and woman and the joining of two families. You must forget your dalliances with the fräuleins and the mademoiselles that you had during your years abroad. And now I hear you toy with the American and British women who frequent our cafés. Enough of that, Alexander. It's time for you to settle down."

"In other countries, men and women choose for themselves. They fall in love," Alexander said patiently. "Patéras, you know in the rest of the world things are changing. Arranged marriages are a thing of the past."

"Not here in Greece. The old ways are the best, my son. And this "fall in love," that is for children. And what about you, Litsa. Do you believe in this falling in love? I am confident that your family also believes a marriage should be arranged for the benefit of the bride and groom and their families. Would your father allow you to choose your own bridegroom, Litsa?"

"When I was in America, I did fall in love. I was to be married, but it didn't happen." Anna pulled up the collar of her woolen coat against the cold wind that blew against them.

Her thoughts returned to her engagement. Would she ever forget Daniel and what happened between them? She was going to have a new life in America. He'd given her a beautiful engagement ring. She'd written to her parents about him, and they gave their blessing, but asked if she could wait until she returned to Salonika for her wedding. She didn't want to wait. Whenever their schedules allowed a free weekend, they shared passionate moments. They both agreed they'd feel more comfortable if their union was blessed by a rabbi. In America, relations between men and women were so much freer than in Greece. But she understood her parents' disapproval, if they were ever to know she had not waited until marriage as was proper for a respectable Greek woman. She looked at Alexander walking next to his father, and she realized again what an attractive man he was. It occurred to her that in the last few months, she rarely thought about Daniel anymore and how he had broken off their engagement. "I can't, Anna. I just can't. It would break their hearts. You know I love you, but I can't."

And so for that last year in medical school, she would only glance briefly in his direction. At first it was too painful, and then slowly the pain subsided. She wrote a letter to her family and said their marriage plans did not work out. She could never have told her father that Daniel's family looked down upon Sephardic Jews.

"Ah, you see. A marriage not arranged by parents is destined to fail or in your case not to even go forward." Kìrios Giannopolous seemed quite pleased with himself.

As they walked past the garden wall of the villa, Anna noticed men shoveling dirt. "What are they doing?" Anna asked.

"They are digging a shelter for us. When the air-raid sirens sound, I don't want our family to have to flee so far down the street," Kìrios Antonios told her. "We have heard Hitler has a love for classical Greece. We must pray he will tell the bombers to spare our Acropolis. But who knows the mind of a madman. I know that Salonika has already suffered bombing from the Italians."

"Yes, it has." She remembered the destruction and the fires. But the neighborhood in which her family dwelled was untouched, so far.

"Let's not talk of bombs this afternoon," Alexander frowned. "There is more to life in Athens than war and bombs. I was thinking that Litsa would enjoy visiting a cabaret with me. A new stage show is coming to the Zocar café. In honor of her arrival in Athens, I think she should experience the fun side of our city. There are many Americans and Europeans at the cafes, having a wonderful time. Litsa, would you like that?"

"I would like that." Anna smiled.

"Yes," said his father, "young people should go out to enjoy themselves, for who knows how long that will be possible."

"I have two charts here, a man and a woman. I have examined them thoroughly and hoped you might have a fresh perspective on their maladies." Alexander handed her the charts, as they sat in the library. He took a cigarette out of his silver case and offered one to her.

"No, thank you. I don't smoke," she told him. "I'd be pleased to look at the charts." Anna was thrilled to be able to put her knowledge to good use.

"If I may be so bold, may I ask you about your love match that did not work out?"

"He was a fellow medical student." Anna took a deep breath. She would make this a short tale, no need to go into details. "It was America, and things are different there. We met. We fell in love. We became engaged. I wrote to my parents, and they were happy for me. I intended to make a new life with my husband in America. Do you know the difference between Ashkenazi and Sephardic Jews, Alexander?"

"There are also Romaniote Jews in Greece, are there not?"

"Yes. The Romaniotes have been in Greece for two thousand years, since the time of Christ. Daniel's family was Ashkenazi, a descendant of Jews from Europe, Jews who speak Yiddish. I'm a Sephardic Jew, and my family speaks Ladino, a dialect of Spanish from our ancestors' years in Spain. When his family met me, a Sephardic Jew, they didn't believe I was truly Jewish, and they forbid our marriage. Daniel's father had a heart condition, and they advised us that Daniel's marriage to me would surely hasten his death. That is my story," Anna said with a finality in her voice that she hoped would alert Alexander that she had said as much as she was going to say about this subject.

"And so it is everywhere. One must marry within one's own group." Alexander continued paging through one of the charts.

Anna said nothing as she opened up the chart about a young woman with unexplained shortness of breath. As they discussed the two cases, they debated back and forth about possible diagnoses and treatment options. Anna found herself wishing this time with Alexander would never end. She was enjoying herself so very much with this intelligent man who valued her medical expertise.

"One more thing of which you should be aware." Alexander looked up from his reading. "After we listen to the radio broadcasts in the evening, you must retire to your room. My father is a leader in the Athens community, and often other men, intellectuals, people of importance assemble in our house for a meeting to discuss the situation in Greece."

"You don't want them to see me?"

"Quite, the opposite. I do not want you to see them."

While the family visited over luncheon with the Nomikos family and the prospective bride for Alexander, Anna had excused herself, saying she was still quite tired after her long trip yesterday from Kos. Alexander had looked up at her with a knowing smile and a look of "you are deserting me."

Anna spent the afternoon composing a letter to her father, urging him to reconsider his decision for the family to remain in Salonika. She carefully delineated everything Alexander had told her. But in her heart she knew her father wouldn't consider uprooting the whole family. There was his mother, her grandmother, to consider. She was too frail for a long journey, and Papa and Mamà would never leave without her.

Anna also wrote to her mother, reassuring her that she'd arrived safely and the Giannopolous family was kind and welcoming. She didn't mention she must masquerade as a Christian woman. When she thought back to her father's words, to obey Kìrios Giannopolous, surely her father knew this might happen. But there was no need to mention she was going to church on Sunday, as there was also no reason to tell them she couldn't be a doctor in Athens. Her father had such high hopes for her professional success; she didn't have the heart to tell him the truth.

That evening, Anna threw an extra quilt on her bed, as the cold of the Athens winter crept inside her room. The tall windows had frosted, and earlier she had closed the shutters. This was her new home now. The home of Michaelitsa Kalodosis.

Her thoughts returned to her morning in church. It wasn't so bad. She hadn't asked if the family went every Sunday. She hoped they didn't. But it would get easier for her. Surely the first time was the most difficult. It would become second nature to her, and while she stood there pretending to worship a God not her own, her thoughts could dwell elsewhere.

She thought again of the hour before luncheon when she and Alexander discussed his two cases. The fact that he considered her an equal to him in medicine made her so happy. She'd be a nurse, but at least Alexander was not dismissive of her expertise and knowledge.

Alexander was so very intelligent and so kind. She was attracted to this handsome man, she admitted that. But it would come to nothing. It could come to nothing. He was Greek Orthodox. She was a Jew.

C H A P T E R 4

Early February 1941: Athens

As the cold days of winter wore on, air-raid sirens regularly sounded each day. The new shelter built in the garden was very convenient. But eventually the Giannopolous household, like the rest of Athens, stopped paying attention to the sirens. Fortunately, no bombs had ever fallen on Athens.

Each morning, Alexander's face sported a small band-aid attached to another area of skin that he had nicked while shaving, as his thoughts were distracted and preoccupied with the woman who had come to live with them. She was beautiful and intelligent. Her smile, when he saw her at the breakfast table, brightened his morning and he found himself humming. He hadn't felt so lighthearted, so alive since the Italians had declared war on his country and his parents convinced him to stay in Athens to care for the wounded instead of going to the Albanian front. And now every day, hospital beds were filled with the wounded and the poor young Greek boys who died clutching his hand in pain. Even the streets of the city were filled with wounded soldiers, the cloying odor of antiseptic and blood everywhere. Since the declaration of war in October with the Italians, his heart had been filled with melancholy. But that had changed when this intelligent, beautiful woman arrived on their doorstep. In the months since she had arrived, his feelings about her seemed to deepen with each passing day.

Most mornings Anna and Alexander walked together to the hospital, and if he went to see patients elsewhere or lectured at the University, he returned in the late afternoon to escort her home. When there was a dusting of snow on the ground, Alexander was quick to offer her his hand for support. Each morning and each afternoon, they talked and talked of nothing and of everything. He talked of his desire since he was a young boy to become a doctor in his family of merchants, and she spoke of wanting an education far beyond what anyone else in her family had achieved. They discussed their first encounters with patients and their successful diagnoses.

Once inside the Evangelismos Hospital, as Alexander had predicted, she was easily accepted as a nurse on the wards. A white uniform and head covering had been found for her to borrow until a new one was sewn. And the wounded Greek soldiers from the Albanian front looked up at her with so much hope in their eyes, waiting for her to stop at their bedside. They wanted to feel the warmth of her healing touch, and the soothing words she spoke to them, in a soft Greek voice so that she would not be overheard.

"Are you ready?" Alexander knocked on her door.

They were going out to the café Zocar, where they would see the new stage show that had just arrived.

"In a minute," Anna called out as she checked her reflection in the mirror one last time. She was wearing her best dress, with fashionable wide shoulder pads, a bright blue color, which brought out the green in her eyes. She had brushed her hair a minimum of one hundred strokes to make it shine. The seams in her silk stockings were straightened. The British had just arrived, and she'd been told there would be Australians and New Zealanders there. She'd seen the RAF soldiers on the streets with their trim uniforms. Tonight she would laugh and dance as she'd done during many evenings in America. She kept telling herself how much she was looking forward to tonight, flirting with the soldiers, dancing, forgetting everything else. Maybe she would meet a man tonight, a man who would make her forget these feelings for Alexander.

Your father sent you here to be safe, she told herself, over and over again. He would be horrified to learn of her growing feelings toward this Greek Orthodox man. There was no future for two such as them. Alexander knew this as well. But why did he look at her so, and let his hand brush against hers? She wasn't an innocent young girl. She was a woman who knew where such feelings could lead, especially living in the same house as this attractive man, this attractive Greek Orthodox man. She realized she was playing with fire. This incredible sense of connection that she felt to him, it made no sense, but it was so very real.

Yes, hopefully tonight, she would meet a charming Brit, and she would flirt with him. Tonight at the café, no one there would care about her identity. She'd just be another girl wanting to have a good time, while the impending specter of German occupation hung over the city. Alexander had told her that if the Germans came…. when the Germans came, that these soldiers they saw in the streets would be fighting a losing battle. They were no match for the Germans. They didn't have enough planes, enough men. And they would have to evacuate from Greece as quickly as possible, leaving the Greek people defenseless against the German onslaught.

Anna walked out the door of her bedroom to see Alexander standing there in his stylish dark pinstriped suit with broad lapels, a welcoming smile on his face, and she forgot about flirting with those soldiers. She fought it truly she fought these feelings, but they overwhelmed her best efforts. She was falling in love with this man, his kindness, his compassion, his intelligence, his good looks. When they were out of earshot of others, he flirted with her and she flirted back. It meant so much more to her than flippant words. But the flirting could never amount to anything more. There was no future, nothing, even though this was wartime and perhaps people behaved in ways that in more normal times they wouldn't even consider. Wartime…. Did that make the thoughts and the dreams she had about Alexander Giannopolous acceptable? She never mentioned him in the letters she wrote to her family. She knew it was irrational, but she feared if she mentioned him, her family would somehow know about these dangerous feelings she had for Alexander, which seemed to grow stronger each day.

"Litsa." Alexander placed her hand in the crook of his arm. "You look beautiful. I'm sure all the soldiers will be fighting over the chance to dance with you and ply you with drink."

"Don't tease," she laughed.

Alexander was eager to introduce her to his friend Dimetri and his wife, Irini. Dimetri and Alexander had been friends since they were mere boys. "So you are the Litsa, Alexander cannot stop talking about?" His friend winked at her, as he politely got to his feet.

Anna looked down at her hands, uncertain of how to respond.

In the doorway were several soldiers, with fashionably dressed young women on their arms. Alexander motioned for them to join the two couples.

The café was filled with gaiety as the soldiers drank with girls perched on their laps. Everyone enthusiastically applauded when the floor show was over. Such happy times, but one could sense the tension beneath those smiles.

"My Bill, my Bill," a pretty blond girl murmured and took another swallow of her drink. She had earlier been introduced to Anna as Emily Brown, a secretary for the American Legation. She was drinking way too much. "Emily, I think you had enough," commented one of the soldiers.

"Leave me be," she protested sadly.

"Poor Emily, she's lost another beau," one of the other women said as she patted Emily's shoulder.

"I'm bad luck," Emily lamented as she downed another glass.

"Come on, mate," an Australian young man commented. "It's wartime. It could happen to any one of us. It was his time, pure and simple. I say it was some Jerry who was responsible, not you."

Emily looked down at the table. "I need cheering up."

"Come up to my room for the evening, Emily. My roommate shipped out this morning. And I've always had a fancy for you American girls. I'll get us a nice bottle of wine, and we can cheer each other up. What do you say?" asked a red-headed soldier with the accent of a Scotsman.

"I do need cheering up." She unsteadily got to her feet.

The Scotsman offered her a helping hand, and they left the café.

"You know," commented a plump American girl, "Bill was the third flier she fancied who was killed."

"Enough talk of those who don't come back. Come here, lovey." A tall Australian with a wide-brimmed hat pulled a girl who was standing next to him onto his lap and gave her a kiss. "How about a whirl?" He motioned toward the dance floor.

"And you?" A Brit with sandy hair was addressing Anna.

"Sure," she answered, totally aware of Alexander's eyes fastened upon her. Ask someone to dance, she thought, as she watched Alexander sitting at their table, not making conversation. He just watched her and the British soldier, who swung her around to a popular Benny Goodman tune. She was having fun, she told herself. And then the tempo of the music became slow and romantic. The lights had dimmed.

As the Brit smiled down at her and began to pull her close, Anna saw Alexander get to his feet and approach them. "I believe this dance has been promised to me," Alexander said in a voice that made the Brit instantly release Anna from his grasp, with a polite bow to the Greek man.

"Of course." The soldier went back to their table.

And so their dance began, as Alexander gathered her in his arms, and she felt herself surrender to his closeness, his touch. She laid her head against his chest, listening to the beat of his heart. It was happening, this powerful connection between them, and she couldn't stop it. She didn't want to stop it, as he held her more closely and murmured her name in her ear. One dance ended and another began. It seemed they couldn't let go of each other. The tempo at last changed to a swing dance, and Alexander released her.

"Come, Litsa," he told her. "There is a very special dessert served here called the Chicago. You must have some with me."

"The Chicago?" She walked back to their table, which now seemed to have even more soldiers and women crowded around it.

"Ah, the Chicago!" Dimetri echoed. "Waiter!" He signaled for the man who attended to their table. "Five Chicagos for us."

"What is a Chicago?" Anna was seated next to Alexander, who had grabbed her hand under the table and was softly caressing her fingers.

"It is a wonderful dessert with ice cream, whipped cream, cherries, and nuts. And it's huge, for sharing. It was brought back to Greece by a Greek who spent time in Chicago," explained Dimetri.

Everyone dug their spoons into the huge mounds of ice cream, enjoying the cold extravagant dessert. Alexander placed his spoon into the ice cream and then brought it to Anna's mouth to share with him. She smiled at him. She didn't stand a chance of resisting this man. Wartime, she told herself. The world is upside down.

"Time for us to go." Alexander helped her to her feet and into a woolen coat. "Litsa and I need to be at the hospital early tomorrow morning." They bid everyone good-bye, and then Alexander drove them home in silence.

He had parked the car in the shadow of the house. And then he put his arm around her and drew her close. His kiss was warm and sweet. Anna slid her arms around his neck and returned his kiss. How could what felt so good, be so wrong? She became breathless as his kiss became more passionate and then he drew away. "Litsa," was all he said, his eyes looking out at the darkened street.

He opened the car door and walked inside with her, leaving Anna at the door to her bedroom.

The following day, the family had finished their Sunday dinner, and Alexander and his father were engaged in a game of backgammon. Kiría Maria had retired early with a headache. Anna noticed how often her hostess seemed to have debilitating headaches, especially when her husband announced they would soon be listening to the radio broadcast about the war. Anna also retired before the words of the announcer told more terrible stories about the bombing of London. She, as well as all of Greece, wanted to hear that the Americans were going to enter the war. Surely then Germany would be stopped. But those words about the Americans never came.

Anna closed the door to her bedroom, but she didn't disrobe. She forced her thoughts away from war, as she reread the last letter she'd received from her family. They were thankful she was doing so well, and she should not worry about them as they were fine. Her sister Sophia had given birth to a little girl, Sirika, and they were both healthy. I want to see my new niece, she thought. Perhaps she could just go home for a visit, and then she'd return to Athens. The years she had spent in America, she missed everyone so much. Even when she had fallen in love with Daniel, it wasn't easy to think of a future in America without her family surrounding her. After she had been in Athens for a month, she had written to her father, asking about a brief trip home. But her father told her no.

Anna decided to read more of the book she'd started yesterday. Yes, she needed a distraction, especially after last night, dancing in Alexander's arms and the kisses they had shared in the car. A cold wind rattled the windows, and although she had placed a shawl around her shoulders, she still felt a chill.

Remembering the blazing fire in the library, she decided to return to read in front of the fireplace, where the two men were playing backgammon.

She opened the door to find Kirios Antonios was not there and Alexander was standing alone in front of the fire. He turned around and smiled at her.

"It was cold in my room, and I thought I'd warm myself by the fire," she explained.

"Come," he extended his hand to her, "it is chilly tonight."

Anna took his hand and stood beside him, in front of the flames that licked high in the old fireplace. She reveled in the warmth from the heat.

And then Alexander was standing behind her, and she felt his breath on her neck and then his lips. No, she told herself. No.

At first she shivered, and then she closed her eyes as his arms encircled her waist, drawing her against him, and he kissed her neck once again.

"Alexander, we…. we…." She lost her words, and she turned around. They entwined with the sweetness of kisses, and then heat spread through her body like a heady wine.

His kisses stopped, and he held her close. "Oh, Litsa," he sighed, "I think of you night and day."

It is wartime, she told herself as she wrapped her arms around his waist and laid her head against his chest. "I should go back to my room," she murmured.

"Yes, of course." He cleared his throat.

"Alexander." She looked up at him and the love she saw in his dark eyes. "Come with me."

Alexander quietly closed the door to her bedroom. "Let's have some light." Alexander struck a match to a taper, and for several long moments they stood gazing at each other.

He held out his arms to her, and she ran to him. His normally agile fingers fumbled with her buttons. He pulled her dress over her head, and his eyes feasted upon her. And then he drew her close.

Their lovemaking was desperate and passionate, their limbs intertwined, their breaths ragged as they explored each other, loving as if each moment was their last.

And when they were done, Anna laid in his arms, a quilt spread across them.

"Alexander, you know this is impossible." She took a deep breath and thought, what have I done? She knew better.

"What is impossible?" He kissed her shoulder.

"You and I. We have no future," she sighed as she nestled against his chest.

"We have the present," Alexander whispered.

They held each other close and again began the movements of love, until, exhausted, they fell asleep in each other's arms.

Dawn was etching its fingers across the room when they awakened.

"I must go back to my bedroom before the household awakens," he told her and gave her a soft kiss on her lips.

"Yes, I know you can't stay here."

He rose from the bed and tenderly covered her. After hastily dressing, he hesitated at the door and turned back toward her. "You know, Litsa, in America people such as you and I can marry. Unlike here, they have civil marriage ceremonies. Religion doesn't matter in such unions as it does in Greece."

"But, Alexander, we aren't in America. You would not leave your family, your country. And after being separated from my family all those years in America, I shall not leave them again. Once this terrible time…. when it is over, I'll go back to Salonika."

Alexander sighed and closed the door.

He started toward his bedroom, only to find his father standing in the hallway, blocking the way, his arms crossed against his chest.

"What have you done?" his father hissed at him, and raising his hand, cuffed him across the ear.

"Let me explain," Alexander began.

"Explain what! I can see only too well, under my very eyes, you have dishonored the Giannopolous name. Kìrios Joseph Carraso sends his precious daughter into my care, and you defile a virtuous woman. Have you no shame, Alexander? You prey on her with not a thought for anyone but yourself!"

"It's not what you think, Patéra. I am not preying upon her, I swear. I love her Patéra. I love her with all my heart."

Antonios' shoulders sagged as he shook his head. "Alexander, that is worse. No, my son, no. You cannot love her. There are women all over

Athens that would be pleased to marry you, to warm your bed. She is a Jew. It's impossible. Have you lost your senses, my son?"

"I love her," he said quietly.

"Then I shall send her away, back to Salonika."

"No, you will not!" Alexander raised his voice.

CHAPTER 5

ALEXANDER DIALED DIMETRI'S number on the telephone.

"It's Alexander."

"So early? I haven't even eaten my breakfast."

"You still have your apartment on Kiphissa Boulevard?"

"Yes, I haven't rented it out yet."

"May I have the key?"

"You wish to use my apartment? It's that Litsa, isn't it? She's seems quite the girl."

"Well, may I come over to get the key?"

"You know, my friend, you could finally consider marriage. It's obvious you are head over heels about her."

"Marriage with her is out of the question. I can't marry her."

"My God, Alexander, does she have a husband? What terrible luck to have fallen for a married woman. My sympathies, old friend."

"May I come over this morning to get the key?" Alexander was impatient to end this conversation. It wasn't going to be easy to find time in his busy morning to meet up with Dimetri. But he had to find somewhere that he and Litsa could be alone.

Anna heard the soldiers singing before she walked through the doors of the ward. They were singing "Hymn to Liberty," the Greek National Anthem, as they did most mornings. One couldn't help but admire the patriotic spirit of these wounded men, who kept begging her to ask the doctors if they could be sent back to their units to fight in Albania.

The singing had stopped, and Anna entered the ward. She waved at everyone and then stood at the bedside of Lucas. "Have something to drink," Anna urged the young soldier. He was always in good spirits despite his wounds. And he was one of Anna's favorite patients. She'd noticed the first signs of infections in his wounds before the other staff members. "Litsa," Antoinette, an Italian nurse, commented, "the training you received in America is so much better than what we receive in Europe. Your expertise is way beyond ours."

"Thank you, but everyone on the ward is so skilled. Our patients are fortunate to have nurses like you, Antoinette," Anna tried to deflect her praise.

"I know you want to do what's best for the patients," Alexander had told her. "But your skills make you stand out as a nurse. Try not to call attention to yourself."

But it was impossible for her not to do what was best for her patients.

"So Nurse Kalodosis," the wounded soldier was addressing her. "You will tell me the truth, won't you?"

"The truth about what?" Anna smiled and sat down on the chair at his bedside.

"I've lost three toes to frostbite after months in the mountains, and when I'm ready to start walking again, I might have a limp."

"That's possible, Lucas. But let's just concentrate on getting well. Your chest wound is much improved." She continued to talk as she gently removed his bandages.

"Do you think I'll ever find an okay girl like you who would love a fellow like me? I want a wife someday. But who would want a cripple as a husband?"

"Lucas, of course, a girl could love you. You're such a sweet fellow." She gently applied the antiseptic over his wounds.

"I want a girl like you but I know you're already taken."

"Taken? I'm not taken," Anna laughed.

"Not taken? Do you think us chaps are stupid and blind? As soon as Doc Giannopolous comes into the room, your whole face starts to glow. And when the two of you are together, everyone can see you are in love."

"Who is in love?" Alexander appeared at the doorway and approached Lucas, placing a stethoscope against his chest. "If your thoughts are turning to love, I think you're soon going to be ready to be released and go home."

"You and Nurse Kalodosis, of course, are the ones in love. All of us talk about it. There isn't much else for us to observe but...."

Anna folded her hands in her lap as Alexander continued his examination of the young soldier. Everyone knows, everyone can see. Anna took a huge swallow, thinking about last night.... it shouldn't have happened, but it did.

The exam completed, Anna left the ward as Alexander proceeded to the next patient. She hurried down the corridor, until she came to the end of the hallway and looked out the window. Was what Alexander said last night true? They had the present and shouldn't think about the future. A future that didn't exist for them, a Jew and a Christian.

She stood by the window, looking out at the orange trees, which stood dormant, waiting for the arrival of spring. The view was bleak, the sky gray, the threat of new snow. Anna shivered.

"Litsa." It was Alexander at her side. "Don't be upset by what he said. Is it really so surprising that we haven't been able to hide our feelings from everyone?"

"What happened last night. It shouldn't have happened," Anna murmured, her thoughts a whirl of confusion.

"But it did happen. I love you. Please don't be upset, my love." He brushed a stray lock of hair from her eyes. "Litsa, I called my parents and told them we will be going to the picture show tonight and won't be joining them for dinner. You like the pictures, don't you?"

"Yes, of course," she told him.

He took her hand in his. "I spoke with Dimetri this morning," he continued in a soft voice. "He has a flat he isn't using, and I asked him for the key."

"Oh." Anna looked up at him.

"We can go to the pictures. But I thought perhaps I'd pick up some dinner, and we'd go to Dimetri's apartment instead. It is for you to choose, of course."

Anna looked up into his dark eyes. She couldn't undo what had been done, and what had been done had brought them even closer. She loved this man. "Dinner at Dimetri's apartment. Yes, let's do that," she told him.

And so almost every day, sometimes in the evening, some days during the lunch hour, they hurried to the apartment, where they fell into each other's arms, so hungry for each other and the passion that ignited between them. Words of love... no talk of the future, and the hopelessness of their situation. As they held each other while the sirens sounded, Anna lay with her head against his chest. He pulled her tightly against himself, and they waited for the all clear to sound. Each moment between them seemed more and more precious. No bombs had fallen on Athens, and people continued to ignore the air-raid sirens. Occasionally, the thunder of far-off explosions thudded through the air. But it was always far away, usually near the port of Piraeus. Although they never expressed their fears out loud, the uncertainty of their future, the approaching German occupation hung over them, like a dark specter.

The war with the Germans was certainly coming closer to Greece. Kìrios Antonios had instructed the servants to enlarge the family vegetable garden and to store several barrels of olive oil and olives from their farm in the countryside. He said with the war upon them, it was prudent to have their own produce. The war between the Greeks and the Italians had already diminished what was on the shelves in the stores.

Anna, Alexander, and Kìrios Antonios were seated around the breakfast table.

"Litsa," the older man addressed her. "I wanted you to know that your father has wired money here to the National Bank of Athens. He is worried about his funds in the Salonikan banks. The money has been placed in your name. And I received several letters for you yesterday. Here." He handed her three envelopes.

Anna put them in her skirt pocket, eager to read them later in the day. Was her father merely being prudent about their funds in Salonika or was there true cause for concern about their wealth? Perhaps he explained this in his recent letter that she had slipped into her pocket.

"Where is Mamà?" Alexander asked as he sipped his dark coffee. "Litsa and I must leave for the hospital soon."

"She doesn't want to get out of bed. She is becoming more distraught every day. I'm at a loss to help her."

"May I go to see her?" asked Anna. "Perhaps I could be helpful. We can bring her back something from the pharmacy to calm her nerves."

"I would be ever so grateful. Please see if you can help her. Just knock on the door, and don't wait for her to answer."

"All right," said Anna as she got to her feet.

Anna sat at Maria's bedside, holding the woman's hand as her red-rimmed eyes stared out at her.

"Kiría Maria, don't you want to have breakfast with us? Or I could have a servant bring you a tray if you prefer?" Anna asked softly.

"I don't want to eat. I'm not hungry. The Germans are coming, Litsa. Everyone says it is true. They will come in the spring, and it is almost spring. The air-raid sirens. Those awful planes screaming at us. It is so hard to wait for the all clear. I can't bear it any longer…I can't." She began to sob.

Anna sat down on her bed and gathered her in her arms. "Hush, Kiría Maria. Don't despair. I think there is something that we can bring you from the pharmacy to help calm you and make you feel better."

"Please, I need to feel better. I need to take care of the household. I keep worrying and worrying. They say the Germans will take the leaders, the men like my Antonios and my Alexander. What will I do? Will you stay with me? If they find out about you, what shall we do? You're so strong, not like me. If you are gone, I will be all alone. I'm only a woman. My children Marco and Delia aren't here with me. Marco is in America, and Delia is in Leonidion. Leonidion is not so far away, but...."

"Kiría Maria, why would the Germans take away your husband and son?"

"I heard them talking," the older woman whispered.

"You heard who talking?" Anna took a deep breath. Was the woman also delusional, hearing voices? Then she was truly seriously ill.

"The men who meet at our house in the evening. They say the Germans often take away the leaders of the community, so they cannot organize the people against them. They talked about torture, making one man inform against the others. Torture! My Antonios! My Alexander!" She dissolved into tears as she clutched Anna's hand.

"Kiría Maria, everything will be fine." Anna stroked her cheek. Who knew what the future would bring? The German occupation.... But clearly this woman needed to be reassured to lift her from depression and anxiety. Anna would have a servant accompany her and Alexander to the pharmacy, and they'd have something compounded, probably some barbiturates.

"I need to feel better. Litsa, I'm so glad you came to stay with us. We have all become so fond of you, especially my Alexander. I can see how you make him smile, and he isn't so serious all the time. I'm tired," she sighed and closed her eyes.

Anna continued to sit at her bedside and retrieved the three letters from her pocket. She knew Alexander was probably growing impatient for her to go with him to the hospital. But she only intended to briefly skim the letters. She'd read them more slowly and savor them when she had time alone, later in the day.

There was a letter from her father, a letter from her oldest sister, Victoria, and a letter still in its sealed envelope addressed to her in Salonika. She looked at the return address.... Daniel.

She opened the envelope and withdrew the letter. He was apologizing for his "cowardly reprehensible behavior." He was sorry. He had not married. He continued to think of her and the love they shared. He was enlisting in the American Navy. He was sure America would soon be at war. He asked her to write to him.

Anna crumpled the letter in her hand and put it back in her pocket. It was too late for apologies now. She hoped he would be safe in the Navy, if America went to war. But he no longer had a place in her life. He belonged to her past. Her heart was filled with love for Alexander, despite the fact that neither a priest nor a rabbi would ever consent to marry them.

Sunday, April 6, 7:00 a.m.: Athens

The sirens began, sounding three times in half an hour. Never had the sirens sounded so frequently in such a short period of time. Anna and Kiría Maria had come out of their bedrooms and were standing in the hallway. The servants had joined them. They were waiting for the all-clear signal, but it didn't sound.

"There is no all clear. When is it coming!" Kiría Maria whispered with anguish.

Anna put her arms around the woman. "Calm yourself," Anna told her in a soothing voice.

"Where are Antonios and Alexander? Where are they?"

"I'm sure they will be with us in a moment. I think they are listening to the radio," Anna told her. And indeed, the two men were coming down the hall.

"War," announced Kìrios Antonios. "Germany has declared war on Greece and Yugoslavia."

"No, no," Kiría Maria said out loud, but it seemed she was talking to herself.

"Maria." Her husband patted her back. "Come, get ready for church. We must all pray for Greece."

Alexander's parents proceeded in front of them, as Anna and Alexander walked beside each other on the way to church.

"The barbiturates are helping her, aren't they?" Alexander commented.

"Somewhat. At least she is sleeping, and she doesn't seem to be too drowsy during the day. But with the war upon us, I don't know how well she'll manage."

The air-raid sirens sounded, and then ten minutes later the sky was filled with the German Stukas on their way to bomb Piraeus.

"So many planes," commented Anna, as she looked up at the sky. "Where are the planes to defend us?" It was a question that she knew had no answer.

They continued walking down the streets filled with the residents of Athens walking to church, while the Stukas protected by Messerschmitts screamed overhead.

"We should be safe in our city for now. The Germans are more interested in the ports," Alexander explained to her. "They want to destroy Piraeus. Destroying Athens isn't so important to them."

The Stukas were forming another black cloud over the Acropolis. Alexander's father held the hand of his wife, a rare instance of affection between them. Kiría Maria, her eyes wide as a frightened doe, clutched his arm.

"I don't know how much longer she can tolerate this. The drugs are helping somewhat, as you said. But just look at her," said Alexander as his eyes narrowed with concern. "I often wonder if the woman who bore me had such a fragile temperament. My mother, Suzanne, died in childbirth. My father married Maria within a few months. He needed a wife to take care of me and of him. I've known no other mother, and she's been a kind and good mother to me. She treated me no differently than the two children she gave birth to. I love her dearly, as a son loves his mother. But especially when I was young, I used to wonder about the woman whose blood flows through my veins. I keep a picture of her on my bedside table."

And then a Stuka screamed low over their heads, and as Anna bent down, Alexander sheltered her in his arms. "Why do they make that horrible noise?" Anna asked as Alexander released her, and she saw his father shaking his head at them with disapproval.

"Hitler thought if he outfitted his planes with sirens, they would be even more terrifying. And he was right, wasn't he?" Alexander smiled ruefully.

As bombs dropped and exploded in the distance, the ground shook beneath their feet.

"And what about my home? Do you think they are only trying to destroy Piraeus? Salonika is also a port," she spoke in a low voice.

"If anything has happened in Salonika, we'll know very soon. I promise we'll tell you whatever we hear." He paused, looking at Kiría Maria, who was weeping, as they continued on their way to church.

"Litsa, soon it will be Easter, and we will enjoy celebrating the holiday together. That's something for us to look forward to."

"I know Easter is a great celebration for you, but it's always a time of travail for Jews."

Anna sighed as they continued up the street to the church. Her family and other Jews usually lived in harmony with their Christian neighbors, except for the days after Easter. Jewish families remained in their houses with their shutters fastened. The sermons of Easter preached about the perfidy of the Jews and the killing of Christ. It was always a worrisome time for the Jews all over Greece. While she was celebrating Easter with Alexander and his family, her family would be inside their shuttered houses, trying not to provoke their Christian neighbors.

"Litsa, you are safe here. Don't worry. No one suspects you are not a Christian," Alexander explained in a low voice.

"But I am not a Christian. I can't forget my family, and I cannot forget who I am," Anna said tersely in a soft voice and walked away from him.

He caught up to her. "Litsa, please," he said in a whisper. "I know this masquerade is difficult for you. I understand."

"No, you don't understand. You can't understand." She turned away from him.

That evening, Dimetri Pagonis, his wife, Irini, and his parents were their guests for dinner. They had finished dessert and were assembled in the living room with after-dinner drinks. The lamps had been turned on, as approaching darkness filled the room, and the blackout shades were pulled down low over the windows.

"What a wonderful dinner," Kiría Paponis complimented her hostess. "One rarely sees such a bountiful feast anymore."

"My husband, Kìrios Antonios, knows how important it is for me to entertain like in the old days before all this talk of war."

"You are a good husband," Kìrios Pagonis told his old friend.

"There are ways to put food on the table. You know this as well as I do. If one has enough drachmas, anything is possible."

All during dinner, everyone talked of Germany's declaration of war. Anna was very conscious of Kiría Maria trying so hard to remain calm, as she nervously played with her food, rearranging it on her plate, scarcely taking a bite. The men talked about the Germans having come down through Bulgaria and now opening a second front. Everyone was convinced the Greek army would soon be overrun.

"But what about the British?" Anna asked.

"The British?" Dimetri sighed. "Didn't you hear that on March eighteenth there was a surprise attack in Epirus on the Parmythia Airdrome. The Germans completely wiped it out and destroyed the eighteen British planes, so that the meager force stationed in Greece has been reduced to almost nothing. The British won't be able to help us."

Anna looked down at her plate. She wanted to ask about Salonika. What did everyone think was going to happen there? Could the Greek army defend her home? What would it mean for the Jews of Salonika? Would they be subjected to the violence Alexander had witnessed in Germany? Would there be harsh restrictions imposed upon them, while she as a pretend Christian remained unaffected? But she kept her thoughts to herself. The Pagonis family were such good friends, but she had so often been reminded by both Alexander and his father to trust absolutely no one. And so she was silent. She ate little more than Kiría

Maria, for she had no appetite, as she was consumed with worry for her family in the north.

There was a pause in the war talk, when Kiría Maria spoke up. "No more talk of this, please, Alexander." She turned to her son. "Your father heard from Kìrios Nomikos. They are waiting to hear of a marriage proposal for their lovely daughter."

Alexander kept silent and took a swallow of his wine.

"Kiría Maria, perhaps we should discuss this at another time," said her husband.

"It has been months since we entertained them for luncheon. It's bad manners to keep them waiting so long for Alexander to express his interest in marriage to their daughter."

Alexander had begun to speak when the sound of air-raid sirens began filling the air.

And then there was silence. No one spoke. Everyone looked nervously about as the silence seemed deafening. And then there was the sound of planes in the distance, growing closer and closer.

Kiría Maria fled the dining room. Kìrios Antonios put down his napkin. "Excuse me." He followed his wife from the room.

Anna thought of her own family. Was anyone suffering from fear and anxiety as Kiría Maria? She envisioned her mother holding two grandchildren on her lap, as her father tried to calm the family with brave words. "God will protect us," he often said when the bombing had first begun in Salonika.

"We aren't observant," her brother Victor voiced his always contrary opinion.

"It doesn't matter, Victor. God will protect us."

The give and take between the members of her family, the good-natured arguments, the teasing, and the hugs and kisses. She missed them so much. If only she could get on the next train back to her home.

"Alexander, Litsa, Irini," Dimetri said, taking a swallow of his retsina, "let's go up to the rooftop and watch the planes. The Germans are going after Piraeus. We are safe for the moment."

"You young people do that," Dimetri's father told them, reaching for the bottle of retsina. "We folks with more sense will stay inside the house. But be careful up there," he warned them as the air-raid sirens went off again.

The two couples climbed up the stairs to the rooftop, as the building shook with the explosions in Piraeus. From the rooftop they could see the Acropolis, brightly lit by a huge luminescent moon.

"It's so bright tonight," commented Alexander. "A perfect night for bombing."

"Look at the sky." Anna pointed south to the horizon that seemed aflame. Blue, red, and green tracer lights plumed across the sky, followed by the thunder of antiaircraft guns.

Another air-raid siren split the air, as a thick cloud of screaming Stukas and Messerschmitts flew over the Acropolis. And then a few minutes later, the boom of explosions, the rooftop shook, and the sound of breaking window glass was loud in their ears.

"Come here," Alexander said softly, extending his hand to her.

Anna walked over to him. He made her feel safe, and she loved him. How could he possibly understand what it was like for her tonight, so worried about her family? But he tried; she knew he did.

Alexander stood behind her, his arms wrapped around her waist. "Look at the other rooftops," Alexander observed. "Everyone is watching." He waved to his neighbors, who waved back in return.

"I think you Athenians are all mad," Anna told them, as they watched searchlights illuminating the sky.

"Greeks do not cower in the face of aggression," Alexander explained. "Look at the Acropolis. Yes, the Nazi planes are flying over it, but it has stood for thousands of years. We look at it, Litsa, and we know we shall endure just as all the generations before us have endured. We think of the time before our independence, when we were subjugated by the Ottoman Empire. Our lives were so hard, but we endured. And years before that, the roof of the Parthenon was blown apart by Venetian explosives, but still it stands."

Anna watched the sky light up again and the pillars of the Parthenon turn pink with the reflected flares. Down below on the streets, British trucks filled with soldiers were rumbling past the houses.

"Litsa," he spoke in a gentle tone. "You are a woman, but be brave. Venetians, Ottomans, Italians, and now the Germans…We are strong, we are brave, we shall endure."

"We women are as brave as you fellows." Irini gave her husband a kiss on the cheek.

"Litsa and I should probably get to the hospital." Alexander started walking toward the stairway. "The wounded from Piraeus will be arriving."

"Yes, we should go." Anna knew the wounded would need them.

"Kìrios Alexander." A servant appeared on the rooftop. "You have had a phone call from the hospital asking that you and Despinis Litsa go there as soon as possible."

Anna and Alexander hurried down the stairs. Tonight they didn't walk through the streets to the hospital, but rode in his car. They careened up the street, sometimes riding on the sidewalk to make way for the trucks filled with soldiers. The trucks were speeding in the opposite direction, screeching to a halt as more soldiers climbed on board, until the trucks could hold no more.

Throughout the night, Alexander and Anna tended to the never-ending stream of wounded soldiers and civilians who were pouring into the hospital with horrific burns and mangled limbs. In the middle of the night, at approximately three in the morning, suddenly there was a huge explosion that shook the hospital and shattered many windows. But the wounded needed their attention, and it wasn't until the next morning that they learned that the *Clan Fraser*, a twelve-thousand-ton British munitions ship, had exploded in the harbor. The entire Piraeus waterfront was on fire.

In the days to come, terrible accounts were being reported from Piraeus, of hospital ships clearly marked with the sign of the Red Cross that were being bombed. The soldiers who tried to escape into the water were machine-gunned by the Germans. What kind of evil was this enemy that would soon occupy their country? On the hospital wards, it was incomprehensible to the staff that this enemy had disregarded the rules of war by purposefully attacking hospital ships.

"There are no rules of war for the Germans." Alexander spat out his words with bitterness. "They are beasts."

April 10, 1941

The sweet fragrance of spring flowers wafted on the air. What a contrast to the worried expressions on the faces of people that Anna and Alexander passed on the street.

Everyone was gathered in front of the newsstand. Alexander took her hand and they made their way to the display of newspapers.

"In only two days!" the crowd buzzed all around them. "It fell in two days!"

Anna caught her breath as she stared at the bold black headline: SALONIKA HAS FALLEN. Salonika had fallen to the Germans in two days. Her home…her family.

Alexander paid for a paper, tucked it under his arm, and led Anna away from the crowd.

CHAPTER 6

April 14, 1941

ALEXANDER LOOKED DOWN at his watch. Where was Litsa? She told him that she couldn't go home with him this afternoon because there was something more she had to do. She'd be home later. He didn't feel comfortable having her walk unaccompanied on the streets, with the German soldiers soon to be arriving. But she protested that she would be fine. Why hadn't she mentioned what was keeping her from going home at the usual time?

"Alexander." His father peered out from his study. "Litsa hasn't returned yet? You know that we must speak to her."

"Has there been any further word from Salonika? She's so anxious about her family."

"We can reassure Litsa that her family is physically unharmed. But you know we need to discuss with her the imminent fall of our city to the Nazis. We all have to prepare as much as possible for what might be coming. I spoke to your mother this morning, and she agreed to travel to Leonidion very soon, before our city falls to the Germans."

"It's the right decision, Patéra. Hopefully Leonidion won't be of much interest to the Germans. Mamà will be happy to be with Delia and her family. She certainly needs to leave before the Germans arrive." Alexander looked at his watch again. "Litsa should be home any moment now."

"I'll be waiting for you." Kìrios Giannopolous went back into his study and closed the door.

Alexander knew it as soon as Anna walked in the door. Something was wrong. He could sense both her agitation and her sadness. "What's wrong, Litsa?"

"How do you know?" She gave him a weak smile.

"You can't keep anything from me. I can feel it."

"Let's go out into the garden. I need to speak with you."

"Can it wait for a little while? My father is anxious to talk to you. He's been waiting for you to come home."

"No, please just a few minutes, Alexander, I must talk to you, first."

Alexander felt very uneasy as he followed her into the garden. She was still wearing her nurse's uniform, which was unusual for her, as if she had forgotten to take it off and change into her street clothes. Something was clearly upsetting her.

Anna stood beside a budding orange tree, threading her fingers in agitation, looking up at him, with tears in her eyes.

"Tell me. It can't be so bad." He took a step toward her, but she backed away. "Litsa?"

"I'm pregnant," she breathed out in a hushed tone.

"Pregnant?" Alexander was incredulous. "But I tried to be so careful." He never thought that this could happen if he were careful.

"I know you've tried to be careful, but it happened. I went to see Georges Samars, the hospital gynecologist. He said I can return as soon as tomorrow to have it taken care of. It's early of course, perhaps only two months, and he assured me it will be a simple procedure." She wiped away a tear from her eye.

He had never seen this strong woman with tears in her eyes. "An abortion?" he said the word she avoided.

"There really is no other choice, Alexander. I won't bring a bastard child into this world." She took a deep breath. "Well, I've said what I needed to say. You said your father is waiting to talk to me. It isn't Salonika, is it? My family?"

"No, your family is fine." Alexander said the words, but his thoughts were spinning. Pregnant? This woman whom he loved was carrying his child.

"At last," said Kìrios Antonios. "What took you so long? Well, never mind. Sit down the two of you."

Alexander didn't want to be here with his father, knowing what he was about to say. Everything had changed now, and all he could think about was this child.

"My family is safe?" she asked anxiously. "Alexander said my family is all right."

Alexander was amazed at the way Litsa was able to focus on this meeting with his father, as if they had not just had the conversation about their baby.

"Yes, my child, I received news from our sources that your family is unharmed. There was little violence when the Germans entered the city, as the Greek army didn't put up much resistance. Some factories, houses have been appropriated by the Germans. It would seem that your father's leather factory no longer belongs to your family. Your father is a clever man, and I'm sure he has made provisions for your family's well-being. I expect that when the Germans arrive here on our doorstep, the same will happen to us and my businesses. In preparation, I had a special room built into our new air-raid shelter dug in the garden. Alexander, when your mother, Suzanne, died, I kept her dowry, fine jewels, and all else she brought with her into our marriage. It's been untouched. Someday I hoped to present it to your bride. But since you haven't yet expressed an interest in marriage, I have hidden it along with other precious stones and your golden coins, Litsa. I've instructed the servants to be canning and preserving food, and this too will be hidden in case of an emergency. I have learned that when the Nazis first occupy a country, they don't enact severe restrictions, but they do take and confiscate anything and everything they desire. And then little by little that changes, until their horrible brutal nature is revealed."

Anna sat with her hands folded in her lap. Alexander knew she was relieved that her family was unharmed. He knew he should be paying attention to what his father had to say, but now there was a child to consider. Why was their country so stupidly dogmatic about marriage between two people of different faiths?

"Litsa, there is more that we've learned. The Nazis come into a town without barracks for their soldiers. They requisition any residences to which they take a fancy. I'm sure our villa will be requisitioned. And requisitioning means having Nazis living in our house. If we're fortunate, we won't be turned out into the streets, and sometimes they allow the servants to remain. I'm afraid this will come to pass for us in Athens, as it has in Salonika. If we are thrown out of our house, our emergency preparations, with our hidden supplies, will do us no good. Let us pray we are not thrown out of our own home."

"My parents, my family? Have their houses been taken?"

"I have no word about that yet. As for us.... do you realize the possible danger to you with a Nazi living here under our roof? Maria and I have come to care for you in these few short months as if you were our own daughter. I made a promise to your father to keep you safe from harm, and I intend to honor that promise." His father looked pointedly at Alexander.

"I know you promised my father. But the Nazis are coming, and you can only do your best. My father will know that you tried to protect me. I greatly appreciate everything you've done for me. But if the Nazis are in Salonika and soon in Athens, is there any reason for me to remain here? I've enough money to purchase a ticket back to my home." Anna looked sad and defeated. Alexander had never seen that side of her before.

"No, no, my child. You are safer pretending to be a Christian here in Athens. Your father had the foresight to send you here for that reason. I know Alexander told you about the terrible treatment of the German Jews that he witnessed when he lived in Berlin. Why wouldn't the Nazis behave in the same way toward Greek Jews? Perhaps not at first, but they are insidious in their persecutions. One cannot trust them. I have pledged to keep you safe, and so I will do everything in my power to keep you from harm. I was at first thinking that when the Nazis come to our house, you will have to learn to cross yourself and kiss the household icons as the other women do, making sure there's no doubt you are a Christian."

"Yes, of course I can do that," Anna sighed. Alexander could see the defeat in her shoulders.

"But there is more. Litsa, as an unmarried woman, do you understand the danger to you? When an arrogant Nazi comes to live in our house, I want to be able to keep you safe. But I don't know how I can do that. A man who has taken away our house, perhaps our valuables and anything else of worth, may set his sights on you. I can't offer you the protection that a husband or father could offer. You are an unmarried woman, and you would not be able to refuse a German's advances. Do you understand?"

Anna said nothing.

"Litsa, I can think of only one solution."

"A solution?" Anna frowned and looked tentatively at Alexander.

"I shall immediately begin looking for another place for you to stay. You'd have to be hidden, of course. There's no other way. And we must do this before the Third Reich enters Athens."

"Patéra," Alexander began.

"Be quiet, Alexander," Kìrios Antonios said sternly.

"Patéra, there is another option," Alexander countered.

"What other option?"

"Litsa and I could marry."

Anna turned to him, her eyes wide.

"She would have to be baptized in order for the priest to marry you." Kìrios Antonios frowned. "Litsa, would you be willing to become an Orthodox Christian?"

"Baptized? No, I can't do that. I won't do that." Anna got to her feet. "I will not go into hiding, and I can't imagine my father would want me to agree to such an absurd idea, having me baptized. I'll return to my family in Salonika. We shall face the Nazis together."

"Litsa, wait." Alexander took her hand. "Please just think about it and what it would mean."

"I'll think about it," Anna said tersely, pulling her hand away and starting to walk out of the room.

"There isn't much time," Kìrios Antonios called after her. "I fear the Germans will proceed down to Athens very soon. If you are to marry, it has to be before they arrive and take up residence in our home. I'll start looking into a place for you to hide, in someone's attic or cellar."

"But there are many Jews living out in the open here in Athens," Anna turned around and protested.

"That's true. But I tell you again, eventually being identified as a Jew will not be an enviable position under the Third Reich. Even with your false identity papers, as an unmarried woman you would have no protection. Your father asked for me to keep you safe, and I decided that you must hide. I did not think of marriage, and of course, a baptism. But perhaps my son knows better."

"I mean no disrespect, Kìrios Giannopolous. But surely when my father asked you to keep me safe, he had no wish for me to be baptized as an Orthodox Christian," Anna spoke sharply and walked out of the room.

"Patéra," Alexander got to his feet, "I'll talk to her and convince her. She just needs time."

"Time? There is no time. You really wish to be married to a woman with such a disrespectful nature?" His father scowled. "I'll start making inquiries about a suitable place for her to go into hiding."

"There is something more, Patéra. Litsa carries my child."

"She what!" Kìrios Antonios began to shout. "And you weren't going to suggest the honorable thing when I spoke to you earlier today?"

"I just learned of it."

"And what were you going to do about this baby? You have brought shame upon the honorable name of Giannopolous. How will I tell her father that you dishonored his daughter?"

"She's going to have a procedure at the hospital."

"My grandchild, murdered? What is the matter with you, Alexander? Is this how I raised you?"

"She will agree to marriage. At least, I think she'll agree to it," Alexander sighed.

"This conversation is over, my wayward son. Come to your senses and convince her to marry you, to save both herself and your child. Do not make me any more ashamed of you than I already am at this moment."

"I'll do my best to convince her. She's not an easy woman to convince of anything. But I do love her, and I want this child, I swear that to you."

Kìrios Antonios took the newspaper from his desk, placed his reading glasses on his nose, and ignored the presence of his son.

Anna stood at the window looking out at the Acropolis and the Parthenon. That magnificent structure had endured for centuries. There was permanence to the beautiful marble columns, a permanence that her life was lacking. Events were spinning out of control. Control, she always relished having control. She was not going to be hidden away, she wasn't! She wouldn't be prevented from tending the sick and the wounded. That was something she would never consider. And this life inside her…She placed her hands across her flat stomach. Would it really be so easy for her to have a procedure? Well, she'd have to. She had no other choices. She'd see the doctor tomorrow, and it would be done. She felt her eyes well up with tears.

Could she possibly consider being baptized… baptism as a Christian, giving up her faith, the faith of her ancestors? How could she consider such a thing? She thought of the stories told about the Jews of Spain, her ancestors. In 1492, Queen Isabella issued an edict that all Jews must either convert or leave Spain, upon pain of death. Her ancestors had left, eventually settling in Greece. But she knew many converted to Catholicism, only to continue practicing Judaism in secret.

"Anna." Alexander entered her room without knocking.

"You're not supposed to call me Anna. I am Litsa." She lifted her chin in defiance, as the tears slipped down her cheeks.

"For this afternoon as I beg you to become my wife, you are Anna," he said with tenderness.

"Why am I supposed to become a Christian in order for us to marry? Why can't you become a Jew! Well, have you not considered joining my faith?" She was angry and didn't want to hide her anger from him.

"I did consider it." He took her hands in his. "I went to see Rabbi Barzilai."

"You did?" Anna looked up at him. "Really, Alexander, you went to see the Rabbi?"

"When my father told me you'd have to go into hiding because you are unmarried, I thought there has to be another way. I saw the Rabbi and our priest."

Anna was overwhelmed with emotion. "Alexander." She caressed his cheek and brushed her fingertips against his soft dark mustache.

"I love you, Anna." He kissed her fingers. "I went to see the Rabbi to ask about marriage between us. Of course, he said I had to convert to Judaism in order for him to marry us. For my conversion, I would need to be circumcised. I agreed, but he advised against it. He said being a circumcised male when the Nazis arrive would not be a smart idea. And he said my becoming Jewish would only put both of us in harm's way. And then I went to see the priest. He agreed to baptize you in the morning and marry us in the afternoon. And now with a baby coming…. we must marry."

Anna let him take her in his arms. "I can't, Alexander. I can't."

"Anna Litsa, listen to me. When I was studying in Berlin, I had a good friend, Carl, who was Jewish. One night Carl told me about a Yiddish word *beshert*. It means fated soul mates. He said the first time he saw his Yetta, he knew they would marry. *Beshert*, Anna…you and I were meant to be together. From the first moment I saw you, I knew." He tightened his arms around her. "I know how hard it will be for you. I shouldn't say such things, but in your heart you will remain a Jew. Of that, I have no doubt. Just go through the motions, say the words, and keep both you and our child safe. I believe that God has brought us together, sweetheart, and he wants us to marry. It doesn't matter what we call our God or how we worship him. He is looking after us."

All week long, the household bustled with preparations for the hasty marriage and celebration afterward. The baptism would be held in secret, without anyone knowing that it occurred. But the marriage would be a wonderful event. The Giannopolous family, aunts, uncles, cousins, and friends all understood that it was prudent to marry before the city fell to the Huns. Anna and Alexander had also invited several of their coworkers, doctors and nurses who smiled and said, "We were just waiting for the two of you marry. It's no surprise to anyone who has eyes to see."

And everyone, both coworkers and family, were aware that there might not be any celebrations in the near future or perhaps for a long time to come. And so everyone was happy to participate in this joyous occasion. They understood that Litsa's family wouldn't be able to arrive in time for the wedding.

Kiría Maria would be leaving for her daughter's family in Leonidion a few days after the wedding, but for now she threw herself wholeheartedly into the wedding preparations. She instructed Anna in the steps of the wedding dances, so no one would suspect that Anna had never danced them before. Kiría Maria and her husband selected the caterer and the musicians. It was easy to find people to work on such short notice, for who else was throwing any festivities with the city on the brink of capture? Kìrios Antonios procured all the foods his wife requested without any hesitation. The cost didn't matter, and those on the black market were happy to oblige this man with such deep pockets for his son's marriage. The trunk with the dowry of Alexander's birth mother was opened, and her wedding dress was found, which had miraculously escaped the moths. It needed little alteration for Anna.

Anna knocked on the door of Kìrios Antonios' study.

"Come in," he said. "Litsa, Ariadne said you wanted to speak with me."

"Do you have any more word from Salonika?"

"The Germans have confiscated the radios from Jews, hoping to cut them off from the outside world. They have also taken over the Jewish hospitals. So it seems your father was wise when he predicted you couldn't be employed at the Salonikan hospitals." He paused and looked at her. "Is there something more, Litsa?"

"The letters you write to my father…. I'm asking that you please don't tell them about the marriage."

"The marriage and the baptism?"

"Yes, please don't tell him now."

"Litsa, you will have to tell him eventually."

"I know that. I don't want to add to the worries of my family in the midst of these troubled times."

Kìrios Antonios placed his hands into a steeple, seemingly deep in thought. "My child, you must tell me if you're having second thoughts. I will cancel the wedding, the baptism. You just have to tell me and it will be done."

"No, I will not go into hiding and stop caring for the sick and the wounded. I refuse to do that." She paused. "and I love your son very much. He is the finest man I've ever known. I want to be his wife."

The morning of her wedding and baptism, Anna looked at the wedding dress made of silk and lace, hanging on the door of her closet. Suzanne, Alexander's mother had been only eighteen years old when she married. Anna ran her hand over the soft material. Can a woman totally close the door to her entire life when she is united in marriage? Her family, her religion, her past all vanished. Was she to forget who she was?

This afternoon after her baptism as an Orthodox Christian, she would wear this lovely gown. There would be no rabbi to perform the marriage ceremony, no *chupa*, the tent-like covering held over the heads of the bride and groom. There would be no shouts of *mazal bueno* as Alexander's heel crushed the glass, which signified the destruction of the temple in Jerusalem. She'd been told that in a Greek ceremony there were no wedding vows exchanged between the bride and groom.

The Giannopolous family had given her beautiful jewels to wear today, but she had a sapphire necklace her mother had handed her the day she left Salonika. "I was saving it for your wedding day. But bring it with you to Athens. Maybe you'll find a nice Jewish man there, and if we can't attend the wedding, you will think of your mother and father, who love you, on that special day."

Anna arranged her hair in front of the mirror. Michaelitsa Giannopolous...that is who she would be from this day forward. Safety, survival, her new life as Alexander's wife: she must focus on all she was gaining, not on what she was losing.

That afternoon, the sky was a brilliant cloudless turquoise, and the air was filled with the scent of jasmine and orange blossoms. Anna stood at the base of the steps of the church and looked up at Alexander, so handsome in his fine linen suit, holding her beautiful floral bouquet. My beloved, her thoughts echoed with the Song of Solomon. I am my beloved's, and my beloved is mine. *Beshert*, Alexander had said. Yes, they were meant to be.

She smiled up at him, as she gathered her gown and slowly walked up the church steps. He was her future. He would be her husband. So many events had led her to this day. But it was her choice, her decision, which led her to walking up these steps and accepting the bridal bouquet from the man she loved.

Dimetri had been chosen as the *koumbaro*, who would act as the religious sponsor during the wedding ceremony. Dimetri exchanged rings between them three times. With their hands joined together, the *stephana*, the flowered crowns, were placed upon their heads. The crowns' attached ribbons were intertwined as their lives were to be intertwined hereafter. The *stephana* were interchanged on their heads three times. Anna and Alexander locked their eyes upon each other as they drank from the goblet of sanctified wine. Each was given a white lighted candle. Their right hands continued to be joined, as they walked in three circles around the matrimonial altar. The priest removed the *stephana* and prayed over the couple who were now man and wife. And so they were married, joined together according to the dictates of the Greek Orthodox Church. The packets of *koufeta*, the sugarcoated almonds wrapped in tulle, were ready for the guests to take with them. These almonds symbolized the sweetness and the hardness of life.

The wedding celebration was joyous, filled with dancing and feasting. Anna barely touched the lamb *yuvetsi*, with orzo and tomatoes covered with *kefalotyri* cheese. She momentarily thought of this morning. The sky had been gray with a thick covering of clouds, as she was baptized. It was a very difficult time for her, but this afternoon her marriage to Alexander filled her with happiness.

The chorus of "How Beautiful Is Our Bride" was sung by all the guests. The *kalamatiano* dance had begun, where the dancers formed a large moving circle. Alexander took her by the hand. "Come, Litsa, let us dance." Anna followed him into the circle and performed the simple steps she had learned from Kiría Maria.

Alexander and Anna left the celebration early. They had arranged to take a short two-day holiday from their hospital duties. Alexander had prepared Dimetri's apartment for their brief time away from everyone. They eagerly fell into each other's arms, loving and reveling in the joy they found in each other.

Each afternoon of their holiday, they took leisurely strolls on the broad avenues of Athens.

In front of a newspaper stand one afternoon, they learned Prime Minister Korizisi had committed suicide after he was asked to capitulate to the German Reich. "A man of honor, gone. Who knows what kind of man will take his place. Such turbulent times," Alexander sighed. "And once the Germans come, who knows what our government will be. But I'm sure it will be a government of collaborators and fifth columnists."

They were enjoying a stroll in the gardens by the palace, when a little boy darted out in front of them. "Pretty lady, can I sing 'Stupid Mussolini' for you? How stupid he was when he made the mistake of trying to defeat the Greeks. I only ask for one drachma, and my voice is so good. And you, sir, a shoeshine so fine you will see your reflection in the shoe leather, for one more drachma."

"Here are your drachmas, young fellow." Alexander tossed coins at the boy, who adroitly caught them in one hand, a big smile on his face. "We have no need for songs or shiny leather."

The young boy ran off as quickly as he had appeared.

Alexander and Anna continued their stroll. "Look, Alexander." Anna pointed at the nearby walls, where shreds of paper littered the street from posters that had been torn down the night before. "The anti-Hitler posters are gone."

"The collaborators are preparing our city for the takeover. We wouldn't want the Nazis' fine sensibilities to be offended by anti-Nazi posters," Alexander said with sarcasm.

"They will be coming soon. Won't they?" Anna gripped his hand more tightly.

"Yes, it's inevitable. But you are my wife now, and I shall keep you safe."

Later that evening, Alexander and Anna lay in bed. The remains of their dinner were still on the table. The window was open, the curtains fluttering in the breeze as the sounds of returning defeated Greek soldiers filtered up from the streets below.

"Litsa…" Alexander trailed his fingertips down her spine as she sat up in bed, hugging her knees tightly against herself. "You seem a million miles away."

"I was thinking about our wedding. I was thinking about my family."

"It was sad that they couldn't attend our wedding."

"You don't understand. They would never come to our wedding in a church. I asked your father not to tell them about our marriage. When I'm ready, I'll tell them."

"Litsa." He sat up beside her. "But you said you are the favorite of your father, surely…."

"It will break his heart when he learns what I have done," Anna interrupted him.

Alexander put his arms around her.

Alexander, she thought. How much did he know about the Jewish people, her people, who had suffered so much persecution throughout the ages? So many times, they were given the choice of conversion or death. When someone marries out of the faith, it's believed all the future generations will be lost to their people. She had a cousin in America who married outside of the faith. He didn't convert, but no one in the family acknowledges his existence or speaks to him.

She grieved for the pain she would someday bring to her family, when they learned what she'd done. But she didn't regret her marriage to this wonderful man. She had made this decision, which she knew would alter her life's path. But she had done it knowing the consequences that would surely ensue for marrying outside of her faith.

April 26, 1941

Antonios' connections brought more news from Salonika. Anti-Semitic newspapers began distribution. The offices of the Jewish Community Council were closed down. Eight of the Jewish Community Council members were arrested, and all community records were confiscated. Then more Jewish leaders were arrested.

Anna, Alexander, and his father were seated before the radio. They knew it would be any day now. Athens Radio was playing their national anthem. And then the announcer's voice: "You are listening to the voice of Greece. Greeks, stand firm, proud, dignified. The righteousness of our cause will be recognized. We did our duty honestly. Friends! Have Greece in your hearts, live inspired with the fire of her latest triumph and the glory of our army. Greece will live again and will be great, because she fought honestly for a just cause and for freedom. Brothers! Have courage and patience. Be stout-hearted. We will overcome these hardships. Greeks! With Greece in your minds, you must be proud and dignified. We have been an honest nation and brave soldiers."

"And so." Kìrios Antonios got up from his chair. "Tomorrow, it will be tomorrow. We must all stay inside the house."

"Our patients," Anna began to protest.

"We will remain inside tomorrow, and then we shall see."

CHAPTER 7

⸙

THAT NIGHT ALL was deathly silent. Not a soul ventured out into the streets. Alexander and Anna lay beside each other, their fingers entwined, no words between them. Neither of them slept as they both wished that either this night could last forever or that dawn would soon break and the waiting would be over.

They ate their breakfast in front of the radio and listened as the newscaster advised everyone to stay inside their houses. It was almost seven in the morning, when the thunder of German artillery boomed. One half hour later, there was another burst of guns. The radio played the "Hymn to Liberty."

At nine o'clock it began; the sound of the troops entering the city echoed through the streets, the roar of motorcycles, the squeal of tires, the rumble of tanks, the tread of heavy boots.

They were sitting in front of the radio, unread books and newspapers upon their laps.

An untouched backgammon board sat on the table between the two men.

Anna put down the pastry in her hand without taking a bite.

"Litsa, you must eat," Alexander urged her. "You hardly ate any breakfast this morning."

"I can't. I'm not hungry." Anna winced at the sound of trucks rattling through the streets outside of their villa.

"I think we have all lost our appetites." Kirios Antonios got to his feet. "We knew this day was coming, and now it is here. Alexander, get the binoculars, and join Litsa and me on the rooftop. We shall not hide in our house like frightened mice. Let us see what is happening. Come, my daughter, we shall watch the barbarian invasion of our city."

Anna followed her father-in-law up to the rooftop. Down below swarmed the motorcycles, the tanks, and the soldiers, who seemed to fill all the streets in every direction. They were everywhere, clogging the broad avenues of their city, goose-stepping troops to the north, to the south. Anna looked up toward the Acropolis. Was that actually possible… the blue and white flag of Greece gone. A large scarlet flag had taken its place.

"Alexander, may I have the binoculars?" She put them up to her eyes and gasped in dismay. "Look at the Acropolis! Our flag is gone. It's that horrible Nazi swastika flag."

"Give me the binoculars!" Kìrios Antonios grabbed them and after a few moments gave them to his son. "Sons of bitches! They have pulled down our flag and put up that filthy swastika, desecrating our sacred hill. Look." He pointed in another direction, toward the Hotel Grande Bretagne, the old Palace, and the Lycabettus Chapel. "More of those Nazi flags. We are occupied, but we are not conquered," he vowed.

They had seen enough. They went back downstairs to listen to the radio again. An announcement told them that people could now go out into the streets, but the Greek National Anthem no longer played. Next a German voice, belonging to a General Von List, announced to Adolph Hitler that he was speaking from *Deutsches* Athens.

"I need to go out for a while." Alexander got to his feet.

"Let me go with you." Anna had an uneasy feeling in the pit of her stomach.

"No, sweetheart, I won't be long. You must stay here with Patéra." He bent and kissed her. Then he hurried out the front door.

"Patéra, Alexander is meeting with the men who come to the house late at night, isn't he?"

"Yes," he sighed. "They will gather in the *kafeneío*, the coffeehouse, to discuss what must be done now that the Germans have arrived."

"But isn't that dangerous?"

"My daughter, it is dangerous, of course. Alexander's skills as a doctor will prevent him from actually putting himself in harm's way. He is needed to do other things than blow up bridges. All the men are dedicated to the freedom of Greece. They'll do anything and everything they can to defeat the enemy."

Anna held her breath. "I don't want him to put himself in danger. I'm afraid for him," she said softly.

"Litsa, with the Nazis in our city, we are all in danger. Alexander must do what a man must do to defend his country. It was a terribly hard decision for him not to join the Greek forces in Albania and fight for our country. I convinced him the wounded soldiers would need him here when they returned. And so the group of patriots began meeting at our house, making plans, plotting their course of action, and Alexander felt he was making an important contribution. He will take care. I know he will."

Anna folded her hands in her lap, the food she had eaten that day rising up in her throat. Courage, she told herself. I have courage. I have to have courage.

And so the Axis divided Greece into three occupation zones, between the Bulgarians, the Italians and the Germans. Germany was given Salonika, Athens and Crete.

Anna was slipping into her shoes, and Alexander tucked his shirt into his pants. "I will bring you to the hospital, and then I'll go to the University to give my lecture," he told her. "Father will go to his factory. The Nazis can strut around the streets of our city like they own them, but we'll continue on with our lives. I heard an incredible story about the flag on the Acropolis. Yesterday, the *Evzone*, the Greek guard on the Acropolis, was ordered by the Nazis to take down the Greek flag. He did it of course, as he had no choice. But he then wrapped himself in the flag and courageously jumped to his death off our sacred hilltop. If the Nazis think the Greeks will just lie back as they take over the city, they'll soon learn that we're a proud people who will not capitulate to these Nazi pigs."

"Oh, Alexander, the Greeks are proud, but the Nazis have the guns, the tanks."

"Their Nazi arrogance will be their downfall. This is our country, now and forever."

Anna sighed and reached for the doorknob.

"Wait, Litsa, your *stavro*. You must always wear your cross when you leave the house." He held out the crucifix in his fingers. "You can't forget, especially now. Come here and I'll fasten it for you."

He clasped the chain and bent to kiss her neck, when there was a thunderous beating on the front door. "Stay here," he told her.

"With your mother gone, I'm the mistress of the household. You can't hide me away." She walked out the bedroom door with him.

They heard the dog barking before the two young Nazis, tall and erect, came into view, Ariadne standing nervously at their side. "*Heil* Hitler!" they chorused, clicking their heels together and raising their arms in the Nazi salute.

Kìrios Antonios walked out of his bedroom and stood before the tall, blond young man who was poised with a pencil and notebook in hand, an arrogant scowl on his face.

"*Sprechen Sie Deutsch?*"

"Yes," said Kìrios Antonios, "we all speak German."

"*Gut!* We have come to your country to join you in friendship and to save you from British occupation." The German glanced down at his paper and then looked up again. He cleared his throat as he continued in an obviously rehearsed monotone. "We have lifted the curfew so that you may go out later in the evening." He stood there, seemingly expecting a friendly greeting. He was obviously perturbed when it was not forthcoming.

"Would you like some coffee, sir?" Anna spoke up.

"*Nein, nein.*" The young man appeared to be flustered. "I'm not supposed to have food or drink with you." He opened his notebook and looked at Anna. "You are the nurse, fräulein?" he asked as his eyes swept from her face, boldly lingering on her figure.

How could he know that she was a nurse? And then Anna remembered hearing about the fifth columnists among the Greek people, those who admired the Nazis and who would gladly sell their souls for a drachma. They were informing on their own people.

"Who is the doctor?" he continued.

"I am the doctor, and this woman is my wife," said Alexander.

"Your wife? It says right here in my report she is an unmarried woman, Michaelitsa Kalodosis, a nurse."

"Your information is not up-to-date. She is Kiría Michaelitsa Giannopolous, my wife."

"Have you any Jews living here?" He paused. "All the Jews are wealthy you know, and this household looks quite prosperous."

"We are a devout Greek Orthodox Christian family. Our servants are also Christian," Kìrios Antonios pronounced in an authoritative tone.

The tall blond man motioned to the other soldier. "Helmut, walk through each room of this house with the dog. The dog has been trained to smell Jews. Any Jews that we find will have to find lodgings elsewhere. Helmut, go. I am waiting."

The other soldier hurried off with the large, tightly leashed German shepherd straining in front of him.

"So back to your so-called wife. We were warned you Greeks might resort to trickery. You cannot be trusted. You have proof of marriage?" He frowned at them.

"We have a marriage certificate and a framed wedding photograph. I'll get them for you," Alexander offered.

"Later, later, there's no time for that. I have many houses to visit this morning. We're in a hurry. So," he turned to Kìrios Antonios, "you are the business man?"

"Yes, I'm in the leather business and also olive oil, the finest in the country. My olive groves are a short drive outside the city on a farm that has been in my family for generations," Kìrios Giannopolous said with pride, staring defiantly at the young soldier.

"Anyone else besides the servants in the house, since obviously my information is not as timely as it should have been." He looked down at his book again. "Where is your wife?"

"She has gone to visit our daughter and her family."

"Hmph." The German made a notation in his notebook.

"Servants, how many servants and how many beds in this house?"

No one said a word.

"Are you deaf the three of you!" the soldier shouted.

The other soldier returned, writing in his notebook, his dog at his side. "Very suitable," he pronounced and then began looking at the artwork on the walls, the statuary, the rugs on the floors, making notes in his book.

"Alexander," Anna whispered in Greek with shocked horror, "he's making notations of our furniture, our rugs, our paintings."

"Sir," Alexander spoke up. "My wife and I are needed at the hospital."

"Go, go," the soldier dismissed them. "The dog has found no Jews, and we have all the information that we need for now."

The streets were filled with tanks, motorcycles, and soldiers. As they passed the Grand Bretagne Hotel and the Palace, large scarlet swastika flags fluttered in the morning's gentle breeze. They displaced the blue and white Greek flags that had once waved so proudly. The scent of spring floral blossoms mingled with the stench of motorcycle and tank exhaust fumes.

As soon as Anna and Alexander reached the steps of the hospital, it was obvious that something was very wrong. Large black cars and motorcycles were parked in front of the main entrance.

"What are those damned Nazis doing here?" Alexander muttered under his breath and swore a Greek oath. "Did they come to make war on the sick? You stay at my side, Litsa. You mustn't be alone."

They walked up the front steps and were stopped at the front door by a soldier with a rifle, barring their way.

"No entry."

"What do you mean no entry! We are a doctor and a nurse, and this is our hospital!" Alexander shouted into his face.

Anna pulled on Alexander's arm, hoping to silence his belligerent tone.

"Names?" The soldier looked down at a piece of paper on a clipboard.

"Alexander and Michaelitsa Giannopolous."

"Yes, you are to proceed on the left to the door of the office over there. Wait until your names are called. Heil Hitler!" He saluted and clicked his heels together.

As Alexander and Anna walked into the office, they saw Despinis Papadakis, the secretary to Dr. Contos, the Chief of the Hospital, seated behind her desk. She smiled up at them. "A great day, isn't it? The Germans will bring us order and civilization."

"What did you say?" Alexander scowled at her. "The Nazis are bringing us civilization?"

"I am now the secretary to Herr Von Steuben, the new head of the hospital. Be wise, Dr. Giannopolous. Embrace the Nazis, and they will be good to you."

Anna tightly clutched at her husband's arm. "Control yourself. Despinis Papadakis is but a fool," she whispered. "And once we are inside the office, please don't argue with anyone who has a gun. I don't wish to be a widow, when I am barely a bride."

Despinis Papadakis led them inside to the office of the hospital chief. Dr. Contos was sitting at his desk, his eyes downcast, not greeting Alexander and Anna in his usually effusive manner. Standing near the window was a tall German officer with thin blond hair, in an impeccably tailored gray-green uniform, with broad epaulets on his shoulders. The secretary handed him two folders.

He smiled broadly at Anna. "Ah, Fraulein Papadakis, you have done well," he told the secretary. "As you promised, surely she is one of the most lovely fräuleins I have seen in Greece. And you said she speaks German, and she will be delighted, of course, to be my private guide to the Acropolis."

"No, no, Herr Von Steuben. That is Fraulein Lekas, who will arrive later today. I promise you will be quite pleased with her. This is the nurse,

Frau Giannopolous, and her husband the doctor. See I've brought you their files."

"You two are married?" He frowned at them.

"May I introduce my wife, Kiría Michaelitsa Giannopolous," Alexander said with measured politeness.

The German officer frowned again and opened the files. "*Ja, ja,* so you are the ones that Dr. Contos told me about: the best doctor, the best nurse. Today you shall both go up to the wards. Our wounded soldiers will be arriving at any moment. See to it that you treat them with the best of your abilities. We are reorganizing the hospital to make it run more efficiently for the good of the Reichstag."

"I'm due at the University to give a lecture this morning," said Alexander.

"Did I not just say you will be going up to the wards? Are you hard of hearing, Doctor!" he shouted, as his face flushed red with anger. "Do you understand you will no longer be giving so-called "lectures" at the University?

Well, was Dr. Contos incorrect when he told me of your skills and intellect?"

"Yes, I understand," Alexander said each word very slowly.

"You both will be receiving notice of your new duties within a few hours. But one more question, Doctor. It would save me a great deal of time and trouble if you could identify any Jews among the doctors and nurses in the hospital."

"I don't know if someone is a Christian or a Jew. I only know if they take good care of the patients. Why don't you just ask who is a Jew or a Christian?" Alexander proposed.

"Because they are liars, Doctor. They try to hide who they are and must be ferreted out with any means possible. And you, Frau Giannopolous? Could you help us identify the Jews? We will not harm them, of course. They just need to be dismissed. A Jew cannot care for a member of the Wehrmacht. It is verboten. We are bringing a new world order to your country and eventually to the world. We cannot have Jews in such positions. So, Frau Giannopolous, will you help make my job easier?"

"Everyone on the staff is a Greek. That's all I know," Anna said firmly, trying not to show her growing fear. Her hands fisted at her sides, as she tried to keep a nonchalant expression on her face.

"So you two are playing stupid like your chief officer. We will find out what we need to know without your help. I was told, Dr. Giannopolous, you are a gifted surgeon. You will care for our wounded soldiers and make them whole again. Choose the best assistants for your operations."

"My wife is a superb operating- room nurse. She had specialized training in America."

"Very well and make sure our soldiers do not die, Doctor," he sneered. "You are dismissed. You may go up to the wards. Heil Hitler!" He saluted.

As soon as they walked out the door of the secretary's office into the corridor, they were met with a scene of total chaos. Patients in their pajamas crowded the halls, clutching their Greek army uniforms, as they hobbled down the hallway. Looks of total panic were spread across their faces.

"What's going on here?" Alexander demanded of a nearby German soldier, whose rifle was trained on the patients.

"They are being evacuated to make room for Germans," he said matter-of-factly. "They're moving too slowly." He prodded his rifle into the back of a man who was hobbling with a wooden crutch under his arm. "Faster! Faster!"

"They are ill! They are being evacuated to where?" Alexander raised his voice, despite Anna clutching at his arm.

"To where? We don't care where they go. They can go anywhere. They need to leave immediately, before the wounded, brave soldiers of the Third Reich arrive."

Anna and Alexander ran up the stairs to the ward for the most seriously ill. The beds were empty. The ward smelled strongly of antiseptic, as several nurses were hurriedly smoothing new sheets on the beds.

"Where are the patients from this ward?" Alexander asked.

"We don't know where they took them, Doctor," one older nurse sobbed. "Some of them screamed in pain, as they were thrown out of their beds. We were ordered to disinfect everything to prepare for new patients. If they find a speck of dirt, we will suffer the consequences."

As they turned to leave the room, Antoinette Ferrara, the Italian nurse, was hurrying inside, her arms piled with blankets. "We have to get everything ready for our new patients," she said breathlessly. "How terrible for our Greek patients, but at least the Nazis are getting rid of the Jewish doctors and nurses. I never felt comfortable working with them."

Anna and Alexander hurried down the hallway searching for anyone who might know where the patients had been taken.

Dr. Massouda, a slight older man with gray hair and a stethoscope around his neck, was talking to a nurse. He beckoned for Anna and Alexander to join them.

"Where are our patients?" Alexander asked with anguish in his voice.

"We have heard they have been piled into the courtyard of the churches or on public squares or in barns or just out into the streets. I'll be going to help them as soon as I can steal some supplies and medicines from under the eyes of the Nazis. Nurse Abarretz will try to pilfer some bandages."

"Litsa and I will go with you," Alexander announced.

"No, no, Alexander, you must stay. You don't have a choice. None of us has a choice. The wounded Germans will be here very soon. Nurse Abarretz and I along with several other doctors and nurses are being dismissed because we are Jews. Early this morning when we were leaving our shift, before they started emptying the hospital of patients, they announced all doctors and nurses must remain at the hospital to care for the German wounded. This did not apply to Jews, who must leave and not step foot in a German hospital again, upon pain of execution."

"Doctor Giannopolous," a soldier approached them, "the wounded are arriving and you are needed immediately."

"I'm coming," Alexander told him, and the soldier turned and walked away.

Alexander embraced Dr. Massouda. "If there is anything I can do for you, get in touch with me, David."

Alexander and Anna walked away toward the stairwell, when he pulled her aside. "Don't worry," he told her in a low tone. "No one knows who you are. I promise you are safe."

"Alexander, I never believed such things could happen here. I thought you were being an alarmist, but you were right. They will come for the Jews here in Athens, just as you predicted. They'll find me."

"Your papers are impeccable, and you're my wife. I promise your identity is safe."

Safe, thought Anna, perhaps for now. But in the future, wouldn't she be identified as Anna Carasso, a Jewish woman?

Within an hour, all the remaining Greek patients had been thrown out of their beds. The empty beds were quickly filled with Nazi patients. Anna and Alexander agreed that when their shift was over, they would seek out their former patients, wherever they were, and try to help them. Anna was thankful she was going to be a nurse in the operating suite, as the thought of smiling and soothing the pain of the Germans was not an idea she relished, in spite of her oath to heal the sick.

They were on their way home for a quick meal, before going to seek out and tend to their former patients.

"We need to pick up some sugar for Ariadne," Anna reminded him.

The streets were clogged with German soldiers, and making the way in their car was very slow and difficult. When at last they pulled in front of the store, the owner, Kìrios Laskaris, was posting a closed sign on his door.

"So early?" Alexander greeted the proprietor, as he helped Anna out of the car.

"Come inside, come inside," the portly man entreated them. "Look." He pointed to the bare shelves of his store. "Just look at this, Doctor."

"You did very good business today," Alexander commented. "We just need some sugar. We'll wait while you get some from your backroom."

"You don't understand what happened today," the storekeeper sighed. "I have nothing in the backroom. For all the storekeepers on this street, it's the same. There are seventy-five thousand German soldiers in our city. Each of the soldiers was issued one hundred deutsche marks. They were told to buy anything they wanted. In my store, I sold the last tin of meat, just now. I have nothing else left. But some stores emptied hours after opening. My friend Georges, down the street, who sells fine furniture and rugs, carries very expensive merchandise. He told me an incredible tale. A young Nazi soldier walked in and took a fancy to one of Georges' most expensive rugs. The soldier didn't have enough money to make the purchase. He told Georges to hold on to this fine rug for two hours, not to sell it to anyone else, because he was going to German headquarters where they would print him as much money as he wanted!"

"My God! What are these barbarians trying to do to our country!" Alexander said in outrage.

"I don't understand," Anna was puzzled. "Isn't it good for businesses to sell so much?"

"Printing German money like that means that our currency, our drachmas, will soon be worthless," Alexander explained.

"Yes, Doctor, the merchants will all be ruined. The soldiers are emptying our shelves of anything they want and shipping it to their homes in Germany. They behave as spoiled children let loose in a candy shop, where they stuff their mouths and their pockets until overflowing. Next week, new shipments will come in, and I venture to guess it will be the same."

At first they sat in silence as Alexander drove toward their home. "Litsa, Litsa," he finally said. "These Germans are plundering our country with their first footsteps on our soil. They're not human, throwing patients out of their beds. They are beasts."

"Do you think they will take our house and throw us out like the Greek soldiers from the hospital?" Anna felt guilty thinking of their beautiful house, instead of her suffering patients. But she couldn't forget this morning, when the Nazis had noted every last bit of furniture. At least she was in good health, not like the poor Greek soldiers. "And the servants? What will become of them?"

"I don't know if they'll throw us out. And the servants? We will provide for them. It is our obligation to them after so many years in our household. If we weren't ordered to stay at the hospital, I would take us to the farm outside of Athens. Once the weather improved, I had intended to take you there, to see our land, our animals, the olive trees, and the olive-oil presses. The family of Nasos Galanis and his wife, Fenia, have worked there for us for generations. In the spring and summer months, we often go there for a weekend. My mother is particularly fond of the simple life on the farm. Don't worry, my wife. We have friends in Athens who will take us in, if need be." He parked the car in front of the villa and put his arms around her, pulling her close. "We are together and you will be fine."

"But what about that veiled threat to you about the soldiers not dying on the operating table?"

"Even the Nazis cannot be that stupid, to kill the doctor who they've identified as the best surgeon."

The next morning, Anna had awoken early. She sat up in bed, looking down at the sleeping form of her husband, the black tousled hair, the dark mustache, the thin white scar above his eyebrow. It was good to be his wife, to have someone to belong to, to have someone who loved her. And there was the child they were going to bring into the world. She had to remember all she possessed that was good, in the midst of so much uncertainty, in the midst of so much evil that had come into her country.

Her thoughts turned to Salonika and her family. Had their house been confiscated? And what of her cousins, who had darted in and out of her house with her when she was a child? The girls had grown to be women, who had married early, to someone in the Jewish community. The boys, who had jested with her, had either become merchants like their fathers or had sought out professional educations as teachers and lawyers. What had happened to everyone since the Nazis had taken over their city?

Anna began to pull off the covers, ready to face more German indignities today. What other terrible changes were the Germans going to enact on the streets and at the hospital?

"And where are you going?" Alexander grinned and pulled her back into their warm bed.

They were seated around the breakfast table, when they heard the screech of a car pulling up and then the thunder of fists beating against the front door.

"And so it has begun." Kìrios Antonios grimaced and took a swallow of dark coffee.

Ariadne hurried down the hallway, escorting an older German man with graying brown hair, a monocle in his light blue eye, and his gray-green uniform resplendent with decorations. Behind him walked a younger soldier.

"Heil Hitler," he saluted them. "*Guten Morgen*, I am Herr Rupert Von Hoffberg." His tone was brisk. He pulled out a small notebook from his pocket. "You are the Giannopolous family. You are the doctor and the nurse. And you are the businessman. Is my information correct?"

Kìrios Antonios responded, "Yes."

"It has been reported that your house is quite suitable. I shall see this for myself. Do not get up. I will go through your house room by room." He strutted out of the dining room leaving the younger man standing at attention in the doorway.

"He's going to take our house," Anna murmured in Greek.

"It would seem so," Alexander agreed. "Bastards," he mumbled in Greek beneath his breath.

"Shhh," Anna cautioned him.

The three of them sat waiting, listening to the echo of Herr Von Hoffberg's footsteps thundering throughout the house.

The young German man stood with his arms crossed against his chest, staring straight ahead, seemingly oblivious to them.

Herr Von Hoffberg was taking quite a long time going through the house. Anna wondered if they'd be given time to collect important possessions before they were ordered out onto the street.

"Very good," Herr Von Hoffberg's loud voice preceded him down the hallway. "Kruger." He entered the dining room and addressed the young soldier. "Go out to the car until I send for you."

"Heil Hitler!" The young man clicked his heels together and left the room.

"So." The older German pulled out a chair and seated himself, reaching for a piece of bread off of their breakfast table. "You are a very fortunate family. We've made suitable plans for you and your house."

No one spoke a word, as he spread quince jam across his bread and took a bite.

"I am a man of fine sensibilities. Many of my fellow officers have taken up residence in your better-than-average hotels. I am a man who appreciates a good home with beautiful furnishings. We will be establishing a clinic for our German officers and soldiers, here in your home, which the two of you will staff. We, Germans, seek friendship with you. We bear you no animosity. If the British hadn't occupied your country, it wouldn't be necessary for us to have come and liberated you Greeks."

What rot, thought Anna.

"This house is large enough so that you all may continue to live here at my pleasure. In the future of course, I may choose to have you live elsewhere. But I understand you are educated people, and you could be appropriate company for me. Before I joined in the service of *Mein Führer*, I was an engineer.

"So the doctor and the nurse will see patients, three days each week. The other days you will perform operations at the hospital. Your duties,

Doctor, as a lecturer at the University will no longer be necessary. That room in the front of your house will be used as a place for waiting. It does not need to be a place of beauty, so all furnishings, save for chairs, will be sent back to my home in Germany. My wife Bertha, will greatly appreciate your paintings and rugs."

And then he droned on matter-of-factly about removing Kìrios Antonios from his bedroom and his office and sending him to a smaller room in the back of the house. The officer would personally be taking over those rooms. Anna and Alexander could remain in their bedroom, but the rugs and the paintings on the walls would be sent back to Germany. All rooms that Herr Von Hoffberg would inhabit could keep their furnishings, but all others would be stripped bare, except for minimal necessities.

"And the servants? I haven't decided what to do with them." He snapped his fingers toward Ariadne, who had been patiently waiting in the shadows. Ariadne immediately appeared at his side. "More bread, cheese," he told her in German.

Ariadne's dark eyes grew wide in panic. Anna translated his request into French, a language of which Ariadne had some knowledge. Anna remembered not to speak Greek lest her accent from Salonika made her suspect. As Ariadne dashed out of the room, Anna spoke to the German officer. "She's a wonderful servant. Very quick and very smart. I will teach her German, and I promise she will learn very quickly. Her husband, Mattheo, speaks German, and he's provided meticulous attention to my father-in-law for many years."

"Well, it would only be proper for the wife in the household to be cooking and cleaning, and there would be no need for servants. But you are the nurse, so I shall excuse you from those duties. These two servants, and only these two, may remain for the moment. I saw their small room. I could place a few soldiers in there, but I prefer not to be surrounded by soldiers from the lower classes. It is my right, as an instrument of the conquering army, to confiscate anything I want in the name of the Führer. Yes, this is the perfect house for me, beautiful surroundings and no children. I despise children."

CHAPTER 8

"I AM NOT going to Leonidion!" Anna spat out in a low voice, as they dressed for their day at the hospital. "I'm staying in Athens."

"You can't have the baby and stay here. I decided you need to leave Athens. That is clear. My family will take good care of you. I need you and the baby to be safe," he tried to sound soothing, as he pulled up his suspenders.

"You will not decide what I will or will not do!" she raised her voice.

"I most certainly will. I am your husband."

"Don't ever say such a stupid thing to me!" She stood in front of the mirror and vigorously brushed her hair. "I never should have married a Greek man," she muttered under her breath.

"What did you say!" He came toward her.

"You heard me!" She turned back toward him.

"And perhaps I should never have married a Greek woman who was educated by foreigners and no longer understands the proper subservient position of a wife!"

They glared at each other and then burst into laughter.

"Oh, Litsa, you are such a stubborn woman." Alexander took her in his arms. "I love you more each day. We'll come up with a plan that will keep you safe. You and I will make the decision together. It's months until you have this baby. We do have friends here in Athens who will take us in. But for now, let's hurry up and grab something in the kitchen. For all we know, Herr Von Hoffberg is seated at our breakfast table in preparation for his move into our home. I can't stomach the thought of eating with him. Though I'm sure we will all get used to it."

"We don't have any choice, Alexander." She followed him to the kitchen, where they both grabbed a slice of bread and a hunk of cheese.

"Dr. Alexander." Ariadne approached him. "May I have a word with you?"

"Of course." Alexander put down his bread. "Litsa, I'll meet you at the car."

Anna took her purse and walked outside to wait for Alexander. The curbside where they had parked their car last night was now occupied by a big black Mercedes brandishing red-and-black swastika flags on the car's bumpers. Herr Kruger stood, whistling a German song as he polished the hood.

"Herr Kruger, where is our car?" Anna asked him.

"*Nein, nein.*" The young soldier shook his head at her. "That car no longer belongs to you. It's the property of the Wehrmacht."

"You're joking!" Anna laughed.

"I do not joke, Frau Giannopolous. All cars and donkeys, all means of transportation belong to the Führer. These are orders from the high command. I understand some buses will remain on the streets."

Herr Von Hoffberg and Alexander approached the car, deep in conversation.

"My wife and I have a surgery scheduled for this morning. If we have to walk, we will be late." Alexander was speaking in a moderate tone.

"It's a beautiful spring day. You should have gotten out of bed earlier, Doctor." The man turned sharply on his heels.

"Let's go." Alexander started walking briskly down the street with Anna at his side.

"Kruger said they've also taken the donkeys. How are people supposed to live without any means of transportation?" Anna asked with anguish.

"That's the point. Maybe they are hoping we will all just die."

That day was long with several operations, and then their attempts to steal and hide supplies to be handed off to people, who would deliver them to the wounded Greek soldiers. Dr. Massouda was working tirelessly to keep the soldiers alive. Many of those seriously wounded had died that first night away from the hospital. The screams of agony from those who no longer had morphine could be heard far from the church courtyard and the barns, where they had been dumped on the ground.

It wasn't easy to hide the supplies under Alexander's and Anna's clothing and make the surreptitious transfer. They knew that time was not on their side. They were well aware the German fascination with order would soon have the Nazis making lists of supplies, and they would realize many things were unaccounted for. That would be the end of their ability to pilfer anything from the supply cabinet. They realized that eventually there would be locks and keys on everything.

It was the third day of the Nazi occupation. Alexander, his father, and Anna were seated around the breakfast table with Herr Von Hoffberg. Ariadne was pouring coffee into their cups.

"*Milch?*" the German asked for milk.

Anna took a deep breath, hoping Ariadne understood him.

"There was no milk available yesterday," Mattheo, her husband, spoke up.

"I need milk for my coffee. See that you have some for me tomorrow morning." Herr Hoffberg frowned.

"The stores don't have much of anything," Mattheo tried to explain.

"Tell Kruger. He will take your wife to where milk is available. Who heard of such a thing? No milk for my coffee." He put down his coffee cup.

"Well, we have much to discuss this morning." The German withdrew a sheet of paper from his inside pocket. "I expect you, Herr Giannopolous, a man who has experience in the ways of the world, to understand the position of the Third Reich as an occupying force in your county and to understand why we have had to take these new measures for the greater good."

Kìrios Antonios put down his fork and straightened his shoulders. "New measures?"

"We have tried to be friends with you Greeks. We came here with the open arms of friendship, and you are hostile and insolent with your nasty attitudes. Therefore, we've had no choice. We have drawn up a verboten list that will appear in your newspapers today. As the three of us are such good friends, I wanted to tell you about this myself."

He inserted his monocle and peered down at the paper in his hands. "You may not possess any firearms. But I assume you don't have any, do you?"

"Why would we possess firearms?" Alexander nonchalantly put a black olive in his mouth. "We are a peaceful family."

"*Gut,*" the German commented and looked back down at his sheet of paper. "Your radio must be tuned to the Nazi station. It is verboten to listen to foreign radio broadcasts. You will not praise any British war efforts. You will turn over to the proper authorities any cars, any bicycles.

"If these rules are not obeyed, you will be arrested or executed. So is that understood?" He nodded at them and took a slice of bread from the plate on the table.

"Yes," everyone answered in a quiet chorus.

"I just don't understand you Greeks. You have heard of course that your General Tsolakoglou wisely signed the armistice treaty with the Third Reich. So everything should have proceeded smoothly. But, no, your blasted church interfered."

"We haven't heard of this. What happened?" Kìrios Antonios asked.

"Your insolent Archbishop Chrysanthos had the nerve to refuse the German Reich. He would not administer the oath of office to the new government! Well, he's no longer the Archbishop of your people. He has been detained and a new Archbishop has been summoned to properly administer the oath of office. You see, your people are making life hard for yourselves, when it really isn't necessary.

"Today is the first day of your new German clinic. I hope everything will go smoothly."

"We took supplies from the hospital, but we'll need more pharmaceuticals. The local pharmacies have little on their shelves," Alexander told him.

"Give me a list, and I shall get what you need." Herr Hoffberg pursed his lips in disdain. "It was thought you and your wife would be able to function very well without our help. But I should have realized you are incapable of functioning without our assistance. I do hope our trust in your competence was not misplaced."

He turned his attention back to Kìrios Antonios. "Now, I understand you have a large leather factory and an olive-oil plant. This is true?"

"Yes."

"Today is a good day for you to show me your properties."

"It's a bit of a drive from here, on the other side of town."

"Hans will drive us. And by the way, I noticed a fine vegetable garden this morning. Very clever of you. I will expect fresh vegetables with my dinner each evening. As I am such a generous fellow, you may have some on occasion, but never the servants. They will have to make due with whatever they can purchase with their ration cards.

"Well, now on to the next matter," the German sighed with exasperation as he slathered jam on his bread. "There are several things that must be done to your home in order to purify it according to our standards; otherwise I cannot live here."

"Purify it?" Anna spoke up, although she felt it was probably unwise.

"Your music, your books." Herr Von Hoffberg frowned at her. "It will be very enjoyable for us to sit in the evening listening to your record player, as it plays Strauss waltzes, "Tales from the Vienna Woods." But I need to know if you possess any Mendelssohn, any Mahler? I'll remove such terrible music, of course. Then we shall go through your library in search of books written by Jews, by communists and other degenerates. If you have many, we shall enjoy a lovely bonfire, as we rid your house of such filth."

Anna felt Alexander stiffen beside her. "Herr Von Hoffberg, may I accompany you to the library when you make your selections?" Anna offered. She knew how strongly her husband felt about book burnings, and she worried about him being able to contain his anger.

"Of course, Frau Giannopolous, if you wish, you may accompany me to my new library. Herr Giannopolous, we shall go to your factories this afternoon." He got to his feet.

Anna put down her napkin and followed the German officer into the library.

"First, the music. Well, show me the phonograph recordings," he said impatiently.

"They're here." Anna stood next to the record jackets stacked beside the record player.

"Mendelssohn." He pulled out several recordings. "Mahler, such terrible music." He selected three more records. He then pulled each record from their jackets, threw them on the floor, and crushed them with his heel. "Make sure the servants clean up this garbage," he instructed Anna.

"Now for the books." He pulled several sheets of paper from his pocket. "There are so many books not suitable for a library. I must consult my list, which is several pages long. I think we shall begin this morning, but I'll have Hans come back later and make sure we don't miss any filth." He opened the glass doors to the bookshelves and started walking back and forth perusing the shelves, pulling out books, and throwing them on the floor.

Anna looked down at the spines of the discarded books. *The Jungle* by Upton Sinclair, books by Ernest Hemingway, *The Call of the Wild* by Jack London, *An American Tragedy* by Theodore Dreiser. "Why the *American Tragedy*?" She couldn't stop from asking. It was one of her favorite books.

"You have read it?" He made a tsking sound. "Your husband should have forbid you to read of low-life love affairs. Once I rid your shelves of such books, he will no longer have to worry about such ideas in the head of his wife."

Anna looked down at the last book he had thrown on to the growing pile. "A book by Helen Keller? Her story is an inspiration to us all," she protested.

"She was a deaf mute, obviously a subhuman, and she became a socialist," Herr Von Hoffberg announced.

Anna watched as the bookshelves were purged of *All Quiet on the Western Front* and *Metamorphosis* by Franz Kafka. And then she could no longer look down at the book spines. She didn't want to see any more. Instead, she stood very still, keeping her eyes down, with a pleasant artificial smile pasted on her lips. There were so many books being pulled off the shelves, so much knowledge deemed unacceptable by these barbarians.

Alexander took a cigarette out of his silver case and lit it. "David Massouda stopped by this morning." Alexander leaned back in his chair.

"Is he all right?" Anna asked.

"He is fine. But, of course, he no longer has a source of income. He wants to leave Greece with his wife and children. He has family in Izmir, in Turkey, and he wanted my advice."

"Is it easy to travel to Turkey?"

"Patéra was at home, and he explained to David what he must do. It certainly can be done, and my father will help him and his family. Patéra has been diversifying our assets because of all the uncertainty. He's purchased many caïques that can be used for all kinds of transport."

Why didn't my father try to leave Greece with our family? thought Anna. But she put aside such thoughts, as it was futile to think about that now.

Alexander blew out a cloud of smoke and closed his eyes. "Litsa, go to our bedroom. There is something I need to give you before the Nazi returns with Patéra. I'll be there in a few minutes."

"But…"

"Just go, now that there are no more patients waiting for us, and we are alone in the house."

Anna was sitting on their bed, when Alexander entered their room. "Here," he handed her two revolvers, "you must hide these somewhere in your dresser drawers."

"But you heard Herr Von Hoffberg. It's an offense punishable by death to possess firearms."

"We are not their puppets on a string. I will protect us, and I won't give up our weapons." He started to look through the drawer with her undergarments.

"Wait, wait," Anna protested. "You're making a mess. I'll hide them deep in the drawer, so no one shall find them." Anna placed them at the bottom of her drawer and covered the weapons with her lingerie.

They heard the car pull up and the footsteps of Herr Von Hoffberg and Kìrios Antonios.

Alexander walked out to the corridor and stared at the liters of olive oil his father was carrying.

"There are more in the car and barrels of olives as well," his father told him in a tired voice.

Anna watched Kìrios Antonios, his shoulders sagging, his face pale. Why was he bringing olive oil and olives into the house?

"I have some reports to prepare for the commandant. It won't take me very long," Herr Von Hoffberg announced as he walked inside the door to the bedroom, which had recently belonged to Kìrios Antonios.

Anna and Alexander followed Kìrios Antonios into the kitchen, where he and Mattheo were placing the liters of olive oil and barrels of olives on the floor.

"Let's go into the garden." Kìrios Antonios walked out of the kitchen.

"Patéra, what's happened?" Alexander asked.

"They've taken it all." Kìrios Antonios sank into a wicker garden chair.

"Taken what?"

"Our leather factory, our olive oil factory," he said in a monotone.

"They can't just take what is ours!" Alexander protested.

"Yes, they can. Their soldiers need the leather for themselves in Greece, on other fronts, and back in Germany. It is their right, Herr Von Hoffberg told me. They view Greece as a supply line for their battles in North Africa. They'll use our olive oil for lubricating their tanks and other machines. The Nazi, of course, offered to buy my factories, at a reduced, ridiculous price. I begged him. Can you imagine that I had to beg him to let me bring some olive oil and olives back to our house? He said yes, but I had to buy it from him, now that he was the owner of the olive oil factory! What I brought home should last us for a while. We must tell Ariadne to use everything sparingly. I don't want to touch what we have hidden in the air-raid shelter room while the Nazi is here. I'll try not to resort to the black market, until we see what, or if, he will provide anything for the household beyond his needs.

"This morning I met with Metsas and Brettos at the *kafeneío*, the coffeehouse. The German pigs are taking our oranges, lemons, cigarettes, our cotton, our leather from warehouses, figs, rice, olive oil, tobacco, even our silk cocoons. Offices are even being stripped of their metal doorknobs. They have gone to houses of the poor and taken their blankets and sheets. These beasts are like locusts. Nothing will be left in their paths. And the two of you, make sure when you're out on the streets that you do not wear any jewelry, even a watch. The soldiers are stopping people on the boulevards demanding watches, earrings, anything of value." Kìrios Antonios put his head down in his hands.

The three of them remained in the garden, while Ariadne brought them refreshments. There was little for them to say to each other, as the enormity and the savagery of this occupation became more real to them.

"So you are here." They heard the voice of their resident Nazi. He helped himself to a piece of fruit. "I am glad to see you outside in the garden. Come, Kruger, the books," he instructed the young man with a large carton. "Bring all the books here. We shall have a lovely bonfire, and you, my Greek friends, can watch and enjoy."

Anna stared hard at her husband. Don't say a word, she silently shouted at him in her mind. His gaze met hers, a gaze of defeat. Thank God, she thought, he was too smart to let his emotions override his good judgment.

And so the days and nights continued for Anna and Alexander. Their days were spent administering to minor ills for three days in their home, and on the other days, they performed operations at the hospital, stitching up wounds, removing bullets, and amputating limbs.

Their afternoons in the home clinic were spent with what seemed like an endless parade of Germans. The soldiers suffered from sunburns they'd inflicted upon themselves from basking, and then burning, on the rooftops of Athens buildings, in an attempt to feel the healthy, healing rays of the sun. Or so they said, as they peeled away their shirts and pants to reveal lobster-red limbs. Anna kept trying to explain to them that, yes, it was true the sun was good for them. But German skin was fair, and they must take the sun with small increasing exposures, not for a long period of time, which burned their pale skins. She gave them ointment to apply and cautioned them to stay inside, away from the sun, until they healed. It was only the beginning of May, but the Greek sun was already strong.

The vast majority of their other patients Alexander had to see alone as they were young men with venereal disease, and they were too embarrassed to show their symptoms to Anna. Alexander administered injections of Salvarsan to one soldier after the other, along with a short lecture of taking care not to spend time with prostitutes. If they could not stay away from such women, that they must use condoms each and every time.

At night, in the darkness of their bedroom, Anna and Alexander shared stories of their childhood. Eventually Alexander knew each of her sisters and brothers by name, their likes and dislikes, their childhood pranks, whom they married, and what children they had. He learned the names of her childhood friends, and he heard of Anna longing for an advanced education, normally reserved for males. Anna listened to the tales of his education in Berlin, his adventures with his German and French friends, and his role in the family as the oldest son with a younger brother and sister. They especially enjoyed their time alone, when they had heated philosophical debates about everything and anything. And then before they drifted off to sleep, they lost themselves in each other with passion and tenderness.

The shelves of the stores had been stripped bare. Hans took Ariadne to special places where ration cards could produce the meat and produce that Herr Von Hoffberg demanded for his meals. For the rest of the populace, their ration cards produced nothing. Housewives arose before dawn to stand in line for produce. After hours of waiting, they might find nothing more than a strand of parsley to bring home for their families. Those people who had wealth could buy food on the black market for exorbitant prices. The store shelves remained bare, because with no donkeys or trucks for transport, goods from the outlying areas could no longer easily be sent to Athens. Grain was being taxed at an exorbitant rate by the Nazis, and if a farmer refused to pay, his crops were burned to the ground. The British, in an attempt to stop supplies from getting to the Nazis, blockaded the Greek harbors. Grain and goods that had been imported to Greece in the past could no longer get into the country. It was apparent to all that soon mass starvation would come upon them.

The days they spent running their clinic were interrupted by knocks on the door from Greek soldiers returning from the front or released from hospitals. They had no clothes save for their uniforms, and the Germans had posted on their verboten list that wearing a Greek army uniform was cause for arrest. And so the Greek soldiers went from house to house. The patients in pajamas pleaded, begging for food and for any clothes that could be given to them. Alexander and his father had gone through their closets, emptying their armoires of anything but the bare essentials they needed for themselves. They were careful to parcel out to the soldiers a pair of pants, one shirt, one jacket, one pair of socks, one pair of shoes. Because no matter how many soldiers came one day, there would be more tomorrow, and then eventually there would be no clothes to give them. Ariadne and her husband sent them to the backdoor, so they wouldn't encounter Herr Von Hoffberg's wrath.

The nights were punctuated with the sound of gunshots from somewhere in the dark. In the morning, a body was found, a German soldier, a Greek man lying in the streets, or a corpse dangling from a lamppost.

It was the end of May, and Herr Von Hoffberg had summoned them to the window of the library. "Look!" he sputtered. "Just look! I couldn't believe it when I heard of it!"

The three of them walked to the window as instructed.

"What are we supposed to look at?" Alexander asked, although he knew as soon as he saw the Acropolis. The large scarlet Nazi swastika flag was gone.

"Our flag, the Reichskriegsflagge is gone! Do you know who did this?" Herr Von Hoffberg demanded.

"We have no knowledge of this," Kìrios Antonios said in a quiet voice.

"We will find these damned Greeks, and they will be executed on sight, do you hear!" He pulled out a crumpled piece of paper from his pocket. "Now listen," he announced, inserting his monocle and looking down at the paper. "This has just been issued by the German Command here in Athens. Because German military flags have been pulled down and torn from public buildings," he read, "because the Greek people are hoarding food and preventing the food from reaching German soldiers, because of the Greek population's sympathy with British prisoners, and because the Greek press refuses to conform to the new order, the German authorities in Greece have decided that in future those found guilty of the above mentioned offenses will be shot. Do the three of you understand this?"

"Yes," they chorused quietly in agreement.

Damn, thought Alexander, what bravery! No one will give up whoever pulled down the flag. Of this, he had no doubt. He only wished he knew who they were, so he could personally commend them.

"I am so upset, so upset," the German muttered. "Dr. Alexander, I hear there are cabarets to attend and hear music and eat and drink. Is this so?"

"Yes."

"Then I think tonight, the three of you and I must go to enjoy ourselves."

"I prefer to stay at home," said Kìrios Antonios. "But thank you for asking me."

"If that's what you wish, of course, stay at home. Doctor, I want to go to the best cabaret, the absolute best!"

"That would be Maxims. They have an excellent floor show," Alexander told him, but his attention was drawn to Anna, who was looking off in another direction.

"A floor show. Yes, that's what I need to lift my spirits." The German left the room.

"Litsa, is something wrong?"

Anna didn't answer.

"Alexander, today we received a letter from Kìrios Carraso," said Kìrios Antonios. "Our Nazi friend intercepted the letter," he spoke carefully as the door remained open. "He told us that his family was well, although his leather factory had been taken over. He asked if the package he had sent to us was in good condition. Von Hoffberg asked about the package, and I told him that it was a wedding gift that had been sent to the two of you, a beautiful lace tablecloth. He demanded to see it and decided his wife would love such a tablecloth. He also told me that there were many Jews in Salonika and asked if this man was a Jew. Of course, I didn't lie and told him that he was a Jew. Herr Von Hoffberg said that I shouldn't be corresponding with a Jew, as that might make me suspect. He said he had seen my name on a list of suspicious Greeks who were being investigated, but he had vouched for my integrity, at least for now."

Kìrios Antonios reached for his newspaper and placed his glasses upon the bridge of his nose. He shook his head with exasperation. "So I am on their list," he muttered beneath his breath. "You two, go off tonight and try to enjoy yourselves in the midst of those Nazi beasts."

"Well, we've been summoned, so we have no choice." Alexander took Anna's hand. "Litsa, let's lie down for a while before we go out to Maxims."

Anna walked away with him, and when they got to their room, Alexander closed the door.

"Litsa," he said, "I'm sorry."

"So now I am a package, and I'll never know what is happening to my family," she said sadly.

"No, no. We have connections, means of communicating, if not by letter then by people who go back and forth. I promise you, we'll keep in touch with them."

"Alexander, but your father.... Will there be a knock on the door one night, and will they take him away?"

"We must remain on the good side of Von Hoffberg, and we can only hope he will continue to vouch for Patéra."

"I don't feel well. It's probably hearing about that Nazi intercepting the letter from my father and thinking about your father on that list. I wish we didn't have to go. Who wants to sit around with a bunch of Nazis laughing and drinking? But I know there's no choice."

"I'll do my best to have the Nazi pig allow us to leave early. After all, I can always plead we need to be up early for a surgery." He kissed the top of her head. How he loved this woman and the feel of her softness next to him. It seemed the two of them could never get enough of loving each other, yielding to each other, caressing each other. But he sensed her tiredness, and he took her to their bed and held her in his arms as she fell asleep, in their room warmed with the afternoon Athenian heat.

Anna and Alexander hadn't visited Maxims since the Germans entered Athens. The small tables were crowded with German officers, the blue-gray uniforms of the Luftwaffe and the gray-green uniforms of the Wehrmacht, their lanky forms hunched over their dinners. At a few tables, Greeks were attempting to have a good time, despite the Nazi occupation. In the back of the cabaret, a huge roulette wheel whirled, as those gathered around it cheered and clapped.

The soldiers greeted Herr Von Hoffberg with "Heil Hitler" salutes, as the three of them seated themselves at an empty table.

The floor show had not yet begun, and as they were seated, they noticed the Germans around them savoring meat dishes, retsina, and ouzo. Alexander observed the same Greek women who had consorted with the British soldiers were now seated next to the Nazis, flirting, laughing, touching them with affection. Alexander didn't sit in judgment of the women. He had heard the brothels closed their shutters on the day the Nazis goose-stepped into the streets of Athens. But three days later, they were again open for business. Food was growing scarce. Survival, everyone had to survive no matter what they must do.

He squeezed Anna's hand under the table, as the waiter appeared to take their order.

Herr Von Hoffberg ordered the meat stew that the other officers were enjoying.

"We'll have the same," Alexander told the waiter.

"Oh no," the waiter swallowed nervously, "there is no more meat."

"You mean there is meat for the Germans, but not for the Greeks?" Alexander took a draught of his cigarette and blew out the smoke, his eyes narrowed with annoyance.

"I'm sorry. I'll bring you the moussaka. It has no meat but is nevertheless quite a tasty dish." The waiter turned and hurried away.

Alexander shook his head with disgust and leaned back in his chair, as the smoke-filled room echoed with the sound of the Germans singing their drinking songs. Anna was looking down at the table, strangely silent. She had said she hadn't felt well, and now he regretted that he had brought her tonight. He should have insisted she stay at home.

"Hello there!" He looked across the room to see Nurse Antoinette Ferrara waving at them. She was seated at a table with several German soldiers.

Anna sighed and waved back at her, beckoning in their direction. Nurse Ferrara, obviously dressed in her best frock and hat, approached them with a broad smile and an exaggerated swing to her slim hips.

Alexander made introductions, and Herr Von Hoffberg indicated a place at their table. "Please sit down with us, fräulein."

"Why, thank you, Herr Von Hoffberg. It's an honor to meet you. I've heard so much about you," she said, settling into her chair.

"You have?" His pale face flushed with color.

Antoinette placed her hand over his. "Of course I have."

"Have you had dinner?" He winked and smiled at her.

"Not yet."

"I hear the beef stew is excellent." He had fastened his gaze on her ample cleavage. "Would you like me to order some for you?"

She smiled coquettishly at him and leaned over, giving him a closer view of the tops of her breasts. "Why, thank you! I love beef stew."

"Excuse me." Anna pushed away from the table and hurried in the direction of the toilet.

"So, fräulein, you are Italian? How long have you been here in Athens?"

"A few years," she told him, as she shifted in her chair and hiked up her skirt, revealing more of her legs.

"When do you think the show will begin?" Herr Von Hoffberg asked.

"Soon, I think." Alexander was about to say more when one of the woman performers came up to the table and bent down toward Alexander.

"Doctor," she said in a low tone. "Your wife needs you." She waved in the direction where Anna had walked toward the toilet.

Alexander jumped to his feet and made his way toward the toilet through the crowd of drunken soldiers. "Litsa." He rapped on the door and opened it.

Anna was sitting there, her face pale. "The baby," she said tearfully. "I've lost it."

"Are you sure?" He bent down.

"I am sure," she murmured, getting to her feet. "I'm having some cramping. Please, can't we go home?"

"Oh, Litsa…" His voice broke, as he put his arms around her. "We'll go back to the table, and I'll convince the Nazi to let Hans drive us back home. I'll find you something for the pain as soon as we're home."

"It's not too bad. It just has to run its course. You and I both know that."

They walked out into the dim hallway. "Alexander, wait." She looked up at him. "In my head I know such things just happen. But in my heart, I think it's my fault. Please tell me I'm wrong."

"How could it be your fault?"

"I wanted this baby." She paused. "But I couldn't help thinking this was such a bad time to have a baby, to bring a new life into this terrible world. I sometimes wished I wasn't pregnant."

"Litsa, if wishes came true so easily, we wouldn't have these fascist pigs in our country. It wasn't your fault. As a doctor, you know such things just happen sometimes. Litsa, listen to your head, my most intelligent wife. I promise you; someday we will have a houseful of children."

"But not…"

"Yes, but not while the invaders are here."

He helped Anna back to the table.

"Frau Giannopolous, you don't look well," Herr Von Hoffberg commented with a frown.

"She is not well," said Alexander. "She needs to go home, right now. Would you be so kind as to instruct Hans to drive us home?"

Herr Von Hoffberg looked down at his food. "Poisoned? Is it poison? Do you think the food is poisoned and they gave your wife the food that was intended for me?"

"She hasn't taken a bite of her food, Herr Von Hoffberg," Alexander tried to keep the irritation out of his voice.

"*Jah, jah*, you are quite right. But today besides the desecration of our flag, I have heard of sabotage, the blowing up of an important bridge by Greek saboteurs. We Germans must be so careful."

"How terrible," Antoinette agreed sympathetically.

"Please, Herr Von Hoffberg," Alexander began again.

"Is it something infectious, something she can spread throughout the household?"

"It is a female problem," Alexander said in a low tone.

"*Jah, jah*, that is good. I know my Bertha, sometimes that happens to her."

"Can you ask Hans…."

Herr Von Hoffberg got to his feet. "He should be waiting outside, somewhere down the street. I will tell him to return you to the villa. Wait here for me. Fraulein, would you like to go outside with me for a breath of fresh air?"

"Of course." She followed him out of the cabaret.

"Are you in much pain?" Alexander asked Anna, as she winced.

"Just a little. I'd been having some pains all day. But I thought it was nothing. I hoped it was nothing."

"Anna Carraso!" Alexander heard the voice and saw Anna take a deep breath as a young man approached them.

Anna stared down at the table.

"Anna, it's me Elias Silva." The man was all smiles.

"Excuse me." She looked up. "But I think you have me confused with someone else." She began to nervously finger her cross.

"Anna," he began, his eyes widening at the sight of her crucifix.

Antoinette approached their table. "The car is ready," she informed them. "The driver is waiting."

"I beg your pardon, sir." Alexander helped Anna to her feet. "You are mistaken. This is my wife, Michaelitsa Giannopolous. She is not feeling well, and we must leave."

"It's amazing." The man took a step backward, as they walked passed him. "You look just like my neighbor in Salonika. You could be her twin."

CHAPTER 9

1963: Salonika

ANNA HAD INTENDED to return to the hotel, but she found herself walking toward the harbor. As she strolled down the familiar streets, she longed to see the sea that she loved so much. Anna walked along the seaside boardwalk, eager to find a place in the shade. There it was, exactly what she was looking for, a café with a broad awning. She sat down in a chair facing the water, watching the whitecaps crashing against the boardwalk. The sound of Greek voices washed over her like a huge wave, pulling her down into a place she had been running from for the past eighteen years. A tall Greek man passed in front of her, the dark hair, the broad shoulders, the easy grace of his stride. Alexander, Alexander…And then the man turned, and, of course, it was not her Alexander. Her Alexander was dead, executed in the mountains by the EDES, the National Republican Greek League.

He had joined the ELAS, the National Peoples' Liberation Army, during the civil war that gripped Greece after the Second World War had ended. When the occupying Germans left their country, the Greeks had turned on each other, communists against fascists, loyalists against monarchists, and so the country continued to suffer a bloodbath after the German boot was lifted. Alexander had joined the ELAS, the communists, for after all, weren't they the same men who had helped Jews fleeing from the Nazis into the mountains? It was the ELAS *andartes* who had escorted them to safety in the mountains of Zakynthos, after Anna had been identified as a Jew. Many Jews had joined the ELAS during and after the war. Alexander knew his skills as a doctor would be welcomed. Men were being rounded up off the streets into the draft, and it was just a matter of time before Alexander was dragged off to the National Greek army. He didn't want to join their ranks. He felt a strong solidarity with the partisans. Although there were many women in their movement, Anna couldn't go with him into the mountains, because of their young daughter.

As Anna sat down at the small table in the café, she was surrounded by the swirl of voices speaking Greek, a language she hadn't heard in so many years. It all came rushing back, those last moments together.

"Don't worry, Anna." Alexander held her in his arms. "I will be fine. I'm a doctor, not a soldier."

"But it's dangerous. Don't go. Stay here with us." It was hard for her to imagine the days, the weeks, the months apart from him.

"Now give me my precious daughter." He smiled down at the one-year-old little girl. "Suzanne, Suzanne," he murmured and kissed the top of her head.

"Baba!" she called out to him.

"When I return, I will ensure that your mamà gives you many brothers." His dark eyes twinkled. "And I shall greatly enjoy making that happen."

"Why are you making jokes?" Anna couldn't help but laugh.

"Because her mother is so serious." He squeezed Anna tightly in his arms. "I love you, Anna Litsa. I love you with all my heart. I promise to return as soon as I can."

She heard him bidding good-bye to his father, Antonios. Her father-in-law would live for only one more month before he was felled by a sudden massive heart attack, leaving Anna, the baby, Ariadne, and Mattheo in their home. Kiría Maria had perished of typhoid during the war years.

While Ariadne cared for Suzanne, Anna started working through the United Joint Jewish Committee, tending to those survivors from the concentration camps who had made their way back to Athens. But she quickly realized that listening to the heart-wrenching stories of the survivors, day after day, was more than she could bear. It was especially difficult to hear about the Nazi doctor Mengele, who took a special interest in using Greek Jews for his horrible experiments. She quickly gave up her duties there and went back to working at the hospital, this time as a doctor, not a nurse. She told herself that her skills as a doctor were sorely needed to care for the wounded from the civil war. She thought about Alexander and if he were ever hurt, hoping someone would care for him.

Seated in the café, Anna took a swallow of the anise-flavored ouzo she had ordered. It tasted so good, and conversing in Greek felt so natural, so right. She didn't belong to this world anymore, but she wanted to. She so desperately wanted to go back in time. Yes, the war years were filled with terrible memories, but she had been Michaelitsa Giannopolous then, and her husband was at her side. They were together as she would never again be with another man. In the United States, she had been married for thirteen years to an American before their divorce. But she couldn't love her husband the way she had loved Alexander. "I'm tired of sharing our life with a ghost!" he had confronted her. But it was more than that. She had lost too much, making her incapable of truly caring again. Her heart was like a cold stone, only able to love her daughter and her son. For a man, even a good man like her American husband, the kind of love he wanted, he deserved, she couldn't give to him. And so instead of facing her inadequacies as a wife, she threw herself into her work at the emergency room. Only when she experienced that rush of adrenaline did she feel alive.

Anna decided against another shot of ouzo and instead ordered a coffee and a piece of baklava. She'd told Suzanne she was going back to their hotel. She knew her daughter thought she'd been overwhelmed by the sight of the marble tombstones from the Jewish cemetery, which seemed to be everywhere, even used as building blocks of the Aristotle University, in the streets, on walkways. She'd seen those tombstones before on that terrible day she'd returned to Salonika. It was the memory of that day when she was confronted with what had happened to her entire family that overwhelmed her. It was after the war was over. She and Alexander and their infant daughter had traveled to Salonika so that she could be reunited with her family. That feeling of terrible agony, horrific loss, and Alexander holding her, trying to ease her sorrow...it all came back to her this morning....

"I'm sorry." The official behind the desk looked up from the long list in front of him. "There is no one with any of those names here."

"Are you sure you checked every single name I gave you?" Anna was impatient with this incompetent bureaucrat.

"I checked twice. Why don't you return to where this family lived? Perhaps the neighbors can help you. Unfortunately, I wouldn't be too hopeful. From our records, it seems over fifty thousand Jews lived here, and perhaps two thousand returned. You know, of course, they were all sent to Auschwitz."

"It isn't **this** family. It is my family!" Anna shouted.

"Anna." Alexander took the baby from her. "Let's do as this man says and go back to your home."

Anna looked up at her husband. "I can tell what you're thinking. I can tell." Her heart began to thunder in her chest.

"Let's go back to your neighborhood, and maybe we can learn something."

"They are alive! I know they are. Maybe they haven't come back yet. It's a long journey, or maybe they decided to go somewhere else. Isn't that possible?"

"Of course, it's possible," he said in a gentle voice.

You're wrong, she wanted to shout at him. I'll prove you wrong.

"Anna!" the Greek Orthodox woman who had lived next door to them greeted her with open arms. "We'd no idea you had survived."

"Kiría Vafiadis, this is my husband Alexander Giannopolous and my little girl." They walked inside the home of Anna's neighbor.

"Sit down, sit down."

"No, thank you." Anna could feel her heart beginning to hammer again in her chest. "My family…Do you know what happened to my family? Where are they living? Have they returned yet?"

"Oh, Anna, I'm so sorry." The woman's eyes filled with tears. "No one has come back. I kept hoping. Your parents gave me some things to keep for them until their return but…I did have a visit from your cousin Moises. He told me that he was the only one who survived. Everyone else is gone. He told me the terrible stories of what happened to everyone. He thanked me for taking care of those things your parents had given to me. I gave him everything, except for the letter your father wanted you to have."

"Everyone… not everyone," Anna whispered as a wave of cold crept over her. "We're a large family, my sister, brothers, their children…. my grandmother, surely someone…."

"No one, Anna, no one. Go to see your cousin Moises. Do you remember where he lives down the street? The family who took over his house are good people; they agreed to return the house to him. You know so many Christians took the houses of your people, and now that these few poor pitiful souls have returned, they refuse to even give them a room to live in."

"You want to know where your family is!" Her cousin Moises stood in the doorway of his home. "Where do you think they are! In the smoke of chimneys from the crematoriums! The ones like your father and mother and my parents and the other aunts and uncles, all sent to showers upon arrival, where they were gassed and then shoveled into the ovens. Our grandmother died on the train, where we were herded like animals for nine days and nights with no food or water. The young, strong people who survived the cattle cars were sent to work for the Nazi beasts. Your sister Sophia was holding her little girl. She was fortunate, for the man who was working for the Nazis was Greek. He told her in our language to give her child to your mother for just a little while, before the selection process began. Those prisoners who met us when we got off the trains knew the meaning of the directions: gas chambers to the left, slave labor to the right. But of this final selection, we knew nothing when we arrived. And so when the selection began, because of a fellow Greek countryman, your sister was saved. A mother with a small child was automatically sent to the showers, to the ovens. Your mother and little Siriki were sent to the ovens, and your sister was saved. Sophia labored for the Nazis and eventually died from typhus. She died only two weeks before the liberation.

"We were looked down upon by the Ashkenazi Jews because we didn't speak Yiddish. 'Ladino,' they scorned us, 'what kind of language is that for a Jew? You're not a Jew.' Can you imagine that! I survived because I was strong and athletic. I was forced to entertain the pigs with boxing matches. And then they selected me for the *sonderkommando* and gave me extra food. Do you know what I did to survive, Anna? The *sonderkommando* shoveled the bodies into the ovens, the bodies of our own people! But we Greek Jews had an uprising. We tried to blow up the crematoriums. I was one of the few who survived the uprising." He was growing hysterical now, as his eyes bore into her and Alexander.

"And you, Anna, we know what you did during the war. Whore! Traitor!" he had spat at her, his eyes bulging out of his emaciated face. "You come back here with a Christian husband and a child. Your father told my father, his brother. Did you think you could keep it a secret? You deserted your family, your people."

"Please," she beseeched him, and then she noticed he was clutching the hand of a small boy, who was fearfully looking up at her. "Is this your son?"

"All my children, my family, my wife are dead. This is Joseph, your brother Victor's son. He was hidden in a monastery and well cared for. To the monks' credit, they never tried to convert him."

"Please, let me take him back to Athens with us. We have means and…"

"To be made into a Christian like your husband?" He laughed ruefully. "No. I'm a Jew. I..,"

"Shut up!" he interrupted her. "Don't you think we have lost enough Jews?" He slammed the door in her face.

Those days in the hotel room in Salonika, Alexander had nursed her and cared for her as if she were a child. The wife of the hotel owner was more than willing to take care of Suzanne, while Anna cried without end for the family she had lost. "I should have been with them. I should have been with them," Anna sobbed over and over.

"Anna, then you too would have died. Suzanne would never have been born. Your parents wouldn't have wanted that. That's why they sent you away."

"They should all have left."

"But they didn't know. No one knew the evil in the hearts of those Nazi beasts. Who could have imagined those death camps and what happened there? It was beyond imagining, such demonic evil. Anna, I took your father's letter from your neighbor. I read it, and I think you should read it."

"I can't." Anna dissolved into tears once more. "Not now."

"Then I shall read it to you," said Alexander.

> *My darling Anna, always our favorite child,*
>
> *If you are reading this letter, it means my darkest fears have been confirmed and that we have not come home; we have not survived. I know you have married Antonios' son, and in order to do this you converted to Christianity. These are hard times my child, when we are forced to make difficult decisions. Do not berate yourself for this choice, as certainly it has saved your life. I have been told this man you married is a good and decent man. In your heart you will remain a Jew. I know this. Keep our memory, the memory of your people, alive, and in this way we will not die.*
>
> *Your Mama and Papa with all our love*

Nineteen years ago and it seemed as if it just happened yesterday. The crushing pain and Alexander there, always there, giving her strength, helping her to heal. She had come back today with her daughter, thinking it was time, time to tell Suzanne about the past, the past she had buried.... the past her American husband encouraged her to keep buried. "Suzanne doesn't need to know. My family has embraced her. I am her father, the only father she has ever known."

Anna lacked the strength to argue with him. He was the only father Suzanne would ever know, and he was a good and loving father to her, ever since that tragic evening so long ago, when he had taken the two-year-old in his arms and she called him "Baba," the Greek word for "Daddy," the word she called to every man she saw. But now Suzanne was a grown woman, and surely soon she would marry and start a family of her own. Wasn't it time to tell her about her father, Alexander? But could Anna bear the pain of telling her what had happened, of reliving that terrible day?

And then Anna's thoughts reluctantly returned to that morning. It had been a lovely spring day, the smell of blossoms wafting in the gentle warm breeze that blew through the open window of her bedroom, as Anna dressed for work at the hospital. She heard Suzanne banging a spoon in the kitchen, when she was interrupted by a knock on her door.

It was Ariadne. "Kiría Anna Litsa, you have a visitor."

A visitor at this time of the morning?

Anna walked into the parlor to see two disheveled men with full dark beards and ragged clothing. She caught her breath as a terrible sense of foreboding enveloped her. One man's eyes caught hers.

"Kiría Giannopolous, your husband.... "

"Yes, Alexander," she interrupted him. No, please no.

"Dr. Alexander," he continued, "was executed by firing squad several weeks ago." His mouth spoke words that at first she couldn't understand. "We witnessed his execution and saw his body in a pit with the others. We came as soon as we could. Could you spare some food for us?"

"No, you're wrong! My husband is a doctor. He was not executed!" The room was growing dark. She felt blood rushing in her ears, and a terrible coldness took hold of her as she crumpled to the floor.

As Anna sat in the café in Salonika, that memory she had buried, never to be remembered, came back to her with startling intensity. This afternoon it was so fresh, the pain, the terrible pain. It was better to wall off that anguish, to let the nothingness, the coldness deep inside her, take hold, numbing her to all that pain. For many years, nothing had been able to penetrate that shell, that wall around her heart. But today the wall began to crumble, and she blinked back tears. It was a terrible mistake to return to Greece, a terrible mistake for her to come back here.

Once she left Greece, she shouldn't have returned.

That night so long ago, it was raining and the streets were filled with a cold mist. Anna had clutched her small suitcase and her daughter, as she and Ariadne made their way down to the docks. Fog had rolled in from the sea, and they could barely see the boat that bobbed up and down in the water. Anna had used the gold coins that had been hidden during the war to purchase passage on the boat that would take her and Suzanne to Cairo. Her father's money in the Athenian bank was lost. In Cairo, she would wait for papers to allow her entry into the United States. She was being sponsored by the American cousins she had contacted. Anna didn't know how long she would have to wait in Egypt for the papers. But the civil war in Greece went on and on, shootings in the streets, one faction against another, the fear someone would also identify her as a communist because of Alexander's membership in ELAS. She had heard of women suspected of communist affiliation who were sent to prison with their children, never to be seen again.

Greece was no place to raise their daughter. There was nothing left for them in this country that was tearing itself apart, with blood and terror.

Anna hugged Ariadne good-bye and instructed her daughter to give her a kiss. "Take care of yourself," Anna told her, so thankful for the woman's friendship during this past year. "I will write to you."

"Kiría Anna Litsa, you have forgotten that I cannot read, and you must forget all this tragedy and make a new life for yourself and the little one. You have given me and my husband the house, which was so generous. I shall never forget you and the child and this wonderful family, who helped us so much throughout the war years, ensuring we did not starve to death as so many others did. You're still young, Kiría. You will find happiness again. Go to America and make a new life for yourself."

Anna boarded the boat and stood at the railing, as she and Suzanne waved good-bye to the middle-aged woman.

She had heard the encouraging words of Ariadne. A future for her daughter, yes of course. That was why she was making this journey. Her daughter deserved to live in a country that wasn't being torn apart by bloodshed. But a future for herself? Her life was over. It was buried with her family and Alexander. There were no tombstones in a cemetery for her family and for her husband. Was he buried somewhere in the mountains or just thrown into a pit, ravaged by wild animals? Happiness? An illusion for fools, not for her. She must give love to her daughter, but that was all her heart would ever manage, if indeed she still possessed a heart.

As the dock filled with other passengers, she watched Ariadne turn and go on her way.

Anna had been one of the first passengers to board. As the time passed, more and more people crowded the decks, until Anna could barely find a small spot for herself, Suzanne, and her suitcase. All around them was the press of unwashed, emaciated bodies, war-weary faces, everyone desperate to leave this war-ravaged country, hoping the authorities in Egypt would allow them entry and not send them back to Greece.

"Your boat is overcrowded!" Anna was startled to hear a voice of American English. It was a man in an American uniform. "Some people need to get off, or you're going to sink!" Anna heard the desperation in this voice, and she was gripped by fear. Could it be true? Who was this man? And inside her wall of indifference, she felt fear, not for herself, but for her daughter. She felt her parents, her family reaching out to her, calling out to her, telling her she must save her child. She clutched Suzanne more tightly in her arms.

"Doesn't anyone speak English?" the man shouted.

"I speak English!" Anna announced loudly, but in the din of Greek voices, the man didn't hear her.

Anna grabbed her daughter and her suitcase and made her way toward the voice. "I speak English!" she yelled as she grew closer.

"Thank God! Tell the captain. Tell him some people need to get off the boat!"

Anna yelled in Greek to the captain who was standing above the deck on the bridge.

"These people have paid good money for their passage. That English is crazy. Mind your own business!" he announced with scorn in his voice.

"He won't listen!" Anna shouted toward the American.

"Then you must tell the other passengers." The voice was coming closer to her. "Tell them there are too many people."

Anna yelled as loud as she could, telling people to get off the boat.

"Do you want to cause panic!" the captain shouted down at her. "Shut up, woman, and mind your own business."

The other passengers looked at her with scorn and exasperation, shaking their heads. "Be quiet…. We need to leave Greece…. We are staying on this boat."

"They won't listen," she began, as the tall man in the American uniform turned in her direction.

"My God!" he exclaimed. "Anna, Anna Carraso?"

"Daniel?"

The boat's horn was signaling its imminent departure.

"Get off!" the captain thundered at him. "Get off my boat! You haven't paid for passage, and you're trying to cause trouble!"

"Anna, get off the boat with me. I was walking past, and when I saw so many people on such a small boat, I knew it was a disaster waiting to happen. I'm telling you it's going to sink. Give me that child." He grabbed hold of Suzanne.

"Baba." She smiled up at him.

"Wait," Anna murmured. "Are you sure?" The fog in her mind was clearing.

"Anna, hurry!" He grabbed her hand and pulled her through the crowd. They proceeded down the gangplank only minutes before it was hoisted from the boat.

They stood on shore as the boat made its way out of the harbor.

"Daniel." Anna frowned. "I paid good money for my passage. I need to get out of Greece. Now I'll be stuck here, until I figure out some other way to get more money. Really, that boat seems to be fine. I shouldn't have listened to you."

"Anna," he ignored what she said. "I can't believe I've found you, that you survived the war. Were you in a concentration camp? I kept thinking about you, especially after the camps were liberated, wondering if you survived. Whose child is this?" he asked as Suzanne nestled against his shoulder.

"She is my daughter." She looked up at this man from her past, who was affectionately tousling her daughter's brown hair.

The lights from the boat were growing dim, as it made its way toward the sea. And then they heard it, the agonizing screams of the passengers. All around them on the docks, people were yelling, "the boat, the boat!" and crossing themselves. Anna started to cross herself and then looked at Daniel, who was watching her, his eyes full of bewilderment. Anna self-consciously moved her hand from her chest and nervously clutched her throat. That part of your life is over, she told herself. She was no longer an Orthodox Christian. Anna told herself she should grieve for those men, those women, those children who had perished, who had screamed before the cold waves welcomed them to their deaths. Those poor people just wanted a better life for themselves. But there was no grieving left inside of the hollowness within her.

She and her daughter had been saved from a terrible fate. If not for Daniel, she and Suzanne would have been on that boat and on their way to a watery grave. Suzanne would never grow up. Gone, gone like everyone else.

"Thank you, Daniel," she sighed. "You saved our lives."

"Anna, you're so thin." He tried to catch her attention, but her eyes were focused on the dark sea. "Anna, I'm here. I'll take care of you now. Everything will be all right."

And so Anna let him lead her off the docks onto another boat. He was a Captain in the American Navy, and he had requisitioned this boat to sail to Athens. He was soon to be shipping out, going home, and he had decided to take a detour to Greece to see the Acropolis.

"I'm so incredibly happy to have found you. It's a miracle that you survived. How long were you in a concentration camp?"

"I wasn't in a concentration camp."

"You're so thin."

Anna didn't explain to him that food had continued to be scarce after the war. She made sure her daughter had enough to eat, and the survivors from the camps that she met were given all the food she could find. Two months ago, after she learned of Alexander's death, food lost all importance to her, and Ariadne had to urge her to eat to maintain her strength.

On the boat, Daniel provided as much food as Anna could eat, all the while holding Suzanne in his arms. The little girl laughed and played with the dog tags that hung around his neck. Anna was so hungry. Here was food she didn't have to share with others who were more deserving.

He asked her why she was going to Cairo, and she told him she was going to the US. and would wait in Egypt until her papers came through. She had cousins in New Jersey who had sponsored her. She had no idea how long it would take, but Greece was unsafe and she had to leave.

Anna shuddered with relief as she watched the man from what seemed another lifetime take care of her little girl. "Your husband, did he survive the war?"

"No," Anna said in a monotone.

"Did he perish in one of those heinous camps like so many other Jews?"

"I don't want to talk about him."

"Of course, Anna, of course."

And then Daniel told her, he never stopped loving her, and how wonderful it was that they had found each other again. She reached for another slice of bread. What he was saying made no sense to her, but the bread was the best she'd tasted in so long.

"Anna, did you hear me?" He was saying in a gentle voice. "Marry me. I can get one of my buddies to perform the ceremony, and you'll automatically be granted entrance into the United States."

"Marry you?" Anna was startled.

"I never stopped loving you, Anna. You need someone to take care of you."

"Marry you?" Anna tried to make sense of what he was saying to her.

"I know it won't be a Jewish ceremony. But I might find a rabbi somewhere before we go home, or we can have another proper Jewish ceremony once we get back to the States," he told her as Suzanne laid her head on his shoulder, her eyes closing with sleep.

And so Anna had agreed to marry this man who had rejected her years ago, in another lifetime.

Daniel, he'd tried so hard, and she'd also tried to make their marriage work; truly she had. He preferred that she didn't talk about her Greek Orthodox husband, and certainly her living as a Greek Orthodox woman. Daniel's Ashkenazi family couldn't believe that there had been Jews in Greece and that they had been annihilated by Hitler. Anna's lack of Yiddish, her stories of a family lost, could not be put into any context they understood. At first when Anna tried to share her story, they murmured a word or two of sympathy, and then they talked about the Ashkenazi Jews, their relatives from Poland who had perished. They were sure the people called Sephardic Jews weren't real Jews, and Hitler wouldn't have bothered with them.

And wasn't Anna proof of that? For if the Nazis had rounded up Sephardic Jews, why had Anna and her husband not been sent to a concentration camp? The Orthodox Christians hid me, Anna tried to explain. "Really?" An elderly aunt frowned at her, the disbelief written all over her face.

Daniel cautioned her about revealing that Alexander had joined a partisan group that espoused Communism. Anna had tried to make him understand that her brother had joined the ELAS, only to return to Salonika when her family was being rounded up for a "trip to Poland."

"Anna, what you're saying makes no sense," Daniel said in a patronizing tone.

"You aren't listening to me!" Anna protested, her hand resting across her swollen belly of pregnancy. "The ELAS controlled the ferry system that helped Jews escape to safety. They provided food when everyone was starving."

"But they were communists." He shook his head at her. "You told me you pretended to be a Christian. Were you also a communist, Anna? Please tell me that isn't so." Daniel's voice was filled with sadness.

"No." Anna sank down into their living-room chair, feeling exhausted. She was weary of trying to explain the war in Greece to her husband. She was so tired of hearing he loved her, in spite of all the things that were impossible for him to accept: her conversion to Greek Orthodoxy, her marriage to a man who was not only a Christian, but a member of a communist organization.

"No, I was not a communist. Daniel, I think it's better if I never bring up the past anymore. No matter what, your family will never accept me as a Jew. I really don't care. We are going to have a child any day now. We need to look forward."

"I love you, Anna." He smiled at her.

"In spite of all you know about me?" she sighed in exasperation.

"It wasn't your fault," he said, magnanimously absolving her of guilt.

Daniel didn't understand. She knew he would never understand. And because he wanted her to close off all that had happened, it formed a wedge between them. He said he loved her, but he didn't love who she was. He loved who he wanted her to be. Their marriage didn't assuage her loneliness. But with a baby coming so quickly, Anna resigned herself to this marriage. She told herself she didn't deserve more, when she alone had survived while the rest of her family perished. Anna never mentioned her family to him or his family again.

And so her family, her life with Alexander, was buried somewhere in a hidden place deep inside of her that still haunted her dreams. In those dreams, she was with Alexander, so happy, so complete, but she would wake up next to Daniel. And on those mornings, she would hug herself and will herself not to cry.

But she had a rewarding position as a doctor and two wonderful children, her daughter, Suzanne, and a son, Joey, named for her father, Joseph, born one year after her marriage to Daniel.

Now eighteen years later, in spite of her bad memories of the war, there were so many wonderful memories. This was her home, where she had grown up. The heat warmed the air... Greek summer, how fondly she remembered it. She watched couples stroll by the café. She suddenly wished she had also gone to Athens, to see the Parthenon perched on top of the Acropolis. She remembered the view from her window in the Giannopolous house. But Salonika had the beautiful sea, and she enjoyed watching the waves and hearing them lapping against the boardwalk, as she sipped her dark coffee.

Greece, her children should know of their Greek heritage. They should experience the beauty of a Greek summer, the brilliant sun, the turquoise blue skies, the sapphire sea. It was a part of who they were. Why not come here every summer? It was the perfect time, especially while her son and daughter would have summer vacation from their college studies for the next several years. Yes, there were painful memories, but also wonderful memories, and it was only right that her children know where they came from.

It was time for them to know about Anna's family and all who were lost. Her son and daughter should know about Alexander and his family and the Giannopolous family heritage. They should learn about the goodness of those Orthodox Christians who had helped protect her and shield her from the Nazis, risking their own lives. Suzanne needed to know her father had joined the ELAS, the andartes who had helped Alexander and Anna escape the clutches of the Nazis in Athens.

Anna put down the drachmas on the table to pay for her refreshments. She signaled to the waiter. "I was on a tour today," she told him. "I was told there was a new Jewish cemetery created after the war, where some of the old tombstones were taken. Can you tell me where it's located?"

Anna decided she and Suzanne would go to the new cemetery together, and perhaps she would find an old tombstone that belonged to the Carraso family. Returning here to her childhood home, she felt the strength to confront the past and share it all with her daughter.

It was a short walk back to the hotel. Suzanne should be returning very soon. But as Anna began her walk back to the hotel, she took a detour, entering the street of her childhood. This was the house she had grown up inside, where her brothers and sisters played. This was the last place her parents and Nona had lived before they were ordered to go to the Baron Hirsch Quarter and to their deaths. She needed to come here by herself. She didn't want to break down in front of her daughter.

She stood on the sidewalk, looking up at the balconies, the window to her bedroom, where she had sat on a window seat looking out at the sea. She would let her imagination roam all the possibilities she thought life might offer her. The house had not changed very much from the outside. Anna took a deep breath and knocked on the door. There was no answer. A young woman peered out from an adjoining house and told her no one was home as the family had gone on holiday. Anna thanked the neighbor and stood rooted to the spot, tears brimming in her eyes. She was alive and she knew her family would want her to go forward, to forget all the guilt for having survived. She needed to talk to Suzanne and tell her of all the wonderful memories that dwelled in her heart. Anna closed her eyes and heard the voices of her family, saw them laughing, dancing, saw them alive. She needed to survive to keep their memories alive, and her daughter needed to know of them and her Sephardic heritage. She needed to heal after all this time. But she wondered if she could ever fill that empty place inside of her.

CHAPTER 10

1941: Athens
Summer

IT WAS A hot summer night, only relieved by a gentle breeze that ruffled the curtains framing the kitchen window.

Anna filled tomatoes and green peppers with the rice and beef mixture she had prepared earlier in the day. It had been a pleasant surprise when her father-in-law presented her with the meat and rice, after his last shipment had arrived.

Alexander was perched on a stool in the kitchen, drinking his glass of retsina, watching her cook. "Isn't it wonderful that Von Hoffberg is so taken with Antoinette that he took her to the seaside for the weekend? Just the two of us tonight."

"Your father is spending the night elsewhere?" Anna wiped her hands on the apron and placed the *gemista* in a pan.

"You disapprove?"

"It's not for me to approve or disapprove."

"It's the way it is for Greek men, and you know that. This woman Cleo has been my father's mistress ever since I can remember."

"Well, it better not be that way for all Greek men." Anna narrowed her eyes at him.

"Oh, Litsa," he laughed. "Don't worry about me. I know full well a woman with your modern ideas would never tolerate such behavior from her husband. You must realize that here in Greece most women are not educated, so a man seeks out other men for intellectual stimulation. A man only needs a woman for taking care of the household and having children.

While I was living in France and Germany, I experienced many relationships with intelligent, educated, free-thinking women. They opened my eyes and my heart to what could be between a man and a woman. Though I must admit having an extra woman on the side is not a terrible thought," he teased her.

Anna threw a dishcloth at him.

"But you are enough for me." He ducked and came up behind her, kissing her neck and encircling his arms around her waist. "While we're on the subject of mistresses…. tell me, doesn't your father have a woman like that for his pleasure?"

"I wouldn't know," she said tersely. "That isn't the kind of thing a father shares with his daughter. But I imagine that it would be terribly hurtful to my mother if he did have such a woman."

"Litsa, my mother knows of Patéra's mistress. Patéra would never be seen in the street with her, never bring her to our house. He wouldn't bring shame to Kiría Maria. And even with my mother gone, he wouldn't bring this other woman to our house."

"How thoughtful of him," Anna mumbled sarcastically and returned to arranging cookies on a plate. "Alexander, I need to finish our dinner. Dimetri and Irini will be here soon. They are bringing their niece. And then there is my brother…."

"No one is coming for at least a half hour." He loosened his arms around her and, after giving her a kiss on the lips, resumed his position on the stool. "Do you want to talk about the visit from your brother?"

"You don't mind if I dismissed the servants for the weekend, do you?" she changed the subject.

"It's nicer for us to be alone. Ariadne and Mattheo will enjoy spending time with their families. And I think it's wonderful to have you cook for me. I know you are a brilliant doctor, but your wifely duties in the kitchen have so far been untested."

"You'll learn tonight that I am both an excellent cook and baker. You, Alexander Giannopolous are very fortunate to have such an accomplished wife in the kitchen."

"If what you say is true, I'll be delighted to have our friends sample the wonderful dinner you've promised me."

"With Von Hoffberg gone, it feels like the bars of our prison have been lifted, if only temporarily. You know, he makes Ariadne account for every grain of rice, every thimbleful of oil she serves to him and to us. If it wasn't for your father's connections with the black market, there would be little for us to eat on those nights when he dines out. Other nights we are supposed to just make do with the food available through the ration cards. I've heard many of the Nazis don't offer any food to the families where they are living." Anna placed the *gemista* into the oven for tonight's dinner and turned back to him.

"Alexander, stop that!" she chastised him as he reached for the plate of *kourabiedes* cookies. "They're for tonight." She smiled.

He popped a cookie into his mouth and pulled her close. "You are such a good baker. I think I shall keep you."

"And you are a mess." She reached up to his dark moustache and brushed off the powdered-sugar residue from the cookie.

"Litsa, your brother will be here soon. We should talk."

"What is there to say?"

"Patéra told me that he thinks your brother Zaco knows."

"Knows?" she questioned. But it was obvious what he meant.

"My father says that, of course, before your brother approached him in the *kafeneío*, he would have asked about our family. He would have been told that I had recently taken a wife, a cousin who had come to live with our family. Our wedding was a celebration of note, and it would have been hard to ignore."

"I hadn't even considered that he might know," Anna said, her head spinning with confusion. "I was trying to decide how to tell him, what to tell him. Do you think I should just tell him everything that happened and why I married you?"

"Everything, Litsa? I would suggest you leave out the part about your pregnancy. Because if I put myself in his place, I would go after me with a knife. He told Patéra that your father sent him to see how you were faring. Apparently he is in Athens to join with the andartes and go up into the mountains."

"Zaco's my favorite brother. We were so close when we were growing up. He never dismissed my thoughts because I was a girl. He encouraged me to travel to America for my medical studies. I just don't know if he'll understand, or if he will be ashamed of me because of what I've done," Anna voiced her fears as she untied the apron around her waist.

There was a knock on the kitchen door. "It's him," Anna sighed, summoning her resolve. Zaco had been instructed that although the Nazi was away for the weekend, it was prudent to go around to the backdoor.

Alexander opened the door, and there stood her brother Zaco, a nice-looking man of medium height, with the copper hair of their mother. "Come in, come in," Alexander entreated him.

Zaco stood in the doorframe, his eyes looking around the kitchen, eventually resting on Anna.

He's not smiling at me, she thought. Isn't he glad to see me? He knows; of course he knows, and he will never forgive me for what I've done.

"Please come in." Alexander offered his hand in greeting.

Zaco didn't acknowledge him. He continued to stand there looking at Anna.

"Your sister has told me so much about you," Alexander began.

Anna wished her husband wouldn't try to make conversation, as her brother obviously had no interest in pleasantries.

"Zaco, please come in." Anna came toward him.

Zaco walked past Alexander as if her husband was invisible. He stood in front of Anna, seeming to study her.

"Don't you have a hug and a kiss for your sister?" Anna asked, continuing to approach him with her arms outstretched.

"*Si, si.* My little sister. You look well." He smiled at her and addressed her in Ladino, the language of their childhood. He embraced her while scowling at Alexander.

"Litsa, should I leave? You'll be all right?" Alexander seemed at a loss to know what to say. Zaco's use of Ladino was an obvious attempt to shut out her husband from their conversation.

"I'll be fine," she told him.

"Does this man think I would harm my own sister? Is that what he thinks of the Carraso family, that we are subhumans as the Aryan Nazis claim?"

"If you spoke in a language other than Ladino, I'm sure he would answer you."

"I'll be in the library if you need me," said Alexander. Anna could sense his reluctance to leave her alone with her brother.

"I'm fine, Alexander."

"I shall leave you two alone." Alexander bowed stiffly to her brother and walked out of the kitchen door.

Thank God, thought Anna. She was concerned that if Alexander had stayed, it might have ended with unpleasantries and harsh words between the two men she loved. It was much better if she and her brother were left alone.

Zaco stared hard at her. "You are well? This family treats you well? He, that man, is good to you?"

"Zaco, you know?"

"Of course, I know. Our father knows. Do you think you could keep such a thing secret for very long?"

"I didn't have a choice," she began and then realized there was really nothing she could say that would explain to her brother what she'd done. Yes, she could say marrying Alexander had been forced by the impending occupation by the Nazis. But all the other reasons for her marriage, the pregnancy and her love for Alexander, her fervent wish to be his wife, she couldn't share with Zaco.

"You didn't have a choice?" he parroted. "Really, Anna? And you obviously chose not to tell us what you'd done."

"Because of the Nazi occupation, our father has so much else on his mind. He sent me here to be safe, and I didn't want to add to his worries. Eventually I was going to tell him."

"Well, what's done is done. Do you remember our neighbor, Elias Silva? He came over after he had returned from a trip to Athens. He told us he had seen a woman there who looked exactly like you. But this woman was a Greek Orthodox married woman who wore a cross. So where is your cross, my sister?"

"I'm not wearing it tonight," she said simply.

"Because you were going to see me? Because you thought you could tell me lies about your life here?"

"Because the Nazi who lives in our house is gone for the weekend. And I wear the stavro, the cross, to make people believe I am an Orthodox Christian. Father asked Kìrios Giannopolous to keep me safe. Zaco, I live in the same house as a Nazi. Once we learned we would most certainly be taken over by the Germans, Kìrios Antonios feared that as an unmarried woman I would be subject to the Nazi's desires. He told me that I must go into hiding. I didn't want to go into hiding."

Zaco's shoulders sagged. "Anna, my little sister, I am glad you're all right." His righteous indignation seemed to have drained away.

It was so good to see him, and she knew him well enough to realize his anger was spent.

"Would you like something to eat? I prepared some *taramasalata*. I have it in the icebox. Dinner will be ready later, and you are welcome to join us. We have some friends coming."

"I do like the look of these kourabiedes. And you know *taramasalata* is my favorite. I'm tempted to stay for dinner." He sat down on a stool.

"Zaco, here." She poured him a glass of retsina and put several cookies on a plate. "Now let's talk. I've missed the family so much. Is everyone all right? Letters don't go back and forth anymore. But we have messengers that bring us news. I believe these young men belong to the underground."

"Everyone is all right. Most people think we Jews have nothing more to fear from the Nazis, but Father doesn't believe that. The Germans proclaimed that all citizens will be treated equally. Neither Father nor your brothers believe that either. They took away our radios so that we are cut off from what is going on in the world. The newspaper offices were closed down, and anti-Semitic papers replaced them. I've heard you have radios and newspapers here in Athens."

"Yes, we do have a radio, but we aren't allowed to listen to anything but the Nazi station. And having a Nazi officer living in our house doesn't allow us much chance to adjust the dial. The newspapers are filled with Nazi propaganda. My hus...." she stopped herself from saying husband. "Alexander and his father have many contacts, and we do receive news from the outside. Kìrios Antonios informs me whenever he hears news of Salonika."

"Your husband Alexander?"

"Yes, my husband Alexander. He's a fine man and he's good to me."

"I could see that he feels protective of you, and it's good for a husband to feel that way about his wife."

"What did our father say when the neighbor told him about me in Athens?" Anna asked, fearing the answer.

"His face grew pale, but he said nothing. I spoke up and said it is truly amazing that two people could look so alike. Father never said a word about it after that day. When I told him I was going to Athens to join the andartes, he told me to seek you out in the Giannopolous household and make sure you are well."

"Anything else? Did he say anything else?" If only he said he understood, that what she had done was understandable.

"He said nothing else. But I will tell you, my dear sister, I am glad you are safe and this man Alexander cares for you." He smiled at her. "You always did whatever you wanted when we were children. Why should you behave any differently now that you are a grown woman?"

"Please stay for dinner. I can't bear the thought that we're only going to have these few minutes together. I've missed everyone so much."

"Has it been hard, Anna?"

"Pretending?"

"Yes, pretending."

"At first, yes. But so much is becoming second nature, which is best, so that I don't inadvertently make a mistake. When I go to church on Sunday, in my mind I am elsewhere. I'm not allowed to speak Greek, for we Jews from Salonika have a definite accent. Instead I speak French.

Tonight, if you stay for dinner, and you must, then you will speak French as well. Friends are coming with a young unmarried cousin. I know you like the ladies, my brother. I hear she is quite beautiful. I assume you've still not married, Zaco."

"No. How could I marry when there are so many beautiful women in the world?" he laughed.

"We're going to play the phonograph and dance. Someone found a Benny Goodman record and the Andrews sisters. They paid dearly for them on the black market. We're no longer allowed to possess the recordings of such decadent, degenerate music in the house. I know you love to dance. Please stay. I'd also like you to get to know Alexander. I'm not asking for your approval. I know that isn't coming. But at least see what a good man he is."

"And all this food?" He inhaled the smell from the oven. "Meat?"

"It's through Kìrios Antonios and his connections. For most Athenians, there isn't an abundance of food."

"It's so in Salonika as well. Any kind of meat is a luxury. We are living with Aunt Mathilda. The quarters are a bit close, and our mother and Aunt Tillie argue about the food or lack of food. But when the Germans took over our house, we were forced to leave."

"Come have dinner with us, please, Zaco."

"And who shall we say that I am, Anna?"

"My neighbor from Kos. We grew up next door to each other. And my name is no longer Anna. I am Litsa."

And so they had a pleasant meal. Everyone praised Anna's cooking and baking. Alexander looked with so much pride at his wife. "She is wonderful, isn't she?" Alexander's words made her blush.

"Where are those phonograph records you promised us?" Anna gathered the plates from the table.

"We'll meet you in the parlor with the phonograph." Dimetri helped his wife out of the chair.

"May I escort you?" Zaco asked the young attractive woman who hadn't been immune to his charms.

Nicoletta looked up at him and batted her eyelashes. "Of course." She put her hand in his.

Anna finished clearing the dishes and smiled as the sounds of Benny Goodman's band filled the corridor. For a brief moment, she could believe it was like old times, before the world had turned upside down.

"Isn't it grand!" exclaimed Nicoletta. "I'm having so much fun this evening."

"Shall we dance?" Zaco took her hand as the music played and the wail of the saxophone filled the room.

"Your neighbor is quite the charmer." Irini smiled.

"We used to say he could charm the birds out of the trees. But don't worry about your niece. He goes home tomorrow." Anna felt so good sitting in her parlor, watching her brother dance, listening to their favorite swing music.

"We haven't seen the two of you in the cafés," Irini, her belly swelling with early pregnancy, commented. "I've heard your Nazi comes at least once or twice a week, with the Italian nurse."

"Anna and I have no interest in sitting with the Germans, watching them eat food we are not served, listening to their drunken songs," said Alexander.

"Well, Dimetri and I don't go all that often. But it's a welcome diversion once in a while. Maybe we can all go to the cinema next week. There is a rumor that a Cary Grant movie is playing, instead of the usual approved German film. We can take a chance that the rumor is true."

"I'd like to go," Anna agreed.

"So, Alexander." Dimetri lit a cigarette with the flame from his silver lighter. "I heard about your father's olive-oil factory. Damn shame, don't you think?"

"The olive-oil factory?" Anna asked.

"You haven't heard? It was blown up two days ago. Blown to smith-ereens."

"But it didn't belong to us anymore. Why would the Nazis do such a thing?" Anna tried to understand. She frowned at the silence between the two men.

"Well, I guess the Germans won't be able to use the olive oil to lubri-cate their machines. What a pity." Alexander leaned back in his chair.

"Oh." Anna suddenly understood. It wasn't the Germans who blew up the factory. It was the Greeks.

"Come, Litsa." Alexander took her hand. "Let's dance and forget fac-tories and the Nazis. Let's have a good time, while our jailer is gone."

As they danced and listened to the music the Nazis had declared verbo-ten, one could almost forget they were an occupied country. Anna danced with her husband, Dimetri, and her brother. She remembered dancing with her brother when she was a teenager. She had been worried about knowing the steps and appearing foolish before the eyes of those boys she'd wanted to impress. And so her big brother Zaco had consented to teach her how to dance. Tonight her head was filled with so many good memories of happier days, when she was together with her family.

Later that evening, it was difficult to say good-bye to Zaco. He prom-ised to send word to their father that Anna was well cared for and safe in the Giannopolous home.

"Zaco, when the war is over, we'll all be together again. Alexander and I will go to Salonika. Do you think Papa and Mama will be able to accept my marriage?"

"I don't know the answer to that, Anna. But I do know he wants you to be safe, and that is the most important thing. And, yes, this Alexander seems a good man. I can see how much he cares for you. He and his father are very generous to the underground with their funds and connections. If he were Jewish, he would have been the perfect bridegroom for you. Now I must go. Stay safe, my little sister." He kissed her good-bye.

Anna was standing over the sink washing the dishes, while Alexander stood at her side, eating an orange, frowning at her. "How much longer will it be before you're finished?"

"A while. There are a lot of dishes to wash and dry."

"If you promise to never tell a living soul that I helped you in the kitchen, I'll dry the dishes while you wash." He grabbed a towel and began drying.

"Of course, I shall never tell a living soul that my husband was so eager to get me into our bed that he demeaned himself by helping in the kitchen." She smiled. "But there is something else I wanted to discuss with you."

"Yes." He put down the dish in his hand.

"When I see Irini so happy about her pregnancy, I think about the baby we lost. You know I was ambivalent about my pregnancy, and I still believe this is a terrible time to bring a child into the world. But if we wait until the Nazis leave, maybe it will be too late. Maybe I'll be too old by then, or maybe they'll never leave. When I walk down the street and see a mother pushing her child in a carriage, I feel an ache inside of me. An ache for the child we lost." She bit her lip.

"Litsa." He took her hands in his and looked into her eyes. "We'll do whatever you want. If you decide to throw away your diaphragm, I won't object."

"But Von Hoffberg wouldn't allow us to continue living here with a child."

"Then we'll go somewhere else, somewhere where we won't be prisoners in our own house. We could leave Athens if need be. Our medical expertise would be welcomed everywhere."

"No," she sighed. "I don't want us to bring a child into this horrible world now. We can wait. Things will get better. They have to."

Anna turned off the water from the faucet and looked toward the corridor. Was that a knock on the front door? There was a sound, a timid knock. Or was it just the wind? "What was that?"

"It's the front door. It's the middle of the night, Litsa. Stay here while I get the revolver from our bedroom. Don't open the door. Good news doesn't come at such an hour." He hurried from the kitchen.

Anna took off her apron, dried her hands on a towel, and walked down the corridor. She stood in the shadows far from the door, waiting for Alexander to return. Maybe it was nothing, just the wind, a tree branch against the door.

Alexander approached the door with a revolver tucked into his waist. "Who is it?"

There was a faint answer that neither of them could discern. "I said, who is it? I shall not open this door until you answer!" Alexander shouted.

There was an answer again, in a louder voice that Anna couldn't understand, but apparently Alexander heard it as he opened the door. "My God, Fenia!"

A young woman dressed in filthy rags staggered inside the door. Alexander caught her as she began to sag to the floor. "What's happened? Litsa, this is the woman who lives at our farm with her husband and children."

"I'm sorry to come here," she sobbed. "But I didn't know where else to go, and my Nasos would want you to know."

"What's happened?" Alexander asked in a gentle voice.

"Is there any food? Please some food. Anything at all. I've barely eaten since I left the farm, and it was days ago. I don't remember how long."

"I'll get something." Anna ran to the kitchen and grabbed whatever she could easily put on a plate. When she returned, Alexander was seated on a sofa next to the disheveled woman.

"Where is your husband, Nasos? You've come all this way alone?" Alexander's voice was filled with concern.

"Nasos is dead." She wrung her hands in despair. "Everything is in ruins. We were inside the house when we heard the tanks. The Nazis banged on our door. They took the food from our larder and began shooting the animals. They machine-gunned the chickens, even the pigeons, as they laughed. They took away our dairy cows. I instructed my children to run out the backdoor and seek refuge with the neighbors. When Nasos pleaded with them not to take our donkey.... there were tears in his eyes as he begged them to spare the donkey, the Germans shot my husband in the head and laughed. They set fire to the olive groves. With so much smoke, I was able to hide in a ravine. There's nothing left. Nothing! A neighbor is keeping my children until I return. I don't know what to do, Kìrios Giannopolous. I didn't know where else to turn. Forgive me for coming like this in the middle of the night. Nasos tried to save the farm, but he couldn't. He was a fine hard-working man. He tried, but the Germans are not human. Ours was not the only farm and groves that were torched." She began to sob.

"Please eat something." Alexander took her hands in his. "I will make arrangements for you and your children. After you eat, you must rest."

"I have clothes, shoes for you," Anna offered. "We have food hidden in the shelter that we can give to her." Anna watched the woman devour the bread and cheese.

Alexander got to his feet. "Litsa, tomorrow at first light, I'll go to meet with the underground. They will find a place for Fenia and her children. Those Nazi bastards! Killing an unarmed man. Shooting animals for sport when famine is licking at our heels."

"Did the soldiers harm you?" Anna asked in a soft voice, looking at the woman's bruises on her arms and the swelling on her face.

"No, no, of course not," Fenia answered fearfully, avoiding her gaze, as tears slipped down her cheeks.

"Alexander, I'll take Kiría Fenia to our room and help her cleanse herself and put her to bed."

"Don't worry, Fenia," he told the woman in a reassuring voice. "It was good that you came here. I'll find a place for you and your children."

Anna escorted the woman to her bedroom.

"Fenia," Anna said as she helped the woman remove her garments, noticing the dried blood on her limbs. "I'm a nurse. You can tell me if there is anywhere on your body that might need special care."

"No, no. Thank you." She closed her eyes and winced as Anna gently washed the dirt and blood from her body. Fenia raised her arms and let Anna pull a clean nightgown over her head.

The two women sat on the bed, and Anna took her hand. "I'll get you an ointment for your wounds. We have something to help you in our medicine cabinet."

"Please stay here with me. Don't go. It feels so good not to be alone. I was so afraid."

"Of course, Fenia. Fenia, you can tell me if the soldiers hurt you."

"No, no," she began to sob.

"It's all right." Anna cradled her in her arms.

"Please, you can't tell anyone. No one must know. I'm so ashamed. At least my Nasos was already dead. If anyone else knows, I shall never be able to remarry. How will I exist as a woman without a husband? My children will never have a father. We shall have to depend on the charity of others, and in these terrible times…."

"I won't tell, I promise. No one will know. Shh, shh," Anna tried to soothe her. "How many soldiers hurt you?"

"Th…-three. I said no. I pleaded and I cried. They wouldn't listen. I should have resisted. I should have killed myself. But who would take care of my children?"

Anna continued to cradle the sobbing woman in her arms. "It wasn't your fault. It wasn't your fault. Kìrios Alexander and Kìrios Antonios will take care of you and your children."

CHAPTER 11

January 1942: Athens

AS WINTER WORE on, the famine in Greece grew more overwhelming. The British, determined not to allow Germany to bring in any supplies to the Greek ports, had blockaded the harbors. The wheat normally imported to Greece was prevented from entering and was diverted to other countries. Railroad tracks between Salonika and Athens were damaged, so moving wheat by rail was very difficult. With all means of transportation confiscated, the farmers taxed beyond their means, fields burned by Nazi soldiers, no food was entering Athens, save for the black market and the meager rations doled out by the Nazis..... the people of Athens were starving.

"I need to leave the hospital early to work at the Red Cross soup kitchen," Anna told Alexander, as their hospital operating gowns were being fastened before their early morning procedure.

"I'll try to get away as early as I can. You'll have to wait for me. It's not safe for you to be alone on the streets. Well-to-do women are being attacked by beggars." Alexander finished scrubbing his hands.

"I know, I know," Anna sighed as she put on her surgical mask.

"While you're doling out soup, I can help with medical care for the people. Medical care, isn't that laughable? Most of what I see is due to malnutrition, and there is no magic cure, save for food of which there is almost none. I've heard they're going to institute new rules. Unless a medical professional pronounces someone to be suffering from malnutrition, they will not be permitted entrance to the soup kitchen."

"Rules and more rules for the poor starving people," Anna said as they walked toward the doors of the operating theater.

"There wouldn't need to be so many rules, if there was enough food for everyone. I've also heard there are many people who supposedly qualify for the soup kitchen but are too weak to get there. How many people must die before this is over?" Alexander swore a Greek oath under his breath as they pushed through the doors.

The sky was overcast and gray. Large snowflakes began to swirl toward the ground. The cold wind whipped at their coats as they hurried through the snow-covered streets, walking toward Syntagma Square, passing the Old Royal Place, where the large scarlet swastika flag waved in the frigid air. As Anna and Alexander walked around the square, they passed the confiscated bicycles and cars tightly packed beside each other, filling the pavement.

While Anna and Alexander continued to make their way to the soup kitchen, Anna tried to keep her gaze averted from the sidewalks and streets. Beggars, children, women, men, ex-soldiers held out their hands, their mouths filled with words of supplication:…. "Please…. *Pinao* … I'm hungry…. some food, anything…. a crumb of bread…. milk for my children." Ex-servicemen were everywhere, many of them amputees, who had made their way to Athens from the Albanian front, lacking both the money and the means to go home. They were forced to camp out in the streets with no means of support and no shelter from the elements and the freezing temperatures of this unusually bitter winter.

Anna and Alexander walked the last few streets to the soup kitchen, careful not to step on the emaciated corpses that littered the sidewalks. The cart to pick up the dead had not yet made its rounds. The line for the soup kitchen stretched all around the block. It was the one meal these people might eat all day or sometimes the only meal for the entire week.

"Kiría Litsa," Mary Agnes, the middle-aged woman who headed the soup kitchen, spoke in a low tone as she took her place next to Anna, who was ladling thin soup into bowls. "I just came back from my meeting with the Nazi commandant. What a foul man! I arranged this meeting in order to plead for milk for the children. I explained the situation was so dire that the Red Cross was identifying only one child to help in each family. Can you imagine having to decide which child to try to save, the healthiest child, who might survive? And with that decision they know they are condemning the other children in the family to a certain death from starvation. I pleaded with the Nazi, in the name of God, to give us milk for the children. And you know what he told me? He said German officers need milk for their coffee, and none can be spared for Greek children. Then as if trying to impress me with his compassion, he said he had notified his higher-ups in Berlin about the starvation situation. He was told not to concern himself with the dire fate of the Greeks, and certainly not to bother his superiors in Berlin again. All that's important is that German soldiers are well fed."

Anna shook her head with despair as she spooned the soup into the bowl of the boy standing before her. Those large dark eyes looking up at her, the stick-thin arms outstretched with a bowl broke her heart. Each time she was here, she tried in vain to steel herself against the sights in the soup kitchen. But it was the children who often brought tears to her eyes.

"Have you noticed there are more and more boys on the streets?" Anna commented to Mary Agnes. "After only three months in session, the schools have all been closed down. The children are now roaming the streets. I've talked to the boys, and so many of them are orphans, living on the streets with nowhere else to go. When there isn't enough food for the family, their mothers go without, so there is something for the children. It's only a matter of time before the mothers die from starvation. And the situation is getting so much worse. In the fall, people dug up grass and weeds to eat. But now in the winter, there is nothing, nothing at all. How many of these people, these children, will survive until spring when grasses will begin sprouting again? And even then, how much nutrition can be found in blades of grass? Children need protein to grow."

"And of course, there is almost no protein to give them," the woman acknowledged as she dipped her ladle into the large pot. "I thought by establishing the soup kitchens that it would help. But sometimes I wonder how much good we can do in the midst of so much hunger. And our new program, where each of us adopts a child to feed one good meal each day, seems like such a small contribution in the face of so much misery."

"I approached other women in our church to sponsor a child," Anna told her. "Not everyone is able to feed another mouth. But many were grateful to learn about the program." Anna looked down as her ladle scraped the bottom of the pot. She would only be able to fill the next bowl halfway.

The soup had been depleted. They had to inform those waiting in line that there was nothing more to give them. "Come back tomorrow," they told the poor souls. Knowing full well, because of the unpredictable suppliers, there might be nothing to offer them tomorrow.

Anna sat down in a circle of wooden chairs, alongside the other women who volunteered in the kitchen. A feeling of hopeless depression hung over the room as they began to share stories of the terrible things they had witnessed and the unbelievable accounts of misery that they had heard. Anna could have gone to the room where the doctors were treating the ill. But she knew there was so much that Alexander never told her, trying to shield her from all the misery. Here among the women, everyone wanted to share the terrible things they had witnessed and the heartbreaking stories they had heard. There was a new woman with them today, whom Anna had never seen before. "That is the Rabbi's wife, Kiría Barzilai," Anna was told.

An older woman with white hair began, "I was passing by Omonia Square this morning, and men were lying on blankets above the vents of the subway, trying to keep warm in this freezing weather."

"Have you seen the women scavenging through the Germans' garbage, hoping to find potato peels?" The Rabbi's wife sadly shook her head.

"I passed a line of what must have been three hundred people who had brought chairs with them, to wait, because of a rumor that one shop had cigarettes."

"A woman was walking beside me this morning. She collapsed on the street. A crowd gathered around her. She was dead, and her two little children sat beside her, pulling on her coat, crying, begging her to get up." The woman wiped her eyes with a handkerchief.

The room was filled with silence. After several minutes, the women arose from their chairs and proceeded to the cloakroom.

Anna was putting on her coat beside Kiría Barzilai. "Hello," Anna greeted her. "I'm Kiría Litsa Giannopolous. We're pleased to have you here."

"Kiría Giannopolous?" She smiled at her. "I came as soon as I heard about the soup kitchen." The woman addressed her in Greek.

"We hope to see you again tomorrow." Anna spoke to her in French. She never spoke Greek anymore. It was easier that way so that her accent from Salonika wouldn't be identified.

"I know of you, Kiría Giannopolous," the Rabbi's wife lowered her voice. "Your husband came to see my husband before you married."

Anna felt frozen and didn't reply as she took a step backward. Please, she thought, please don't say anymore.

"Do not worry, Kiría Litsa. It's good to have met you." She smiled at Anna and patted her hand. "I'll see you again tomorrow."

As Anna and Alexander walked back toward their villa, the silence was heavy between them. "Please help me. *Pinao*, I'm hungry." They heard the desperate plea over and over again. Despite their heartfelt concern, they were growing so used to the pitiful pleas that they barely heard the tearful voices. And that made their sorrow at what was happening in their country even more profound. As they made their way toward their neighborhood, they had to walk around the memorial displays, which marked the ground where demonstrators had been shot and killed while taking part in protests.

"What's going on over there?" Anna pointed her gloved hand across the street to where a swarm of boys had descended to an area below the balcony of a large well-appointed house.

As they neared the crowd of boys who were looking up at the balcony, and then down at the street, Anna caught her breath and blinked back tears.

Two German officers, snug in their winter coats, were standing on the balcony looking below at the children dressed in tatters. The men took turns popping an olive into their own mouths and then tossing the pit down to the street. As the mob of boys fought each other in hopes of retrieving a pit and sucking it dry, the Nazis roared with laughter.

"Litsa," Alexander said to Anna as they undressed before bed. "We can't feed all of Athens."

"But we have food left over from our meals with Von Hoffberg, and your father has easy access to everything in the black market. I know he owns many caïques that transport blackmarket goods from all over the islands back to Athens."

"My dear wife," he stepped out of his trousers. and placed them neatly across the back of a chair "The black market should not be of concern to you. Patéra's business dealings provide us with what we need. With his factories confiscated, it was necessary for him to look for other businesses to sustain our family. But it's a precarious enterprise for him, and at any time he could be in danger. My father can't supply enough for everyone we see on the street. And you know you can't take the food that Von Hoffberg has ordered for our own table."

"So many are suffering, Alexander, while we have food to eat."

"Is it better if we were also to starve? And, Kiría Michaelitsa Giannopolous, I'm not pleased to see you eat only half the lunch you bring to the hospital. I know you go down to the backdoor and give away half of your food. Do you think I haven't noticed you are losing weight?" He watched her unbuttoning her dress.

"I've always been a little plump." She hung her dress in the armoire.

"Have you heard any complaints from me?" He smiled at her. "You have such a good heart, Litsa."

"It's cold in here." She reached for her nightgown. "I guess it's too much to wish for an early spring."

"Come into bed under the covers with me." He helped her pull the flannel nightgown down over her head. "I will hold you. *S'agapò.* I love you."

"*S'agapò.*" Anna smiled up at him. She turned down the lamp and followed him into their bed. "I'm having so much trouble sleeping. I keep seeing the beggars, hearing their cries."

"I know." He pulled the layers of quilts over them and held her close. "You toss and turn all night."

"I try to be strong and not let myself break down. But..." Her shoulders began to heave with silent sobs.

"You're safe here with me. You don't have to be strong all the time." He gathered her tightly in his arms, as she quietly cried against his shoulder.

As he held Anna close, his worries about her raced through his mind, as they did every night. He was the man. He was supposed to keep her safe from harm and safe from the pain that wracked her heart. But promising to keep her safe might well be an empty promise in the face of Nazi brutality. Since the Nazi storm troopers had marched into Athens, the Jews hadn't been treated differently than the Greek Orthodox. However, there were instances when the Nazis decided to execute suspicious "political activists." There always seemed to be Jews in the group who were shot, supposedly as an example to others. While Anna's dreams were haunted by the famine in Athens, his dreams were often of the horrors he'd witnessed in Germany during the 1930s, and the terrible things that had happened to Jews.

As they lay in the darkness of their room, the silence was broken by the sound of adolescent girls with cardboard megaphones who stood on the rooftops and shouted anti-Nazi slogans and encouragement to the Greek people.

"Those girls are so brave," Anna murmured. "If the Nazis catch them, I shudder to think what might happen."

"It's you I worry about," he told her. "Litsa, I could send you out of Greece. Patéra has been transporting Jews to Turkey, to Palestine, to Cairo."

"There is too much to do here. How could I walk away from this suffering? I'm no longer a Jewish woman. I go to church. I wear a stavro. And now that we aren't only treating Germans, but the hospital has again opened our doors to Greek people, I need to be here to help them."

"I understand, but I worry about you. There is something more that I can do. I'm going to see Archbishop Damaskinos. I want to obtain a new baptismal certificate for you." He sighed with resignation.

"What's wrong with the one that I already have?"

"You need to be issued one that is dated from the year you were born."

"I don't understand."

"Being a new convert will not keep you safe from the Nazis."

"Jews aren't being singled out for persecution."

"Not yet. But I told you what I saw when I was a student in Germany. The Nazis hate your people for some unknown reason, and I must do everything I can to keep you safe."

It was morning, and Herr Von Hoffberg, Anna, and Kìrios Antonios were seated around the lace-covered oval breakfast table. Alexander had been called away for an early-morning emergency at the hospital. Herr Von Hoffberg was frowning as he ate the *pfannkuchen*, the pancakes he had insisted that Ariadne learn to prepare. They had learned his frown always preceded an outburst of displeasure, sometimes about something trivial and occasionally about something more serious. They could only hope this morning's lecture to them would be about a matter easily resolved. Anna was hoping he didn't dislike the pancakes. He usually was quite satisfied with Ariadne's cooking. But when he didn't like something, he yelled at her and frightened the poor woman, who feared she'd lose her position and be thrown out into the streets.

"It's too cold in here. Are you trying to freeze me to death?" the Nazi sneered at them.

"There was a problem getting coal," Anna tried to explain. "I assure you that none of us enjoys being cold."

Herr Von Hoffberg glared at her and turned to Kìrios Antonios. "Herr Giannopolous, has your son not taught his wife to show respect?"

"Excuse me." Anna tried to appear contrite. "Please, excuse my outburst, sir. I meant no disrespect. I'm out of sorts this morning, for indeed it is too cold in here. Mattheo has been promised a large shipment of coal this afternoon."

"See to it that the coal is delivered by the time I return from my meetings." He cut a forkful of pancake and swallowed it. Herr Von Hoffberg took another piece of pancake and narrowed his eyes at Kìrios Antonios. He looked down at his plate of untouched food. "Because I am so kind hearted, I ask that we eat together, and I see that you do not eat."

Kìrios Antonios smiled at him. "Yes, of course I am eating." He took a large piece of pancake. "We are so fortunate that you instructed Ariadne to make pancakes. They are delicious."

"Yes, they are good. The woman is learning to cook like a German, and that's good. But living in this country is becoming so dreary," he mused. "Yesterday, the weather was a bit more moderate, and I attempted to walk to my meeting at the Grande Bretagne Hotel. Exercise is good for one, you know. You Greeks don't realize that not having cars and buses keeps you in good condition. Relying on cars makes you soft."

Herr Von Hoffberg took a swallow of his coffee. "Your home is proving most satisfactory to me, but this city of Athens is such a disappointment. Yesterday when I walked to my meeting, I had such an unpleasant experience. Athens has become totally disgusting, and I shall not walk through the streets of your city again. You people don't even know how to care for your dead. Corpses littering the streets, until the cart comes to take them away.… Don't the Greek Orthodox believe in a proper burial?"

"Herr Von Hoffberg, I'm afraid it costs money for a proper funeral and burial," said Kìrios Antonios. "Money is necessary for fuel to transport the dead. Families have no money, and there's no fuel to purchase even if they had the money. I can assure you, it is a great shame for a family to not be able to properly bury their loved ones."

"Well, it just proves you people are inferior if you can't solve this problem. Walking your streets has become a vile experience, and it offends my German sensibilities. Can a man like yourself do nothing to solve this problem?"

"Unfortunately, I have no influence on the public policy concerning the dead."

"Have you influence on these people who are protesting and marching in the streets, demonstrating against who knows what, clogging the avenues, singing the Greek anthem? Don't they understand they are now part of the Third Reich and should proudly be singing *Deutschland Uber Alles*?"

"I don't concern myself with demonstrations. I'm occupied with my business for importing goods. Shortly after our breakfast, I'll be leaving for a few days."

"I look forward to your return, when you of course will provide me with a substantial portion of your shipment. My Antoinette especially likes chocolates and perhaps some nylon stockings. My wife, Bertha…I probably should send her something as well. Her letters to me are filled with so many complaints; it has become an onerous chore for me to read those letters." He paused. "I think she'd like some jewelry. A pity, Frau Giannopolous, that you did not have any treasures to share with me."

He turned toward Kìrios Antonios. "I assume your wife took all her jewelry with her?"

"Yes, she did."

"Well, there is a large collection of confiscated jewelry from the political prisoners who have been executed. I shall stop by the warehouse and see if I can find something suitable for Bertha. The last time I went to the postal office to send a package back to Germany, the workers were on strike. I don't understand why they are not executed on the spot for such insubordination. They better be back at their jobs when I have my package ready to send to Bertha. Herr Giannopolous, how soon can I expect your return?"

"Four or five days at most. I'll do my best to get what you requested." Kìrios Antonios ate a piece of the pancake, which he definitely disliked, preferring a Greek breakfast. "I'm sure the postal workers will have returned to their offices by the time your package is ready for shipment."

"Hmph." Von Hoffberg finished his pancakes and got to his feet. "It's too cold in this house. I'm going to the office of Herr Waldheim, where it is warm."

Anna and Kìrios Antonios watched him leave and heard the sound of the front door closing before they spoke.

"That arrogant bastard, having the nerve to talk about our dead. Corpses wouldn't be all over the streets if those Nazis weren't starving our people," said Kìrios Antonios. "I have heard that often when a family member dies at home, the body is brought to the cemetery and thrown over the wall of the graveyard. No one reports these deaths because the family needs to keep the ration card to purchase more food. To not have a proper burial with a priest is terrible, so terrible." He crossed himself and uttered a prayer. "Litsa…" He paused and pushed away his plate of unfinished food. "You must be more careful about what you say to him."

"I'm sorry. I know it was wrong. I know that."

"He often seems like an affable buffoon, but he holds dangerous power over us. Do you think the groveling I must do to this Nazi, in my own home, is pleasing to me? You must not give him any reason to be provoked. My son seems to find your independent, outspoken ways to be very charming. But speaking without thinking will get you into trouble. We must all be very careful, Litsa."

February 1942: Athens

Anna sat across the table from the young girl she had "adopted," in order to provide her one meal each day.

Today, when the child had taken off her threadbare coat, in the warmth of the Giannopolous kitchen, Anna was pleased to notice that the boils that had covered her arms last month were healing. The administration of proper nutrition and the vitamins the child's body so desperately needed were easing some of the signs of severe malnutrition. The girl, with her head shaved to control infestations of lice, finished her last mouthful of stew and smiled at Anna.

"*Epharisto*—thank you, Kiría Giannopolous. My father said not to forget to say *epharisto*. And the parcel of food I bring home makes everyone so happy. My mother, my father, my brothers, they are so hungry. My mother cries all the time. I wish she would stop. I tell her, 'Don't cry; I'm bringing food from Kiría Giannopolous.' But since my little sister Adonia died, she cries all the time. Yesterday I heard her talking to my dead grandparents, as if they were standing before her. It scares me. But my father says, 'Don't be scared. Soon everything will be all right.'"

Anna swallowed hard. What could she say to the child…. that everything will be all right? Anna realized her mother, like so many others, had begun hallucinating and lost touch with reality, one of the last stages before death from starvation. Perhaps that was better than facing the horrors around her, her family starving and dying before her very eyes.

Anna motioned for Ariadne to bring over the parcel of food that had been prepared for the family. "And your father?" Anna began to inquire, knowing the man had been unemployed for months, ever since the factory closed for lack of raw materials.

They were all startled by the kitchen door slamming open and the sound of Herr Von Hoffberg's leather boots on the tiled kitchen floor.

"So! What is this?" he shouted, as his eyes opened wide at the sight of the young girl.

"This is Barbara Likatsa, Herr Von Hoffberg. The women of Athens have organized a special program…. "

"A special program?" he interrupted her. "A special program to allow unwashed vermin into the kitchen where my food is prepared!"

The child leaped out of her seat and hid behind Anna, seeking protection at the sound of Von Hoffberg's loud angry voice.

"It's only one meal a day for a starving child," Anna tried to explain with a sinking feeling in her stomach. This was not going to end well. But at least the child didn't understand German.

"This program!" he thundered. "Have I approved of such a thing for my household? Did you ask my permission? Of course not. You know I would never acquiesce to such a terrible idea. And the doctor and his father, do they know of these goings-on?"

"No, no, of course not," Anna lied. "What goes on in the kitchen only concerns women."

"I do not want filthy children in my kitchen!" He raised his hand and hit Anna across her face.

"Get out!" he yelled at the child, who stood frozen in fear.

"Leave now. Take your basket," Anna told the girl in Greek.

Von Hoffberg glared as the child grabbed the basket and ran out the kitchen door.

Anna fought the urge to touch her cheek that smarted from his blow.

"You!" He turned to Ariadne, who was nervously fingering her cross. "Scrub this kitchen from top to bottom. I shall eat in a taverna tonight. I've lost my appetite for eating here. Before breakfast tomorrow, I will come to inspect the kitchen. Make sure there were no lice brought into my house by that disgusting child."

"Yes, Herr Von Hoffberg," Ariadne answered in a timid voice.

"And you, Frau Giannopolous." He raised his hand in a threatening gesture.

Anna met his gaze with defiance. "Yes?" She knew she should be cowering, but she hated this man with every fiber of her being.

"You insolent little bitch!" He slapped her again.

Anna caught her breath and looked down at her shoes. She had gone too far. Patéra had warned her, and she hadn't listened. If she were injured and Alexander learned of it, there would be a confrontation that Alexander couldn't win. She'd swallow her pride to protect her household. "I am sorry," she said with contrition. "Very sorry, Herr Von Hoffberg."

"You are a nurse! Do you know nothing about hygiene! Never, never, never is there going to be a piece of trash like that girl allowed in my kitchen again. It is almost more than I can bear to have the soldiers with their unclean uniforms come to the clinic in the parlor. But I make pains to never enter that room, and the servants know to clean it thoroughly at the end of the day. But the kitchen where my food is prepared!"

"You are quite right. I was foolish, and it was stupid of me. It shall never happen again. I promise you." She hung her head in what she hoped would appear to be shame.

Anna and Ariadne watched him stomp out of the kitchen. Both of the women let out a collective sigh of relief.

Anna gingerly touched her burning cheek. "Some ice, please, for my cheek," Anna asked the older woman. "Ariadne, I ask you not to tell anyone that he hit me. Do you understand?"

"Yes." Ariadne handed her ice wrapped in a cloth. "I understand, Kiría Litsa."

CHAPTER 12

July 1942: Athens

A SMOKE-FILLED HAZE hung over the room, as Anna stood beside Alexander, who was rolling the dice in the gambling establishment frequented by Nazis and those with connections to the black market. These were the people with money to spend, money to lose, and hopes of money to be made. Intermingled with the fashionable men and women were young boys hawking currants and cigarettes, who had the good fortune to possess something to sell. On the other side of the room, Kìrios Antonios was drinking his ouzo as he chatted with friends, other middle-aged men, who were playing cards around a small table.

Earlier that evening, Anna had protested against attending the gambling tonight. "I'm really not keen about going." She stood in front of the mirror, straightening her white linen dress with puffed sleeves and a cinched waist. Satisfied with her appearance, she slipped her feet into her white pumps and began to apply her scarlet lipstick.

"Litsa, we need to go out on occasion. Staying home every night will just make us both more depressed." Alexander fastened his cuff links.

"We could go to the cinema," she offered.

"Litsa, haven't you ever gambled?" He opened the front door for her.

"No, I've never gambled, and it doesn't sound appealing to me."

"It's fun. There is so much excitement in the air…. the rush when the roulette wheel begins to spin. It's exhilarating."

"People losing money is fun?"

"People winning money is fun. Litsa, these days since the occupation, many men have lost everything overnight. So they throw caution to the winds. Does it matter if they lose everything to a Nazi or at the roulette table?"

"You don't find that depressing? And how much are you prepared to lose?"

"I have a set amount in my vest to wager, and I won't go beyond that," he tried to reassure her as they walked out the front door. "And I also want to go because there are people, my friends, who I haven't seen for quite a while."

"I still think it sounds like a stupid waste of time. I'd rather go to the movies."

"It's better to waste your time pretending to live in another world?"

"Yes." Anna stopped walking and placed her hands on her hips.

"Are you coming with me or not?" he asked her, watching her stand on the sidewalk without moving.

She looked up at the wall beside her, which was plastered with anti-Nazi posters as well as painted slogans. The posters would soon be torn down only to be replaced the next night. And the slogans, after being painted over, would also appear again. "Some of the graffiti is quite beautiful, don't you think?"

"Litsa, don't change the subject. Do you want me to take you back home? If you're going to be so down, I'd as soon go alone. Lady Luck doesn't like a sourpuss. What's wrong with you tonight? You aren't yourself."

"Maybe you'd like me to stay home. I bet Lady Luck isn't the only woman there tonight that might interest you."

"Litsa, stop that."

She could hear the exasperation in his voice.

"I heard something today," she began. "Something bad happened in Salonika. That's all I heard. There aren't any details yet. My family is there. Going to a gambling den for fun when something terrible may have happened to my family...."

"Litsa," he softened his tone and took her hand. "I've heard the same rumors. I didn't want to say anything to you until the rumors were confirmed, until we know what actually happened. Come here." He pulled her close.

"We're in the middle of a public street," she protested.

"I don't care. You're my wife." He enfolded her in his arms.

Anna leaned against him. "I need to go home to Salonika, Alexander. I need to go back to my family, to my people. I need to help them."

"This isn't your home? My people haven't welcomed you as one of their own?"

"Yes, of course, but…. I feel so torn."

"You can't go back to Salonika, and you know that, Litsa. Your father sent you here to be safe. When you were still writing letters back and forth, you asked to go home, and he always said no. Do you think now that something might have happened he'd want you there? Things have improved here in Athens over the spring and early summer, and you know that. Not so many beggars on the streets anymore, not such terrible famine. I promise you the gambling and people having fun will take your mind off your worries for at least a while. When we learn what actually happened in Salonika, maybe we can do something to help. But until then, can't we enjoy this night out? All right?"

Alexander was clearly enjoying the diversions of the roulette wheel. He kept urging Anna to drink more ouzo. And she knew he was hoping that if she continued drinking, she would start to enjoy herself. She'd been correct about tonight. She wasn't having a good time. There was a crowd gathering around Alexander, cheering him on, excited by his good fortune. Anna didn't want to drink anymore. She was feeling a bit light-headed, and she thought she already had too much to drink this evening. She nibbled on some currants Alexander had purchased from a tattered street urchin, whose eyes were now fastened on her husband. The boy clearly seemed to be enjoying the excitement of the evening. Alexander overpaid him and told him to keep the change. The child had given him a brilliant smile and now seemed to have attached himself to Alexander, mesmerized by the roulette wheel and the spinning ball.

Alexander continued to bet on winning numbers, and as the wheel whirled again, Anna left his side and made her way across the room. He was so engaged in his game, she doubted he'd even notice she was gone. As for her, watching people wager, win, and lose did not engage her interest for very long.

"Please sit down." An attractive, well-dressed Greek man whom she didn't recognize got up and offered her his chair.

"Thank you," she answered in French, grateful to no longer be standing on her feet.

"Ah, mademoiselle, you are French?" He smiled down at her. "May I introduce myself, Theo Horiatis."

"Litsa Giannopolous. No, I am Greek. But my mother was French, and so it was my first language, the language we spoke at home, and I'm most comfortable with it." She repeated the same lie she needed to tell over and over again.

"Hi, Litsa!" Anna recognized the voice she knew belonged to Antoinette.

"Hello," Anna answered. The woman had appeared at her side, with a drink balanced in her palm.

"Haven't seen you out in a while. I don't think I ever saw you here before. My Rupert is in the other room finishing off his dinner."

The Nazi was here? Anna smiled at Antoinette all the while thinking, Can I never get away from that man who keeps us prisoner in our own house? He never stops telling us what to eat, controlling what stations to tune into on the radio, what music we can listen to on the phonograph, what books we may read. She so did not want to see him tonight. The one good thing about tonight, being away from him, had vanished.

"Hello, Theo." Antoinette rested her hand on Theo's shoulder. "So you have met Litsa, the super nurse?" She was slurring her words. The woman definitely had too much to drink.

"Super nurse? Someone so beautiful is a nurse, working with the sick? She was just telling me she prefers to discourse in French, the language of her mother."

"French, German, Italian, even English. Litsa speaks them all it seems, except for Greek. Isn't it odd that I've never heard this Greek woman uttering a word of her own language, except when she spoke in a soft voice to the Greek soldiers, so soft that I couldn't even hear what she was saying."

"English? You speak English?"

"I received my education in the States. So I'm fluent in English, or probably one would say American English."

"And I as well. What a coincidence. I also attended university in the States. A wonderful country, isn't it?" The man easily conversed in English.

"Yes. I quite enjoyed my time there. Let's hope that now with the Americans in the war, that the tide will turn for us," Anna spoke in a low tone lest one of the Germans at a nearby table overheard her words against the Nazi regime.

"Litsa." Antoinette pouted. "Don't you enjoy having Rupert in your house? He'll be so disappointed when I tell him."

"Please, Antoinette. It is just that having someone, actually anyone, living in the house for such a long time is uncomfortable."

"So my Rupert makes you uncomfortable?"

"Antoinette, I think you've had too much to drink," Anna tried to sound concerned for her welfare.

"Yes, enough of that." Theo pried the glass out of her fingers. "Why don't you get something to eat?"

"I don't think you like my Rupert." Antoinette ignored Theo and frowned at Anna.

"That's nonsense, Antoinette. You know we are all very fond of Herr Von Hoffberg. He treats us so well," Anna managed to say.

"He won't like it when I tell him you are pleased the Americans are going to war against us."

"Why would I be pleased about the Americans?" Anna was rapidly losing patience with the woman. "Antoinette, your friend Herr Von Hoffberg has arranged through my father-in-law to get some chocolates and nylon stockings for you. It would be a shame if you never got them because you aggravated the relationship between us," Anna threatened her. This evening was rapidly going from bad to worse. Why had she ever agreed to come?

In addition, Anna was starting to feel somewhat uncomfortable about this man whom she knew nothing and to whom she had lacked the good sense to censor her feelings about the Nazis in her country. Yes, the man was Greek. But many Greek people were fifth columnists, Nazi collaborators, who had the advantage of blending in with everyone else. Antoinette wasn't the only one who'd had too much to drink tonight. Indeed, too much ouzo had loosened her own tongue.

Antoinette sat down in a chair and closed her eyes. "I don't feel so well. I've had too much wine. What's keeping Rupert?"

Theo turned his attention back to Anna. "What years were you in America?" he asked her.

Theo Horiatis was quite a charming man, and Anna soon forgot her concerns about his loyalty to the Greek nation. She thoroughly enjoyed her conversation with this pleasant, well-spoken man. They talked about their favorite restaurants in New York, those interesting places that all tourists like to visit: Central Park, the Statue of Liberty, the Empire State Building. They exchanged memories of the interesting restaurants in the area called Astoria, where many Greeks had settled and where one could get the Greek food that both of them longed for after their prolonged stay in America. She found herself laughing at the engaging tales of his life in New York. For a little while, she could forget about her family in Salonika and what might have happened there.

Antoinette sat drinking her wine in a chair next to them. Anna didn't know if she understood English, which made her conversation with this educated Greek man even more enjoyable. There was something about Antoinette that always made Anna uneasy.

She told herself it had nothing to do with her role as Von Hoffberg's mistress. In these desperate times, there were few options for women to help themselves survive. There were so many women and young girls prostituting themselves on the street corners of Athens, with the hope of earning enough to get food for their families. Desperate families never asked where their daughters had gone for the evening. Greek shame no longer seemed to exist in the days and months of terrible famine. Antoinette had a position as a nurse, but it didn't pay well, and having Von Hoffberg as her special connection gave her many luxuries that seemed so important in a world without them.

"How brave of you," Theo was saying.

"Brave?"

"To have left your home in Greece and to live in America on your own, without the protection of your family. Very unusual for a Greek woman."

"I have family in New York, so I wasn't all alone."

"Theo." A husky blond man in a blue-gray Luftwaffe uniform resplendent with metals approached them. "And who is this lovely woman at your side?"

"Kiría Litsa Giannopolous," Anna introduced herself.

"The wife of the doctor? I've noticed he's doing very well tonight. A most fortunate man."

"Yes," said Anna. Her interesting conversation with Theo was now at an end. She'd need to watch every word she said in front of the Nazi.

"Kiría Litsa and I were just talking about our experiences in America. We both studied in the city of New York."

"Soon the Third Reich will have our boots on the neck of the Americans. It's just a matter of time. As we now take photographs standing at the Acropolis, we shall soon have photographs of us standing by the Statue of Liberty. I was in America once for a visit. Americans are soft. Their armies cannot compete with our disciplined troops," the officer told them with great pride.

A great whoop of excitement broke out across the room. Kírios Antonios had joined Anna. "My son has good luck, doesn't he?" The older man smiled and introduced himself to the two men at Anna's side.

Anna decided she should return to Alexander, as her conversation with the Nazi was not one she wished to continue.

As she began to arise from her chair, her chest constricted by what she saw across the room. There was a young woman who had seated herself on Alexander's lap, whispering in his ear, and he had his hand on her thigh where her dress was hiked up past her knees.

Anna sank back down in the chair.

"Litsa." She heard the sound of Patéra's voice.

Anna looked up at her father-in-law, but words failed her.

Kìrios Antonios' gaze fell on Alexander, with the woman perched on his lap who was whispering into his ear, as a broad seductive smile spread across her face.

"He is a man, Litsa. This is what men do," her father-in-law told her in a soft voice. "He probably should show more discretion. I will speak to him about this. It isn't seemly to behave so when one's wife is in the same room."

Anna tried to turn away, but she couldn't help but stare at her husband and this woman. Take a deep breath, she told herself, as she felt all the ouzo she'd had to drink tonight turning over in her stomach. She vowed not to make a spectacle of herself, but she was overwhelmed with the feeling that she was going to vomit all over the floor.

And as she watched Alexander and this woman, who was now laughing at whatever clever words her husband had whispered to her, Alexander focused his gaze on Anna. It was as if his eyes were boring into her and wouldn't let go. He kept one woman on his lap, while he was trying to capture the gaze of his wife? Anna boldly met his stare. Was he daring her to interrupt his fun with this woman? But he wouldn't do such a shameful thing. Not the man who was her husband. Alexander pulled his gaze away from Anna, took his hand from the woman's ample thigh, and whispered something else in her ear. The woman kissed his cheek and rose from his lap.

Anna watched as Alexander gathered his money. "It's time for me to go," she heard him say. "For you," he pointed at the boy who had sold him the currants, "this is for you." He pressed money into his hand. "I have had incredibly good fortune tonight. And I'm sure it was your wonderful currants that gave me such good fortune. Perhaps the rest of you should also buy some currants from this young lad. I'm sure it will bring you luck," he spoke to the others gathered around the roulette wheel.

Alexander slowly made his way across the room toward Anna, as men congratulated him and clapped him on his back. Anna sat in her chair, her thoughts spinning in turmoil. What had she just witnessed between him and that woman? Was he really so brazen as to have another woman sitting on his lap with all the world to see, including his wife?

"We need to leave," he told her and extended his hand to help her up from the chair.

She shoved her hands into her dress pockets. "I'm not ready to leave, Alexander," she said defiantly, as she could think of nothing else to say with so many people standing around them.

"We are leaving." He pulled her up out of the chair. "Good night," he called out to everyone and tugged Anna across the room.

Once outside in the humid, oppressive night air, Anna extricated her arm from his hand. "I'm not going anywhere with you! How could you, Alexander? How could you behave like that, with me right there in the same room?"

"We are going to the Atlas Hotel," he said, looking down at her. "Really, Litsa, do you have so little trust in me?"

"Trust in a man who behaves like that..." She paused. "The Atlas Hotel? That's where many Jews are staying. Are you going to deposit me there with my people?"

"Litsa, you're so obstinate." He shook his head at her. "We're going to see your brother Zaco. He's staying at the hotel. He was afraid to come to our house, with Von Hoffberg there. He delivered a message to me by way of that woman, indicating that he needed my help. I know it looked as if I was engaged with her, but it was a ruse. In truth, she and I enjoyed each other's company before our marriage. I think it was her way of having fun at my expense. But she had a message from your brother, and so I needed to go along with her plan. Again, I'm sorry for causing you distress. Did you really think I wanted to shame you like that in public? As for your brother, I knew you wouldn't want me to go alone, without you." He started walking ahead of her in the street.

Anna didn't answer as she followed him toward the hotel. She was relieved about Alexander and that woman, but at the same time she was so worried about her brother. Why did he need help, and did he know what had happened in Salonika?

They waited at a street corner for armored troops to pass. Alexander turned to her and spoke in a soft voice. "I'm sorry to have upset you. There was no choice, and I had to play the game Eleni had concocted to deliver the message from your brother." He paused. "However, I must say, I wasn't pleased with your behavior this evening."

"My behavior? What are you talking about?"

"You behaved in a most common manner. Flirting with a man, laughing."

"You can't be serious."

"You didn't behave as a respectable married woman. You aren't in America anymore, and you mustn't bring shame to the name of Giannopolous."

"I won't listen to such ridiculous talk. No, I'm not in America. But you know I'm not a Greek woman who accepts her lowly place. I'm educated, and though we are married, I haven't given up having a mind of my own or having a stimulating conversation with someone. That man was very interesting. We shared much in common as we both were educated in the United States, and I enjoyed talking to him. And I told you I didn't want to come tonight."

The trucks had passed, and they proceeded down the broad avenue toward the hotel.

"Is my brother all right?" Anna asked. She didn't want to argue about these petty, foolish Greek notions with him.

"I know nothing except he asked for me to come to the hotel to see him." He looked down at her, his eyes narrowed with annoyance.

"Don't look at me like that." She glared at him and proceeded to walk in front of him. Their usual manner of holding hands was deliberately ignored by both Anna and Alexander, as the tension simmered between them.

Zaco opened the door and smiled at his sister. "I didn't think you'd also be coming. I'm so glad to see you. Both of you, come inside." Zaco was looking haggard, his arm bound in a sling, bruises on his face.

"You're hurt!" Anna probed the purple discolorations all over his cheek.

"It's nothing. Please sit down." He indicated a chair for Anna.

"I need help. I need money." Her brother turned to Alexander. "I apologize, but I didn't know who else to turn to."

"Of course." Alexander eyed Zaco's injuries with concern. "You are family. Your sister is my wife. Have you seen a doctor?"

"Yes, yes…I saw a doctor in Salonika before I escaped."

"Before you escaped? The rest of the family…Zaco, we heard rumors. What happened?" asked Anna.

"Here." He reached to the top of a worn dresser for a newspaper. "After we talk and I tell you everything, I want you to see what is printed in the papers of Salonika. Anti-Semitic articles fill the newspaper. It's the Jews who are behind all the woes that have ever befallen Greece." He handed Alexander the newspaper.

"Our brothers Victor and Paul have been conscripted for hard labor. Father escaped conscription because he's too old. All the women and children in the family remain unharmed."

"Tell us what happened, Zaco," Alexander prodded him.

"I will tell you everything, and you'll know why I escaped and ran away to Athens." He sank down on the small cot in his room.

"When I saw you last summer, I was going to join the andartes, the guerrilla movement in the mountains. I'd wanted to join in the hopes I would make a difference. But at that time, they weren't well organized. And every time they engaged in sabotage, the Nazis used collective punishment on nearby villages, killing everyone and burning everything to the ground. After a few months, I returned to our family. But I never thought I would need to leave Salonika for my own protection. Since the Nazi occupation, the Jews hadn't been treated more brutally than other Salonikans. But now that's all changed.

"It was one Saturday morning, and many of our people were dressed to attend the synagogue on that Sabbath morning. All Jewish men between the ages of fourteen and forty-five were summoned to Plateia Eleftheria, Freedom Square, to register for civilian labor. If you came from a Jewish family but now had converted, you were still considered a Jew and had to report. We were supposed to be there early in the morning. It was brutally hot that day, even so early in the morning. Once there, we were instructed to remove our hats, which you know was a problem for the more religious among us. And with our heads uncovered, there was no relief against the scorching sun, which beat down without mercy. I believe there were at least ten thousand men. Once we were assembled, we were made to do calisthenics, squats, somersaults, and other demeaning exercises. Because of my fair skin, I was overcome with the heat. I collapsed, and they threw cold water on me, ordering me to get up. When I couldn't get to my feet, they beat me, hence, my broken arm. It was forbidden to smoke a cigarette, to have a sip of water. And there we were until the afternoon. The Nazis are sadistic beasts. Never have I witnessed such senseless brutality. Many men were carried out of the square unconscious. Every man was given a number, and within a few days' time, they started publishing the numbers in the newspaper, telling you when to report for a labor detail.

"We were going to be used for construction projects in Macedonia. I told Father I was going to flee, and he agreed. How can this happen?" He spoke almost to himself. "We Jews are powerless, totally powerless, against the Nazis. As we were standing in the square, Germans, men and women, were standing on the surrounding balconies taking pictures and laughing as if it were a great entertainment."

"How terrible, Zaco. Are you sure you're making a good recovery?" Alexander asked. "I'd be glad to look at your injuries."

"There's no need. I'm healing."

"Do you want to stay here, Zaco? Of course, you can't stay with us. But I can find you another place if you prefer. I know many Jews are staying here at the hotel. I can finance your stay for as long as necessary. I can help you leave the country. Tell me what you need."

"Thank you, Alexander. I intend to go back up into the mountains to again join the andartes as soon as my arm has healed. I don't want to leave the country. I want to fight for Greece. But I have no means of paying my hotel bill or purchasing supplies to take with me."

"Stay here in Athens at the hotel as long as you like. Anna can't come back here again. It would be too dangerous for her. Bad things aren't happening yet to the Jews of Athens, but surely we know it's just a matter of time."

"Anna?" Zaco turned to his sister, whose face had paled as she listened to his story. "Come give your brother a hug." He smiled at her. "I'll be all right. I promise you."

Anna made her way across the floor toward her brother. She didn't believe he was going to be all right. She didn't believe anyone was going to be all right. And for the first time, she began to doubt if the subterfuge created by the Giannopolous family would save her from the Nazis when their attention turned to Athens.

They stayed with Zaco for several hours, until Alexander cautioned them that they mustn't stay with him too long. It was hard for Anna to bid him good-bye. Alexander removed his winnings from his vest pocket.

"You carry so much money with you?" Zaco asked in astonishment.

"I just won it all at a roulette wheel. Tomorrow, I'll bring you gold. I'm not sure if our drachmas are worth very much in the mountains."

After Zaco closed the door, Anna and Alexander made their way to the staircase. Alexander stopped and looked down at her. "Litsa, let's forget all the bad words we had tonight between us. Such things aren't important."

"No, they aren't." She took his hand in her own. "Alexander, I'm afraid for my family."

CHAPTER 13

1964: Salonika

ALEXANDER HAD REACHED out to Suzanne, but she kept her hands fastened at her sides resting them on the examining table. The girl looked up at him, her brown eyes wide. "What you're saying is impossible," she told him.

Alexander let his hands drop as he feasted his eyes on her, the smile so like the photograph of his mother. Her face, of course, was darkened by the sun as was the fashion for American tourists, but he assessed that her skin was naturally darker, like the olive complexion of many Sephardic Jews. He didn't know what to say, for fear he would say something that might frighten her away. He decided to say nothing. Anna, he thought, Anna, Anna. *Doxa to Theo,* thank God…. You are still alive….

"Well." Suzanne crossed her arms across her chest, her brow furrowed, seemingly deep in thought.

He knew her crossed arms were a defensive gesture so that he wouldn't reach out to her again. He understood her shock and reluctance to believe him.

"Let's say you were telling the truth," she began. "And just so you know, Dr. G, I don't believe a word you've just said to me. So if you are telling the truth, how do you explain why my mother has been lying to me all my life, telling me my Greek father was dead? My mother wouldn't do such a thing. If you knew my mother like you say you do, you'd know she wouldn't have lied to me."

"Your mother didn't lie to you. She was told I was dead, and she'd no reason to believe otherwise." Anna, my Anna is alive. After all this time….

"Well, very nice to have met you." Suzanne started to get up from the examining table. "I'm leaving. I can't imagine what you expected to accomplish by telling me such an unbelievable tale. Good-bye."

"You need to have your ankle bandaged." He tried to stop her from getting up. "The nurse will do that for you. Suzanne, my child, all I ask is that you give me a few more minutes of your time. Just a few more minutes. Would you meet with me in my office? It's much more comfortable than the examining room. Would you like a cola?" He desperately searched for something to delay her leaving the hospital. How would she not want to flee from this strange man who'd just told her he was her father, her dead father? He sought in vain for words to make her feel at ease.

"Well," she paused. "Yes, I would like a Coke. You don't actually have Coca-Cola, do you? I miss Coca-Cola," she said wistfully. "You do seem like a nice man. I should be going, but I could stay and talk to you a little more. Maybe I can help you figure out why you're thinking I'm your daughter when that's totally impossible. I'm sorry, but you're mistaken."

"I appreciate your willingness to talk with me just a little more. Would you like something to eat?" Why was he rambling on like an idiot?

"No," she said guardedly. "I'm just thirsty. I really don't have much time, so you better make this quick. Five minutes and I'm sure I'll be able to convince you that I'm not who you think I am."

Alexander turned to the nurse and spoke in Greek. "Bandage her ankle. Please take your time. Provide a cola for her. Bring her to my office, but not for at least ten minutes. Don't let her leave the hospital until she has come into my office. That's very important."

"You have other patients waiting, Doctor. I know she was supposed to be your last patient, but Dr. Vlachos asked if you could see two more before you leave."

"I'll see no one else today. Find someone else to see them."

"Yes, Doctor."

He turned back to Suzanne, who was impatiently swinging her uninjured leg back and forth as she sat on the examining table. "There are also papers to sign for your release," he told her. "Instructions to care for your injury. I'll have them in my office for you." He fought the urge to reach out to her, the overwhelming need to have physical contact with this young woman who surely was his daughter.

"I told you my mother is a doctor. She'll know how to take care of a simple sprained ankle."

"Well, it's hospital procedure that you are properly signed out," he lied to her. "I'll wait for you in my office. The nurse will show you the way."

Alexander reluctantly took his eyes from her, left the examining room, and hurriedly walked down the corridor toward his office. Several of the medical staff tried to capture his attention by calling out to him, but he impatiently waved them away with his hand. Anna, Anna, Anna…, Her name echoed in his thoughts. And then he could hear nothing but the sound of her voice, saying his name, whispering words of affection, and her eyes filled with love. Once inside his office, he locked the door. He looked at his watch. He had ten minutes.

Anna, my Anna is alive. Our daughter, all grown up, and beautiful and smart. It was impossible but true. Not only did he see the date and place this girl was born, but those things she said about her mother Anna being a doctor. Of course it was his Anna. In his heart he knew it was true; he felt it.

Suddenly totally exhausted by his emotions, he sank down into an armchair. Alexander put his head into his hands. And then he broke down and wept. He hadn't allowed himself to weep since that day he returned to Athens and was told that his wife and daughter were on the overloaded boat that sank in the harbor. The boat that had no survivors. Since that horrible day, he had locked all emotion inside of himself, erecting a stone wall around his heart. But with the sight of this girl, the wall crumbled, and all the pain he'd been shielding from himself for so many years wracked him with fury. His shoulders heaved as the tears ran down his face. His sobs broke the quiet of his office.

Enough, he told himself; he needed to pull himself together. Suzanne would be here soon, and he didn't want to frighten her. He pulled out a handkerchief from his pocket and wiped off his face.

Thoughts spun through his mind. Of course, he wanted to see Anna, if only briefly. After all, she had a husband and a new life in America, and it wasn't his place, not his right to interfere. She was another man's wife, no longer his Anna Giannopolous. He had to focus on his daughter, Suzanne. Maybe he could make some kind of arrangement with Anna for their daughter to visit with him on occasion, to get to know him and for him to get to know her.

Alexander got to his feet and unlocked the door, waiting for Suzanne to come into the office. He pulled off his white coat and straightened his tie. He glanced at his flushed face in the mirror, noting he looked like hell. Then he sat down behind the desk trying to regain his composure. No, he told himself, he shouldn't sit behind the desk. That would be too formal. He rose to his feet and sat down in an armchair. Then he pulled another armchair next to him. Not too close, not too far away.

He tried to think of what to say to her, but thoughts of Anna kept flooding his mind, until he could think of nothing else. She was alive! His wonderful Anna was alive. She had been alive all these years, safe in America. She hadn't endured the years of Greek civil war and all the unrest that had plagued the country since that time. He saw her that first day, when he had looked up from his newspaper and there she was, so lovely. And he had immediately felt an inexplicable, strong connection between them. He remembered their wedding day, as he stood on top of the church steps waiting for her to join him. His bride, his beautiful Anna Litsa… *Beshert*, he had told her: they were meant to be. They would be together forever, he had foolishly thought. And he remembered her face, exhausted but beaming with happiness, after she gave birth to their daughter. And they both rejoiced in the perfection of their tiny girl. So many wonderful memories.…

There was a knock on the door.

"Come in," he said, getting to his feet.

The door opened, and Suzanne stood there. What a beautiful young woman she was, with straight, shoulder-length dark brown hair and a lovely face. She was much taller than Anna. She had the height of the Giannopolous family, his family.

She walked toward him with a slight limp, and he could sense her unease. "Please, sit down." He indicated the armchair. "Do you need assistance with walking? Are you in any pain?"

"It just hurts a little. I'm really fine."

And she stood there for a long moment, looking at him. Her eyes took in the office, his desk, the books lining his shelves, and then he saw her catch her breath. He turned to see what had captured her attention. The photograph. It was the silver-framed wedding photograph that he kept on a shelf next to his books.

"Would you like to see it?" He retrieved it from the shelf and handed it to her as she collapsed into the armchair.

"It's my mother," she said with astonishment, her face draining of color as she studied the portrait. "It's my mother, and she is wearing a cross around her neck. How could that be? She is younger, but that's her, and I think that's you, except that now you don't have a mustache. What's your name? I know it isn't Dr. G, is it?"

He watched her take a large nervous swallow. She knows the name of her father. Of course, she would know the name of her father.

"I am Alexander Giannopolous."

"That's the name of my father," she said meekly. "Giannopolous was my last name before Dad adopted me and changed my name to Caplan."

"This was our wedding photograph. It's all I had left, and I keep it with me always."

"I just don't understand. That's you and that's Mom. How could it be a wedding photograph?" She looked down at the framed portrait and traced her fingertips against the glass.

"Because I am not a Jew and your mother was wearing a cross? Those were desperate times, Suzanne."

"I don't understand," she repeated in a soft voice. "You said that Mom was told you were dead, but obviously you weren't."

"I was gravely injured, and those who witnessed the firing squad and my supposedly lifeless body presumed I was dead."

The young woman stared hard at him. "My father…. I always thought you died in Greece, and Mom hardly talked about you. This is incredible."

"Yes, Suzanne it is incredible, but for me so wonderful. Be assured I would never want to take the place of the man who raised you as his own daughter."

"I don't look like you." She frowned. "I used to wonder if I looked like my father, since I didn't look much like Mom."

"You resemble my mother. Her name was also Suzanne."

"I…I know. Mom told me I was named after her." She shook her head in disbelief. "How can this be true?"

"It's true. And you, Suzanne, how did you and your mother survive the sinking of the boat?"

"You know about the boat?" She hugged the portrait against herself.

"Of course, I know. I ask you again, how did you survive? Did your mother grab you and swim for shore? I was told there were no survivors. I shouldn't have believed what I was told. I should have searched for you. Your mother must have taken refuge with you somewhere in Piraeus." He was trying to make sense of what she was telling him.

"We weren't on the boat that sank. I know all about it, because I loved hearing the story of how Dad saved me and Mom from drowning, and then they got married. When I was a little girl, it sounded like Mom and I were saved by a knight in shining armor in a grand fairy tale." She smiled and handed Alexander the wedding portrait.

Alexander turned around and placed it back on the shelf, glad to have this momentary distraction. Her dad, a knight in shining armor. He told himself that he needed to be grateful that someone had saved his family from a watery grave. But the word "Dad" stabbed like a knife in his chest. Don't be a fool. Would you have preferred to have them drowned? he asked himself.

"Your dad has been a good father to you?"

"Sure, he's the best. I'll tell you the story about the boat, if you'd like to hear it. It's so melodramatic. When I tell people, they think I'm making it up."

"Yes, I'd like to hear about the boat."

"Well, Mom and I were on this boat. I really don't remember, because I wasn't very old."

"You were eighteen months old."

"Yeah, that's right," she acknowledged and continued with her story. "So this boat was totally filled with all these people who wanted to leave Greece. When we first got on, Mom said there weren't many people on board. But before the boat was scheduled to leave, more and more people got on. Mom didn't think much about it. She said she was just glad to be leaving Greece. Then she heard this man speaking English, saying the boat was overcrowded and people had to get off. And just like in a fairy tale, this man was someone whom Mom had known many years ago in America. Dad liked to say they had always loved each other, and it was just a big mistake that they parted. They were supposed to get married, but something happened and Mom went back to Greece. So Dad said he looked at Mom, and he recognized her right away, even though she had gotten so thin. You see there wasn't a lot of food to eat in Greece back then. Dad said I looked at him and called him 'Daddy.' Well, not actually 'Daddy.' I called him *baba*, which is Greek for 'Daddy.' So he took Mom and me off the boat. The boat sailed away without us and it sank. Mom and Dad knew they loved each other from the moment they saw each other again, and so they got married. Isn't it a great story? It was the bedtime story I loved hearing when I was little, how Dad saved us and we came to America."

"That's a very nice bedtime story, and it does sound like a wonderful fairy tale." He smiled ruefully. Was it that fellow Daniel who had spurned Anna because she was a Sephardic Jew? That was her husband? "Your mother is well?"

"Sure. She's fine."

"Our servant Ariadne saw your mother board the boat, and then she left the pier. It was the next day she heard the boat had sunk with no survivors."

"So you thought we drowned?"

"Yes." He paused. "Suzanne." He reached out to her hand, and this time she allowed him to hold her fingers. "I know this is a huge shock to find out the father you thought was dead is alive."

"Yeah." She smiled at him, and that smile melted his heart.

"I'd like us to get to know each other. I hope you'd like that as well."

"Yes, I would. Mom's going to be surprised to see you again, don't you think? After all, she thinks you're dead."

"Yes, she will be surprised. How long are you here in Salonika?"

"Just a few days, but I'm sure we could stay longer. My friends might want to leave sooner, but I could catch up with them. I bet Mom might like to stay longer and spend some time with you after all these years. At least I think she would."

"Your dad is here as well?"

"No, he's home. Joey, my brother, is home with him."

"You have a brother?"

"Yes, he's three years younger than me. He's finishing up high school next year."

"Other brothers or sisters?"

"No, just Joey. I always wished I had cousins like my friends did. Dad is an only child, and Mom's family died in the war. Do I have cousins or aunts or uncles here in Greece who are your family?"

"I have a brother in America in San Francisco, with children, and a sister in Greece. She also has children, your cousins."

"Wow, I want to meet everyone. Do you think they'd want to meet me?"

"Of course, you are family, Suzanne." He paused. "There is also someone here in Salonika that I think you and your mother would want to meet. You have a cousin Joseph. He is the son of your mother's brother Victor."

"I'm sure she'd like to see him. She told me everyone in her family had died in the war."

"Almost everyone, save for your mother's cousin Moises and her nephew Joseph, did perish in the war. We met Joseph after the war when he was a little boy. Your mother wanted to take him with us, but her cousin who was caring for him wouldn't hear of it." Alexander remembered that terrible day when Anna learned the fate of her family, and her cousin Moises had been so angry and said such hurtful things to Anna.

He turned his attention back to Suzanne and forced himself to have casual discourse with this young woman, when all he wanted to do was hug her and embrace her as a father embraced his daughter. "What kind of medicine does your mother practice?"

"She's an ER doctor. That means she works in an emergency room. Is that what she did here in Greece?"

"No, she worked as a nurse during the war. Sometimes she was my assistant in the operating theater. It wasn't safe for her to draw attention to herself as a doctor. Has your mother told you much about those days? Has she told you much about me?" he asked tentatively.

There was a knock on the door, and the nurse came in with a bottle of cola and a glass filled with ice. The nurse left, and Alexander poured the drink for Suzanne. He handed her the glass, all the while thinking, did Anna tell his daughter nothing about him save for the fabrication that he was a Greek Jew? She must have had her reasons. He couldn't sit in judgment for the woman he had abandoned so many years ago, his head filled with noble patriotic ideas when he should have stayed home with his family. Surely he could have found the money to buy his way out of the draft into the Greek National Army.

Suzanne took a large swallow of her drink. "It's not the same as our Coke, but it's OK," she commented. "Mom hardly ever talked about her life in Greece. It was almost like she didn't exist before she came to America. I never thought about it much till I got older. It seemed to me that she barely talked about Greek stuff except how being a Greek Jew was different than being the kind of Jew that Dad and his family were. She only talked about that Greek stuff when Dad wasn't around. I got the sense that Dad didn't like her to talk about it with us."

"Your mother is a Sephardic Jew."

"Yes, she said that. Anyway, maybe my dad thought being a Sephardic Jew was a bad thing. I don't know." Suzanne seemed thoughtful. "Once in a while, Mom would take Joey and me to this Greek area in New York called Astoria. We'd go to a restaurant, and Mom had us sample her favorite dishes. We'd go to one of the bakeries and bring home a giant baklava."

"I'll take you to the best place for baklava here in Salonika." He smiled at her.

"I'd like that. I bet the baklava is really good here, since it comes from Greece."

"Yes, it does originate in Greece. Your mother made very good baklava."

"Really? She never made it for us. We just bought it at Greek bakeries. It was on those outings in Astoria that she talked a little about her life in Greece. She said her family and you died in the war. She told us she had lots of brothers and sisters, three of each, and she missed them. She said she missed her parents and her grandmother, Nona. She said things were bad in Greece. There was a civil war going on, and it wasn't safe for us to stay here. And that's why she decided to leave. Mom had lived in America when she went to medical school, and she had distant cousins in New Jersey. That's a state close to New York. I didn't like it much when she talked about that stuff because it seemed to make her really sad." Suzanne took another swallow of her cola.

"You asked what Mom told me about you," she continued. "She said you died in the war, not World War II, but a civil war and that you were a fine man. Yes, 'a fine man' were the words she used. You were a doctor, and once in a while, like when I graduated first in my class from high school, she'd say your father Alexander would have been so proud of you. I'm wondering if I should just call you Dr. G? I can't call you Dad, since I already have a Dad."

"You could call me 'Patéra.' That's Greek for Father."

"Let me think about that. I could call you 'Alexander.'"

"I'd prefer Patéra. It is disrespectful to call a parent by their given name."

"OK, I'll think about it." She looked down at her watch and then back up at him. For a long moment, she seemed to study his face. "Did Mom not really ever talk much about you because you and her..., well, it wasn't so good between you, and she just wanted to forget you?"

"I don't think so." He felt a tight band squeeze across his chest. "In America she had a new life, and I was part of her past. Suzanne, have you plans to see the islands?" He tried to change the subject.

"There's this island close to Athens called Hydra. Have you heard of it?"

"Yes, it's a charming place with no cars, only donkeys."

"My friends and I are going there, because we wanted to visit an island. It's the closest one to Athens, so the ferry to get there doesn't cost much."

"There are so many beautiful places to see. Sometime it would be my pleasure to show you Greece and its beauty."

"Maybe."

"I know today has been overwhelming for you."

"It is overwhelming. I have so many questions. I do believe you're my father. I should have known more about you, don't you think?" She looked back at the wedding photograph. "You know what I said about you being Jewish? Mom said so little about you that I think I just assumed. I couldn't have imagined in my wildest dreams that Mom would have been married to a goy. That's a non-Jewish man. And I certainly can't understand why Mom would have been wearing a cross. Wow, how did that happen?"

"That's something for you to ask her yourself."

"I sure will ask her. When I was growing up, my Bubbie, that's my grandmother told me not to ask my mom too much about her life in Greece. Bubbie said people who lived through the war didn't want to be reminded of those terrible days." Suzanne looked down at her watch again. "I think I need to get going. Mom will be expecting me back at the hotel. She's going to be so surprised when I tell her that I met you. It's going to be a big shock to her. I hope she doesn't faint or something."

"I don't think she'll faint. She's a strong woman." He remembered Anna's extraordinary strength and courage when she was living as a secret Jew with the Nazi in their house.

"Yeah, I guess she is, being a doctor and all. Do you want to see her?"

"Of course, I want to see her." How eager he was to see her one more time. He smiled at Suzanne, his daughter, so full of life like her mother. "Let's arrange to meet this evening."

"Sure. That sounds like a great idea.

"Patéra." She smiled at him. "I'm so glad I found you, and I think Mom will be glad to see you, don't you think?"

"Yes, I hope she would be glad to see me." Alexander took a deep breath. Could Anna ever forgive him for leaving them in order to join the andartes?

"Do you have other children, a wife, who might like to come and meet me and Mom?"

"I have no children…except for you. I don't have a wife," he told her.

"So where will we meet tonight?" she asked him.

"I know of a very nice taverna, wonderful food and music." He picked up a pencil and paper and wrote down the address. "Give this to the taxi driver, and he will take you there. Have you ever tried Greek dancing?"

"No, I haven't."

"It's great fun. When your ankle has healed, I'm sure you will enjoy it. Your mother loved to dance. And I shall contact your cousin Joseph to see if he can meet us there."

Alexander escorted her outside to summon a taxi that would drive her back to the hotel. "Your mother is traveling with you and your friends?" he asked.

"Not really. She just wanted us to come to Salonika."

"Of course, this was her home, where she grew up."

"Really? I didn't know that." She frowned, and Alexander sensed she was wondering what else her mother hadn't told her. But it wasn't Alexander's place to say any more.

"I suppose you are also from here. Is this where you and Mom met?"

"No, I'm from Athens. I came here to Salonika to help the Jewish community that had suffered so much in the war. Those people who survived the camps needed a great deal of care and support. Unfortunately, they weren't welcomed with open arms by the Greek Christians who were living in the houses and occupying the shops that had once belonged to the Jews, before the Nazis took them away. I wanted to do something to help, to make a difference to your mother's people. I've been practicing medicine here since that time. Will your mother be staying in Salonika for a while?"

"I don't know. We're only supposed to meet up here for three days, and then I'm supposed to be off to Athens with my friends."

"Perhaps your dad will be joining her."

"That's unlikely," she laughed.

"Unlikely? I don't understand."

"They're divorced."

Alexander stopped in midstep. "*Ti eípes!*"

"Hey, you're speaking Greek to me." She smiled. "I don't know what you said."

"I'm sorry. I asked you to repeat what you just said."

"They've been divorced for at least four years, right after Joey's Bar Mitzvah. Dad has a new wife, Sarah. She's got one kid, so I have a stepbrother. Before I went to college, I spent weekends with them."

Alexander felt lighter than air. Anna no longer had a husband. She was no longer another man's wife.

"I'll see you later tonight." He handed the taxi driver a fistful of drachmas and closed the car door.

Back in his office, he placed his papers into his briefcase. Today after his weekly visit to the monument in the cemetery, he would take a walk along the sea wall to help gather his thoughts. But first he called Joseph, who was elated at the opportunity to meet his aunt. Joseph was now a solicitor for a prominent law firm. While he was growing up, Alexander had arranged with the Salonikan Jewish community to pay for his education as an anonymous donor. Moises Carraso would not have accepted a single drachma from Alexander, even though it would have provided Joseph with an excellent education. He remained tormented by the loss of his entire family and the horrors of his life in Auschwitz. Alexander couldn't fault him for his bitterness. He himself was not able to move past the loss of Anna and his child. When Joseph was close to fifteen years old, the truth about his benefactor had been revealed. Moises was not pleased, but he didn't interfere, and Alexander and Joseph developed a warm relationship.

Alexander walked to the parking lot where he'd left his car this morning. This morning seemed a lifetime ago. The events of today threatened to overwhelm him again and now the news about Anna being divorced. He hurried to his car, rolled down the windows, and rested his head in his arms on the steering wheel.

That terrible day came flooding back, blocking out the here and now. He was no longer in his car at the parking lot. He was back in the mountains, a member of the ELAS.

He'd been ready to slip away from his unit in the ELAS before he was injured. They weren't the group they had been during the occupation. There was talk of conscripting children, taking them away from their parents for a "communist re-education." In addition, they were committing atrocities just as the Germans had done, and he wanted no part in it. The groups loyal to the new government were hunting them down and executing them. Alexander hoped if he successfully returned to Athens that the money and the connections he and his father had established would keep him safe from prison. But on that fateful day, his ELAS group was ambushed and lined up before a firing squad. It had been a miracle that the silver cigarette case in his breast pocket had deflected the fatal bullet. But he had not escaped unscathed, and it was months before he had the strength to travel back to Athens and his family.

It seemed to have taken forever, until that day when he found himself totally exhausted, knocking on the door to the Giannopolous villa.

Ariadne had opened the door and shrieked, "A ghost!" After he calmed her and convinced her he was indeed alive, she related that the andartes had come to the house and told Anna he was dead. The servant explained how Anna seemed unable to recover from the shock of his death. Anna had decided to return to America. She and Suzanne were on a boat that sank when barely out of the harbor. There were no survivors. And then to his horror, he learned that his father had died. He'd never felt so alone.

Now all these years later to learn Anna was alive, their daughter was alive. And Anna wasn't married. But did that really matter after all this time? Surely he and Anna had both changed. They were no longer the same young man and young woman who had fallen in love and endured the war years. He was approaching fifty, and Anna was just a few years younger. Too much time had gone by to recapture what they once had between them.

Today was Wednesday, the day each week that Alexander visited the new Jewish cemetery. This was where he had financed the erection of a marble monument to all the members of the Carraso family who had perished at Auschwitz. It hadn't been easy for him to obtain permission from cousin Moises. He burned with anger at the death of his family. Why would a Christian like Alexander concern himself with such things? "Because these people are the family of my wife," Alexander had said. "That's why I came to Salonika," he told him, as for the umpteenth time he stood in front of Moises's door, not being invited inside the house. "I came here to be a doctor, to help Anna's people, your people. To do what she would have wanted me to do. Design the monument as you like; I'll provide the funds."

He also went to the Orthodox Church three times a year for the Saturday of All Souls, where he prayed for Anna and his daughter. Every Wednesday, he drove to the new Jewish cemetery that was erected after the war. Among the cedar trees, he would stand with his head covered, as was necessary for Jewish prayer, before the headstone of the Carraso family.

There were no bodies, of course, for they had burned in the ovens of the concentration camp. But the headstone listed the names of Anna's family, her parents, her grandmother, her brothers, sisters, and their spouses and children. On the monument was carved a long list of names, with the dates of their births and the final statement of their death in Poland, at the Auschwitz concentration camp.

Before he left, Alexander would place a small stone on the headstone, as was the custom in a Jewish cemetery. He would spend many minutes standing there, reading each name, most of whom he remembered from the stories Anna had told him. You are not forgotten, he would pray silently. He had learned the Kaddish, the Jewish memorial prayer for the dead. And so he would recite it each time, and he would then envision Anna and say the prayer again.

There were no names on the monument for his wife and daughter. He didn't want their names on the plaque with all the others. His wife had been Anna Giannopolous, not Anna Carraso. He needed no monument to his wife and daughter, for he carried them in his heart each and every day.

And today at the cemetery, as he stood in the same place as he had countless times before, he placed his hands on the marble and said the words of the Kaddish, the prayer for the dead, and he smiled. "She's alive," he whispered to those souls who had perished almost twenty years ago. "Our Anna is alive."

CHAPTER 14

1942–1943: Athens
Winter

FAMINE, ALTHOUGH STILL rearing its ugly head that winter, was somewhat diminished. Not as many people were felled by its relentless fingers that now crushed mainly the ill, the poor, and the young.

No special measures against the Jews in Athens had been taken. People like Anna kept their identities secret with the use of false identity papers, including false baptismal certificates. But most Jews lived out in the open, going about their daily lives, suffering the same restrictions and indignities imposed upon both themselves and their Christian neighbors by the occupying armies.

Antonios spent time with his contacts at the *kafeneíos* and tavernas where he listened and gathered information about what was happening in the rest of the world. Especially for Anna, he tried to learn the news of Salonika. Some of his contacts were well-to-do Greeks whose houses had been occupied by Nazis, whose radios were permanently turned to the Nazi propaganda channel. They were men who at great risk to themselves had hidden radios where they listened to the BBC. These were men who knew if their radios were found, they would face a revolver to their heads, hanging in a public square, or the firing squad. All these measures were preferable to Gestapo interrogation at the infamous house on Merton Street. As the months wore on, the group of his contacts changed, as one by one its members heard a pounding on their doors in the middle of the night. Their families watched helplessly as the men were dragged off, sometimes never to be seen again. Sometimes a body would be found in the street or hanging from a lamppost, after suffering an interrogation that made death a welcome relief. The lucky few returned home, their bodies broken, but alive. And in their place were new Greek patriots eager to help their country.

On occasion, Von Hoffberg made an offhand comment about Antonios being watched for anti-Nazi activities. But Patéra strongly believed, while Von Hoffberg continued to enjoy his company with backgammon, chess, and drinking, that he wouldn't be hauled off in the middle of the night. He also knew when the day came that the Nazi grew tired of him, or for some reason became offended by something he said, then Antonios would also be marked for interrogation. It was just a matter of time.

At Antonios' insistence, Alexander could no longer be seen in the company of their kafeneío compatriots. "I am old. What will be, will be. For you, you are a young man. I won't permit you to take unnecessary risks."

Alexander had protested. He was a proud Greek, and he was ready to sacrifice everything for his country. But his father forbade Alexander to take part in any sabotage of German assets. Alexander could no longer participate in plans for blowing up bridges and railroad tracks.

The news from Salonika was very upsetting to Anna. But Alexander honored his promise to her, that he would share whatever he heard from his father or from members of the andartes.

The Jewish men who were registered by the Nazis that terrible day in Eleftherias Plateia, Liberty Square, were sent to do hard labor building roads for the Third Reich in Macedonia. They were given meager rations and were exposed to malaria and typhus. Some men, including her brothers Victor and David, were eventually released, because their ill health rendered them useless. They arrived home weakened by malaria and starvation rations. Antonios learned that her brother David had been nursed back to health. Her brother Victor was somewhat better, although he continued to suffer from malaria.

The Jewish community in Salonika reached out and begged the Nazis to release their sons, husbands, and brothers. They proposed to pay for Greek laborers to replace the Jews. The Nazis, in response, demanded the outrageous sum of three billion drachmas. After raising as much as possible in Salonika, the Jewish community sent representatives to Athens to plead for contributions. Surreptitiously, Alexander and his father had generously contributed. But still the huge sum of three billion couldn't be raised. The Jews needed one half billion more to meet the Nazis' demands, and it could not be found anywhere.

"They chose the living over the dead. They've taken your cemetery," Alexander informed her in a soft voice, as they strolled through the botanical gardens, careful to remain out of earshot of any passersby.

"What do you mean they've taken my cemetery?" Anna hurried to match his stride.

"The Jews were short half a billion drachmas to pay for the release of your men. They were forced to agree to give up the land of the Jewish cemetery in payment. There are hundreds, thousands of marble tombstones. The Greek government has always wanted that land, in a prime location, for its own use."

"Alexander, that isn't possible. What of the bodies? My ancestors, my grandparents except for Nona, are all buried there. It's against Jewish law to disturb a body once it's buried." Anna had stopped walking and was hugging her arms against herself although the day was not very cold. "How will my family go to their graves to say Kaddish?"

"Kaddish?"

"The prayer for the dead. I can't believe my people would have agreed to the desecration of the cemetery."

"What other choice did they have?"

Anna swallowed hard, continuing her walk through the gardens, which used to be a place of solitude but today couldn't ease her agitation. "And what of the tombstones that date back to the sixteenth century?"

"I don't know for sure. But marble is valuable building material," Alexander told her in a quiet voice.

"Building material!" Anna yelled before Alexander's tight grip on her arm silenced her.

"Your family is safe. Surely that's the most important thing."

Anna wrested her arm out of his grasp, as she defiantly looked up into the dark eyes of her husband. "So making war on the sick and the children is not enough for these evil beasts. Now they must make war on the dead!"

Alexander put his hand over her mouth, fervently hoping no one had heard her outburst. "Shhh!" he cautioned her before taking his hand away. "Let's go home," he told her.

"I don't want to go home to that vile Nazi, pretending, pretending. I'm tired of pretending to be an Orthodox Christian, and I hate that man."

"Litsa, calm down. Please," he beseeched her.

Anna was silent as they proceeded down the broad avenues toward the Giannopolous villa. They were rounding a corner and making their way down a small street when they saw a gathering of young boys playing in the street. "*Psomi!* Bread!" one of the boys shouted and pointed to where they heard the sound of a truck rumbling toward them.

"*Psomi! Psomi!*" the boys shouted in an excited chorus. As the large truck came into view, the boys pressed back onto the sidewalk. The truck rambled down the street, and indeed it was loaded with loaves of bread. Bread was such a rarity for the poor of Athens. But this truck was commandeered by a German in his helmet, looking straight ahead, on his way for a Nazi delivery. As the truck passed the boys, one of them jumped into the back and began tossing loaves to his friends, who screamed in delight. The German driver was oblivious to what was happening. The truck went over a pothole in the street, causing the boy to tumble down, somewhat stunned by his unexpected fall.

Anna and Alexander watched in horror, as a Nazi tank behind the truck sped up the street, crushing the body of the young boy. His friends clutched their loaves of bread, as they stared at the tangled mass of blood and pieces of coat. "Nikos! Nikos! Where are you!" they cried.

Alexander and all the other adults on the sidewalk crossed themselves and mumbled a prayer. "Litsa, Litsa, cross yourself!" he urged her in a fervent whisper.

"Yes, yes." She crossed herself and wiped away the tears in her eyes.

When they reached their doorway, he pulled her inside and gathered her in his arms as she wept. "You must be careful to make the sign of the cross. I know you were stunned, but we never know who might be watching."

She cried, weeping for the little boy who was so crushed that there was nothing left to return to his family, and she wept for her own family in Salonika.

"Alexander, how much longer can this go on?" she sobbed against his chest.

Alexander had no answer as he held her tighter. The news of the cemetery, and then the brutal crushing of a boy who was hungry for bread, had overwhelmed his wife. Anna had shown so much strength, but as he listened to her sobs, he understood she was approaching the limits of her endurance.

Anna tried to erase the terrible image of the graves of her ancestors being desecrated, the tombstones that recorded their names, their years of deaths and births, and their occupations chiseled into the white marble that were now destroyed. Were their coffins opened, their bones strewn about like garbage? And then she would see the crushed remains of the boy, no longer recognizable by his friends, who gasped with disbelief at his sudden disappearance. She woke up at night in a cold sweat and sought the sleeping form of her husband. Often she would press her body against him, closing her eyes, trying to take comfort from his warmth. But coldness seemed to permeate her very being, no matter how much heat emanated from Alexander's body.

In February 1943, more news from Salonika, far worse than the desecration of the cemetery, reached their ears. It was Antonios himself who sought out Anna one evening. Herr Von Hoffberg had requested Alexander accompany him to a local taverna, a request Alexander, of course, could not deny.

Anna was reading before the fireplace. She knew even though Alexander was scheduled for an operation quite early in the morning, he was at the mercy of the Nazi, who was fond of staying out to all hours, drinking retsina and raki. Von Hoffberg had developed a fondness for those Greek drinks in the almost two years he had lived with them. He often asked Alexander or Antonios to accompany him in the evening.

"Litsa," Patéra called to her from the doorway. "May I come in to speak with you?"

"Of course." Anna put down her book. Something was wrong. She could see it on her father-in-law's face. "Alexander? Has something happened to him?" Her voice caught with fear.

"No, no," he sighed as he sat down on a chair across from her. "It's Salonika, your people in Salonika. I'm afraid the news is not good."

"Tell me," she said calmly, although she wanted to shout out, "Tell me what's happened!" Her thoughts darted crazily from her father being arrested, her brothers sent back to forced labor, Victor succumbing to malaria.

"All Jews were told to abandon their houses, take a small suitcase and be ready to assemble in several areas, but principally in the Baron Hirsch quarter. Your family has already gone there."

"All the Jews? There are over fifty thousand Jews in Salonika. The Baron Hirsch quarter is the area where the poor Jews live. There's no room for so many thousands. What have the Jews done so that they are forced to leave their homes? Couldn't we have my family come here to Athens now? Jews aren't being persecuted here." Anna's thoughts spun madly, trying to think of a solution. Yes, have her family come here. Surely now her father would see the wisdom of this.

"Litsa." Patéra leaned over and took her hand in his, a kind gesture meant to reassure Anna. Never had he initiated any physical contact between them, and his hand on hers somehow scared her more than his words. "It's said the Jews of Salonika are subversives. They are no longer allowed out of Salonika. Travel is forbidden."

"Subversives? Why would anyone say such a thing? We're good people, no different than any other Greeks."

"I know that, Litsa. But the Nazis believe they must invent some kind of excuse for rounding up Jews."

"Can't they refuse to go to Baron Hirsch?" she asked, although she knew the answer.

"They would be executed on the spot. They have no choice. Litsa…" He paused. "This Baron Hirsch Quarter, where is it located?"

"It's near the train station," Anna told him.

"I see."

"Patéra?"

"I, of course, do not know. But I think your family won't stay in Baron Hirsch for very long," he said sadly.

"The railroad?"

"I think so. I think they'll be sent away on the railroad."

"Sent where? Patéra, I don't think you understand. There are over fifty thousand Jews in the community. It is impossible for the Nazis to make so many people leave their possessions, their homes, and go to this small area of the city," Anna protested.

"Ah, but have we not learned how the Nazis can do the impossible? Even before the Jews were forced to leave their homes, they were made to wear large yellow stars pinned to their clothing. They were forbidden to use the telephone. They were forbidden to talk to anyone outside of the community…At first they could come and go from the quarter. But now it is sealed with barbed wire.

"In Salonika, do you know of a Rabbi Zvi Koretz?"

"Yes, of course. He's the chief rabbi at the Grand Synagogue. He must be trying to help my people. I'm sure he'll find a way to stop this madness."

"The andartes have told me he has cajoled your people into believing no harm would come to them and that they should show no resistance against the Nazis."

"Why would he say such a thing?" Anna was incredulous. Had her people been betrayed by their trust in a holy man?

"No one knows. Is he in collaboration with the Nazis? Was he or his family threatened? Is he not a good man? Is he not a strong man? Is he a fool? But nevertheless your people listened to him. They believed his lies, and now things look very grim. I'm sorry. No one can leave Salonika now." He pressed her hand in his. "We will take care of you, my daughter. I promise you. Here in Athens, the Jews have been safe."

"Patéra, Alexander has told me over and over that he's afraid for the Jews in Athens. That eventually the Nazis will turn their attention to this city."

"You are Kiría Michaelitsa Giannopolous; your identity papers are impeccable."

"How can I continue to live in safety when my family is in danger?" Anna's voice filled with despair. "Money could be used to buy their safety. Can't we send them the money my father has deposited here in my name?"

"It's too late for that. Such funds would be confiscated by the Nazis."

"Should I go back to Salonika to be with them?" she asked in desperation.

"Litsa, Litsa." He shook his head at her. "You belong here with your husband. And you know your father wouldn't want you to place yourself in harm's way."

"I feel so helpless. Please know how thankful I am for your protection. Someday my father will repay you for your many kindnesses toward me."

"You are my daughter, the wife of my son."

March 1943: Athens

Every day Anna waited to hear the fate of her family. How were they fairing in such cramped quarters in which they were forced to live? Her ninety-year-old Nona, her brothers and sisters with their spouses and children. Her parents…how she longed to see them. If she hadn't listened to her father, she would be with them now. Surely it was her duty as their daughter to be with her parents at such a terrible time.

Herr Von Hoffberg was entertaining his fellow officers and their women tonight. It was a large dinner party of sixteen, and Anna was pleased to help Ariadne prepare in the kitchen.... anything to keep her mind off her family. In the hospital, at the Nazi clinic in her home, all she could do was think of her family living in filthy, unsanitary conditions, crowded together. Was there enough food, enough medicine?

Herr Von Hoffberg enjoyed impressing his friends with Ariadne's culinary talents. For such occasions, he seemed to be able to track down any and all foods that he wanted her to prepare.

Anna was chopping an onion when there was a tap on the kitchen door. Mattheo, who was assembling the china in preparation for tonight's dinner, answered the door. He opened it a small crack and peered out, exchanged some words, and closed the door.

"Who is it?" asked Anna.

"An andarte," he said with agitation, "has come to see Kìrios Antonios. It's so dangerous for him to come now. Within an hour all the Nazis will be here for dinner. I'll find Kìrios Antonios, and they can talk briefly outside in the back of the house. I keep hearing of so many men who are arrested and interrogated for the most minor suspicions. If anyone should see this andarte coming to our backdoor...."

"It must be important if he came to see Kìrios Antonios," said Anna, wondering if there was any news about her family.

"I apologize, Kiría Litsa. It's not my place to judge your father-in-law. Forgive me." Mattheo made a slight bow.

While Mattheo hurried to find Patéra, Anna opened the door to see a stocky, full-bearded man, in the uniform of the andartes.

"Do you have any word of Salonika?" Anna asked him.

"I've come to speak with Kìrios Giannopolous," he said and pulled the door closed again, leaving himself out in the cold night air.

Kìrios Antonios, Alexander, and Anna had been requested to make a brief appearance before the dinner, to which they were not invited.

Anna smiled and made meaningless chitchat with several blond, blue-eyed members of the Wehrmacht and the Gestapo. She knew the Gestapo were those Germans who brutally interrogated Greeks who were suspected of anti-Nazi activities. Their looks of innocence did not betray the savage natures that caused terror in the hearts of the Greeks. Did belonging to the Gestapo bring out the sadism in these men, or were sadists recruited for the Gestapo? Anna hated attending these gatherings where she had to be polite to such men.

Antoinette Ferrara was making her way toward Anna.

"Excuse me." Anna turned away from a young officer and smiled at the Italian nurse.

Antoinette stood next to her and spoke in conspiratorial tones. "Litsa, Rupert told me he received word that his wife, Bertha, is unwell. Has he said anything to you?"

"No, he hasn't," Anna told her, a frozen smile on her lips. She wanted to know what the andarte had told her father-in-law. She didn't want to be here talking to Nazis and Nazi sympathizers.

"Just imagine, Litsa. If that old battle-ax dies, Rupert would be free to marry me. When the war is over, we'd go back to Berlin. I'd have a fine house and servants, just like you have here in Athens. I know you must have thought yourself so clever to have caught a man from a rich family. But the tables turn, don't they, Litsa? You should have waited until the Nazis arrived and found yourself a fine German man like my Rupert. The Giannopolous family will be penniless once the Nazis win the war. But how foolish of me. It's frowned upon for Germans to fraternize with Greeks, and certainly they would never consider marriage to a Greek woman. And you have that olive-skin complexion. The Germans like fair-skinned women like me. Where do Greeks like you with darker complexions come from, Litsa?"

"I'm from the island of Kos, where many people have olive complexions. You're right, Antoinette. It would have been impossible for me to set my sights on a Nazi. So it was just as well that I married a Greek. You're very fortunate, Antoinette. I'll tell you if I hear anything about his wife." Anna tried to change the subject. "It would be such a pleasure to attend your wedding," Anna continued to make inane conversation with this woman she disliked. She counted the minutes until the family would be alone, and Anna could hear what the andarte had reported to Patéra.

"You really mean that, don't you? I used to think you were kind of stuck up when I first met you. And then you set your cap for Dr. Giannopolous, and just like that you end up his wife. But I see what a hard worker you are in the hospital, and unlike the other nurses, you don't spend time gossiping or saying mean things about me and my special relationship with Rupert."

"It's not my place to judge you or anyone else. We live in a world turned upside down, and we do what we need to survive." Anna took a swallow of her drink.

"That's true for all of us, isn't it? Now, for those Jews, it's different."

"What do you mean?"

"Ah, the Jews." A middle-aged officer approached them. "I overhear you speaking of the Jews."

"I've heard from Rupert that eventually the Jews will be made to wear yellow stars here in Athens," Antoinette continued. "The Italians said it would be demeaning for the Jews to wear yellow stars. I must say I'm not proud of the attitude of my own people. Imagine feeling compassion for Jews. But demeaning a Jew? They are already so lowly, how could they be demeaned?"

"You're so right, Fraulein Ferrara. And now we have learned the Jews in Salonika will finally be getting what they deserve." The officer smiled.

"Getting what they deserve?" Anna asked nonchalantly, trying to keep her composure.

"Salonika will be *Judenfrei*. No more Jews in Salonika. This will happen very soon."

"How's that going to happen?" Antoinette asked.

"They are going away," the middle-aged officer laughed.

"To where?" Antoinette asked while Anna forced herself to keep smiling.

"Don't you women worry your little heads about such things." He raised his drink in a salute and walked away from them.

"Has Rupert told you anything about the Jews of Salonika? What that officer said is so intriguing?" Anna tried to sound casual and only minimally interested.

"Once people wear stars, they won't be able to blend in, not that they really can anyway. Rupert says all the Reichland, not just Salonika, will be *Judenfrei*. The Jewish scum will be gone from the face of the earth, and all of humanity will have Herr Hitler to thank for it."

"Do you know any Jews, Antoinette?" Anna asked her, trying her utmost not to show any reaction to what the officer had said.

"Just the ones who used to work at the hospital. How can you trust people who haven't accepted Christ?"

"*Guten Abend*." A young blond officer approached them, interrupting their conversation, which was starting to make Anna feel sick to her stomach. "Fraulein Ferrara, who is this charming creature?" He smiled at Anna and put his arm around her shoulders.

"I am Frau Giannopolous," Anna informed him as her body stiffened.

"A married woman? That's of no concern. This is wartime," he slurred his words with too much drink. "A small thing like marriage cannot get in the way of two people who would seek out a passionate tryst. I especially like a woman with skin that has the touch of darkness, so exotic. Olive skin, I believe it's called. Is it not so funny a woman with olive skin in the land of olives!" He laughed at his joke and trailed his fingertips down Anna's neck.

"I think you've had too much to drink, sir," Anna spoke in a soft voice, desperately trying to prevent a scene and becoming the center of attention.

"Isn't there a bedroom in this house where you can spread your legs for me? We will return before dinner is served, before anyone will notice. Your husband won't even know you're gone."

"Please," Anna began to protest, pushing away from him.

"You will obey me as an officer of the Third Reich. What I want, I will take!" His voice became threatening. "You Greek bitch, who do you think you are? To the conquerors go the spoils."

"Dieter." It was the sound of Herr Von Hoffberg's voice. "Go find another woman. This one is not for sport." He shoved the young officer away from Anna.

"And you are dismissed." He turned to Anna and scowled. "I try to be kind and friendly, inviting you to have drinks with my colleagues. And all you do is cause trouble, flaunting yourself like a slut in front of my officers. I'll know better next time."

Patéra had surreptitiously handed her a letter before the Nazi gathering, which she had tucked into her dress pocket. And now Anna sat in her room reading the letter over and over again, as she waited for Alexander and his father to join her. She would soon learn what the andarte had reported.

She immediately recognized her mother's handwriting, as she unfolded the envelope. How wonderful to have a letter from her mother. Her mother had never written to her before, even in the days when letter writing hadn't been so fraught with danger to Anna's false identity.

Her mother wrote that she had pleaded with her father to try and smuggle this letter to her. She sent all her love and wishes for Anna's health and safety. She said she wasn't sure how soon they would see each other again because the family was going to be sent to a new life in Poland. Her father, Joseph, had traded their last remaining valuables for winter coats, so the family would have protection from the Polish winters. The Jews had exchanged their Greek drachmas for the Polish zloty in preparation for their lives in Poland. The women were making aprons for their lives on farms. It would be hard to give up life in the city, but with the cramped conditions in which they now lived, perhaps life on a farm would not be so bad. Her brother Zaco had come home from the mountains when he heard the family was being sent to Poland. He and many other young men had returned, so they could be with their families. Her father was more pessimistic about prospects for their new life. He didn't think the Germans could be trusted. But what other reason could the Nazis have for gathering us all together? Her mother wrote…

And our rabbi, Rabbi Koretz, has assured us that the Germans will not harm us if we just do as they say. Father grumbles about him, but he is the rabbi who married your sisters and brothers, and I trust him completely. Stay safe. When the war is over, you shall visit us in Poland.

Anna folded the letter and put it back in her pocket. Was her father right? Of course, the Nazis couldn't be trusted. It was so wonderful to read her mother's words, as it summoned the sound of her gentle voice in Anna's memory. The letter was dated last month. Perhaps by now, her family would have started on their journey. She should be going with them. She should make her way to wherever they were in Poland, as soon as she knew where they were. Alexander would come with her. The family would learn to accept him and their marriage. As her optimistic thoughts swirled around her, the darkness of reality pushed them aside. Her family would never accept her husband. And this new life for her family in Poland? Did it really make any sense?

When Alexander and his father finished socializing with the Nazis and came inside the room, she immediately sensed their somber moods.

"The andartes have a source for information from Salonika," her father-in-law began. "It is a Jewish man who escaped. He tells that after the Nazis loaded the Jews into the cattle cars, designed for five horses, now transporting fifty Jews, there was no food, no water, only one bucket for human waste. This man managed to escape after only two days when the train had come to a brief stop, and so he was able to report this terrible news. For those who could not walk fast enough into the cars, there was instant death from a revolver. Babies, old people, the sick, everyone crammed inside with no room to sit down. A new life on a farm in Poland? It doesn't seem likely. Litsa, I'm sorry, but that's all I know."

In sorrow, Anna turned away from the two men. She wiped away her tears and straightened her shoulders. Her family was strong, except for Nona. They would survive whatever hardships they might face. At least they had each other.

She heard Patéra leave the room and close the door.

"Litsa," said Alexander as he placed his hand on her shoulder.

"No, please." She stepped away from him. "I need to be alone."

She heard the sound of her husband leaving, as she pulled out the letter from her mother and clutched it in her hands.

"Mamà," she whispered, choking back her tears.

The next day, Anna sat in her bedroom at a small desk and wrote down the Hebrew names of her entire family. She tried to write as fast as possible before Alexander returned to their room.

He opened the door, and she stuffed the sheet of paper inside a drawer.

"What are you doing?" he asked.

"Nothing."

"Litsa, you are such a bad liar when it comes to hiding something from me. It's fortunate I'm the only one who can so easily tell when you're trying to conceal something. Now, what is on that paper you shoved into the drawer? And why don't you want me to know about it? Are you writing love letters to another man?" He tried to lighten her mood.

"Yes, of course it is a love letter," she sighed. "It's a list in Hebrew of all the names of my family."

"What would you do with such a list?"

"When I go to the soup kitchen tomorrow, I'll give it to the rabbi's wife. She's there, helping on most days."

"Why would you do such a thing?"

"Alexander, my family…. I need to do something for them. I'm going to ask the rabbi to pray for my family. There is a special prayer, the *mishe-beyrach*, to say in the synagogue."

"It could be dangerous for you to give her that list. What if someone saw you?"

"Please understand. I have to do this. There's nothing on the list of Hebrew names that identifies me in any way."

"We pray for your family on Sunday in church."

Anna looked down at the floor and said nothing. Praying for my family in a church? She wanted to tell him how impossible that was. How it didn't make any sense. "My Jewish family must be prayed for in a synagogue. Can't you understand that?"

"You can pray for them in front of our icons here in the house. I pray for them every day before I leave for work in the morning."

Anna was unable to meet his gaze. "I can't do that," she said softly, continuing to look away. She couldn't pray before an icon. She just couldn't. "I can't do that."

"All right," he acquiesced, "but please be careful."

"The rabbi's wife already knows who I am. She spoke to me months ago and said she knew who I was."

"Litsa!" His tone was sharp. "The more people who know that you are a Jew, the more danger there is for you, especially when the Nazis turn their attention to Athens."

"I know, Alexander. But the rabbi's wife would have no reason to inform on me. I have to do this. There must be prayers said in the synagogue for the well-being of my family. I have to do something. We aren't a religious family, but what else can I do to help them? Well, Alexander, do you know of something else I can do?"

CHAPTER 15

THE FOLLOWING LETTER was sent by Archbishop Damaskinos to the Prime Minister of Greece in March 1943, after the transport of the Jewish people from Salonika began.

Mr. Prime Minister,

The Greek people were rightfully surprised and deeply grieved to learn that the German Occupation Authorities have already started to put into effect a program of gradual deportation of the Greek Jewish community of Salonika to places beyond our national borders, and that the first groups of deportees are already on their way to Poland. The grief of the Greek people is particularly deep because of the following:

According to the terms of the armistice, all Greek citizens, without distinction of race or religion, were to be treated equally by the Occupation Authorities. The Greek Jews have proven themselves not only valuable contributors to the economic growth of the country but also law-abiding citizens who fully understand their duties as Greeks. They made sacrifices for the Greek country and were always on the front line in the struggles of the Greek nation to defend its' inalienable historical rights.

The law-abiding nature of the Jewish community in Greece refutes a priori charge that they may be involved in actions or acts that might even slightly endanger the safety of the Military Occupation Authorities.

In our national consciousness, all the children of Mother Greece are an inseparable unity: they are equal members of the national body irrespective of religion or dogmatic differences.

Our *Holy Religion does not recognize superior or inferior qualities based on race or religion, as it is stated, "There is neither Jew nor Greek" (Gal. 3:28) and thus condemns any attempt to discriminate or create racial or religious differences. Our common fate, both in days of glory and in periods of national misfortune, forged inseparable bonds between all Greek citizens, without exception, irrespective of race.*

Certainly, we are not unaware of the deep conflict between the new Germany and the Jewish community, nor do we intend to become defenders or judges of world Jewry in the great sphere of world politics and economic affairs. Today we are interested in and deeply concerned about the fate of 60,000 of our fellow citizens, who are Jews. For a long time, we lived together in both slavery and freedom, and we have come to appreciate their feelings, their brotherly attitude, their economic activity and, most important, their indefectible patriotism. Evidence of this patriotism is the great number of victims sacrificed by the Greek Jewish community without regret and without hesitation on the altar of duty when our country was in peril.

Mr. Prime Minister,

We are certain that the thoughts and feelings of the Government on this matter are in agreement with those of the rest of the Greek nation. We also trust that you have already taken the necessary steps and applied to the Occupation Authorities to rescind the grievous and futile measures to deport the members of the Jewish community of Greece.

We hope, indeed, that you have clarified to those in power that such harsh treatment of Jews of other nationalities in Greece makes the instituted measure even more unjustifiable and therefore morally unacceptable. If security reasons underlie it, we think it possible to suggest alternatives. Other measures can be taken, such as detaining the active male population (not including children and old people) in a specific place on Greek territory under the surveillance of the Occupation Authorities, there by guaranteeing safety in face of any alleged danger and saving the Greek Jewish community from the impending deportation. Moreover, we would like to point out that, if asked, the rest of the Greek people will be willing to vouch for their brothers in need without hesitation.

We hope that the Occupation Authorities will realize in due time the futility of the persecution of Greek Jews, who are among the most peaceful and productive elements of the country.

If, however, they insist on this policy of deportation, we believe that the Government, as the bearer of whatever political authority is left in the country, should take a clear stance against these events and let the foreigners bear the full responsibility of committing this obvious injustice. Let no one forget that all actions done during these difficult times, even those actions that lie beyond our will and power, will be assessed someday by the nation and will be subjected to historical investigation. In that time of judgment, the responsibility of the leaders will weigh heavily upon the conscience of the nation if today the leaders fail to protest boldly in the name of the nation against such unjust measures as the deportation of the Greek Jews, which are an insult to our national unity and honor.

Respectfully,
Damaskinos
Archbishop of Athens and Greece
This letter was also signed by the heads of major cultural institutions and organizations. (Source Chronika, *the newspaper of Greek Jewry 1984)*

Alexander put down the paper, having read the Archbishop's edict for a second time. He stubbed out his cigarette in the ashtray, as he waited for his father to join him. Alexander pondered what else he heard about this incredible letter. Archbishop Damaskinos when asked why he wrote such a letter had said that he had taken up the cross. He had spoken to the Lord and made up his mind to help as many Jewish souls as possible. Alexander knew what the reaction of the Nazis would be. Perhaps if religious leaders all over Europe stood in solidarity with the Jews, these persecutions would stop. But as far as he knew, not one other religious leader has tried to stand up against Jewish persecution.

Kìrios Giannopolous walked inside the room and closed the door. "We are alone?"

"Yes, the Nazis are not expected back until after dinner, and I will be on my way to take Litsa home from the soup kitchen within an hour." He took out another cigarette and lit it. "News of reaction from the Nazis to this brave edict?"

"They were furious." His father wearily sank into a chair. "They threatened to execute the Archbishop by firing squad. And you know how he responded? He said that according to the traditions of the Greek Orthodox Church, an archbishop should be hung, not shot. What bravery! Well, it seems that the Germans have backed off on their threat to kill him."

CHAPTER 16

AFTER THE FIRST Salonikan transports began in March, the Nazis proceeded with the deportations until all of the Jews were gone. The streets with Jewish names were renamed. And now in Salonika, it was if those tens of thousands of Jews had never existed. And in the towns of Ionnina, Arta, Preveza, Larissa, and Trikala, as well as countless others, the Jews were all taken away.

All through the spring and summer, Anna waited for news of her parents. But there was nothing, not a word. Anna asked Alexander to send money to them as soon as their new location was made known. She wanted to help them in any way she could. But there was only silence. She knew it must be difficult to receive communications from Poland. After all, the country was engulfed in war.

It was late summer, and the air was hot and still. Night was falling as Anna sat on the sofa in Dimetri and Irini Pagonis' living room holding their friends' three-month-old infant girl. The young Nazis who lived in the Pagonis' house were out carousing as they did on most nights.

Alexander was seated on the floor helping the two-year-old little boy struggle and delight at building a tower of wooden blocks and then knocking it down. Anna and Alexander had eagerly volunteered to watch the two young children, so their parents could have a night out at the cinema.

Anna smiled down at the infant in her arms, who smiled back at her and gurgled, the girl's brown eyes fixed on Anna's face. The baby put her thumb in her mouth and sucked, her gaze still fastened on Anna, and then her eyes began to close as she fell asleep.

Anna held the baby closer as she watched her husband crawling on the floor with little Thanos. The young Nazis who lived in the house thought the children were great fun, especially the little boy. They often played with him and related stories of their own younger brothers and sisters back in Germany.

Alexander helped the boy try to build a tower of wooden blocks. He smiled as the child knocked it down and laughed. "Litsa." He looked across the room at Anna. "I also miss this."

"I want our own child to hold in my arms," Anna said wistfully.

"I know you do, Litsa. I see it when you look at children. I also wish for a child."

"To have a son, of course, to carry on the Giannopolous name?" She tried to lighten the seriousness of their conversation.

"A son or a daughter," he answered, meeting her gaze.

"But we'd have to leave our house if we had a child. Von Hoffberg would never permit us to stay."

"We wouldn't have to leave until a child was born. I assume a pregnant woman could be tolerated by Von Hoffberg. Recently, I've had several letters from Adamos, an old friend, who married a woman from Zakynthos. He has told me that the island needs doctors. With so few medical supplies, people are hoping for hands that can perform miracles. And if we chose to stay here in Athens, I have many friends that would take us in. I've mentioned the possibility to Dimetri, and he said they would find a way to accommodate us."

Anna bent and kissed the sleeping head of the infant. "I do want a child of our own. It's been so horrible during the occupation. It seemed having a baby was a terrible idea. But look at these children. They haven't suffered. They're healthy. I don't want to wait any longer."

"I agree, Litsa."

"We aren't being foolish, are we?"

"To want to have children?" Alexander picked up the little boy and sat beside Anna.

"But there's still so much danger, and what if the terrible famine returns?"

"Our ports are no longer blockaded by the British. No matter what, I would find the means of feeding a child of our own. Food aid continues to trickle into Greece, and we have the means to pay for what we want on the black market. With my father's connections, I feel confident in my ability to take care of a child. And my father has a good steady income from the Greek Jews fleeing the country on his caiques."

"Does Patéra charge them very much?" Anna asked.

"He charges, but only those who can afford it. For the poor, he charges nothing. He must pay the captains and crews of his many boats, and he must pay them well to ensure their loyalty. And you know if the Germans should discover what he's doing, it would be death for him and his crews. There are many unscrupulous men who charge exorbitant fees and then report those trying to flee to the Nazis. They pocket the money, and the Jews are taken away by the Germans."

"We live in a terrible world," she sighed.

"Not everyone is evil," he tried to reassure her.

In September 1943, Italy surrendered to the Allies. The Italian troops in Athens were glad to end their participation in this war. They were eager to sell off their equipment and items such as blankets, boots, typewriters, which the Greeks were eager to buy. Some Italian soldiers joined the andartes in the mountains. But most gave up their weapons to the Germans and were told they were going to be evacuated back to Italy. This however was a lie, and they were sent to POW camps.

Before the Germans took over, Alexander had been told by an Italian commander that Italians believed in a code of conduct and followed specified rules of behavior during wartime. They didn't want to take hostages, and burning down whole villages for reprisal was repugnant to them. He told Alexander, for the Germans, it was another matter. The Germans believed that massacring an entire village would act as a deterrent to others. The Italian conduct of war was at odds with the Germans, who had been issued the following edict from Field Marshall Keitel on December 16, 1942, following instructions from Adolph Hitler.

The troops are therefore authorized and ordered in this struggle to take any measures without restriction against women and children if these are necessary for success. Humanitarian considerations of any kind are a crime against the German nation.

Most of the Italian soldiers tried to evacuate, but on the island of Cephalonia, the Italians refused to give up. Nearly two thousand soldiers were killed in the fighting. Five thousand surrendered and then were summarily executed by the Germans.

Nazi Germany was poised to occupy all of Greece, without having to contend with the Italians and their noncompliance relating to the Jewish question. And so the new regulations against the Jews were instituted.

On October 8, 1943, the Greek newspapers published the rules pertaining to Jews of Athens. All Jews had to return to their permanent homes in which they had resided prior to June 1, 1943. Jews could not change their residences. All Jews must present themselves for registration. Jews who did not comply would be executed. Non-Jews who hid them, offered them shelter, or aided their escape would be sent to a concentration camp or worse. Jews could not go out in public from five in the evening until seven in the morning. Greek police must arrest anyone who did not obey these orders. A Jew was anyone who was a descendant of three generations of Jews, regardless of the religion now practiced.

As a consequence of these edicts, Archbishop Damaskinos of Athens instructed his bishops to tell their parishioners from the pulpit that they must hide and protect their Jewish neighbors. He began giving out falsified baptismal certificates, and he married Christians and Jews together without conversion. Mayor Evert of Athens issued false identification papers to anyone who requested them.

"Do you remember that quote by the philosopher Edmund Burke?" Alexander asked one evening as he exhaled the smoke from his cigarette.

"He said the only thing necessary for the triumph of evil is for good men to do nothing." Alexander sighed deeply. "If only there were more such men as these, the Nazis would have been stopped years ago from their brutal rampage."

Anna swallowed hard.

"You are safe," he told her, reaching out and covering her hands with his own. "Your papers are impeccable."

"But how do I prove my parents and grandparents were also Christians?"

"Only if you fell under suspicion would you be asked to prove such a thing. You are safe," he said again, hoping it was true. With the Italians gone, there would be no buffer from Nazi brutality. Now that the Germans were in total control, Alexander regretted their decision to start a family. But Anna was clearly delighted with the new life growing inside her. He saw the difference it made to her. Here was something positive, in the midst of so much death.

The next evening, as he was about to join Anna in their bedroom, his father stopped him and motioned for him to follow into the shadowed corridor.

"I heard something alarming at the kafeneío today. Vasco said there are rumors about Litsa, rumors that she is not what she seems, that perhaps she is a Jew. Everyone laughed and said what an outrageous rumor that my daughter-in-law, the devout woman who attends church every Sunday, could be a Jew. My son, it's no longer safe for her in Athens."

During the night, Alexander had awoken in a cold sweat, after dreaming the Nazis had pounded on their door and dragged off Anna and their baby. Anna was screaming, and he was powerless to help her, as the Nazis pointed their German lugers at his head.

Anna had shaken him awake from this nightmare. "Alexander, wake up, *agape mou*, my love. You are dreaming."

He grabbed her and held her tight. "A bad dream," he murmured and held her closer. He vowed he'd find a way to continue to keep her safe. He and his father had always talked about what might happen if the Germans turned their attention to the Jews of Athens. And now that it had indeed come to pass, they needed to complete the arrangements for their escape.

"Have you heard about Rabbi Barzilai," Von Hoffberg inquired over breakfast.

"What about him?" Anna asked casually, trying to feign disinterest.

"SS officer Dieter Wisliceny summoned him to his headquarters and demanded a list of all the Jews in Athens. And then, of course, all those men on the list will be compelled to register even if they don't want to. The rabbi has three days to put the list together."

Von Hoffberg then delighted in telling them that since Adolph Eichmann had taken a personal interest in the Greek Jews, soon all the Jews would be taken care of. "Eichmann is in charge of the Jewish question, and I have it on good authority that he has been thoroughly disgusted by the lax attitude of the Italians. Well, we don't have to put up with that anymore. By the way, Herr Antonios, if you hear of anyone thinking about taking in an Italian soldier, make them understand that would be most unwise. The Italians are now the enemy, and if they haven't been able to escape, they will be regarded as prisoners of war. I have a great deal of work to do at headquarters today. Now that those lazy Italians are no longer in charge, there is so much for us Germans to accomplish. Once we get the list of the Jews from the rabbi, that will be our first step in taking care of them. Remind all your friends the punishment for hiding a Jew is death. Germans are now in charge, and we will clamp down on any infringement. Have you heard that we opened up the Haidari Prison, just outside of Athens? I understand it formerly was an army barracks. Woe to the Greeks who are sent there. The commander in charge is particularly brutal. Finally, you people will understand you cannot fight against us with protests, with your futile sabotage. We shall start filling up the prison with your communists, your Jews, and your saboteurs." The Nazi wiped his mouth with a napkin and got to his feet. "I must say, it's days like today that make me so proud to be a member of the Third Reich."

The time that Alexander had always predicted had come to Athens for the Jews. There were those who remained blind to what the registration of all Jews meant. They hoped, they prayed it would be different for the Jews of Athens. After all they were assimilated into the fabric of Greek society, unlike the Jews of many other towns, who lived apart from their Christian neighbors. But for those who understood the terrible nature of the Nazi regime, it was apparent this was the first step in the transport of all Jews out of Athens, just as it had been for the Jews of Salonika.

This afternoon at the soup kitchen, the chickpea broth was almost depleted, although the line of children still stretched beyond the door. The supplies they had received today were so meager. Everyone hoped this wasn't a sign that the soup kitchen's rations were being decreased. The children desperately needed protein, so they could grow normally, so their bodies wouldn't be stunted. But finding any protein for the broth was usually an impossible task. The children, their heads shaved to control lice, stood in front of the women. Anna and the other volunteers had to force themselves to smile and make eye contact with the gaunt faces and the stick arms they saw day after day, lined up with their empty bowls. And so the women steeled themselves and smiled at the children and offered them kind words with their small ladlefuls of broth.

"Kiría Litsa, come with me." The rabbi's wife motioned for Anna to leave the line and follow her. They went to an empty storage room, and Kiría Barzilai locked the door to the outside.

"I wanted to say good-bye." She took Anna's hands in her own. "It's a shame we couldn't be friends. But I understand your perilous situation, especially now."

"Good-bye? Where are you going?"

"I came today, pretending all is normal in my household, not wanting to arouse any suspicion. Tonight my husband, my daughter, and I are being taken away by the andartes. We're going to hide in the mountains."

"Why?" was all Anna managed to say, but horrible suspicions swirled in her mind. Had the Nazis threatened the rabbi's family? Was he being asked like the rabbi in Salonika to tell the Jews not to protest against the Nazis.... that the Germans meant them no harm?

"The Germans have demanded a list of the Athenian Jews."

"I've heard that."

"My husband, Elias, destroyed the list. But even without the list in Elias's possession, we know the Nazis will demand he recreate it. The Nazis have methods to make someone reveal secret information." Her voice caught. "We must leave," she continued, "and we are hoping our flight will be a signal to the Jews of Athens that they all must flee. And you, Kiría Litsa, you must take care. No Jews are safe. I have heard some of the women here speak of you, and their suspicion that you are not a Christian. I believe they are good women. But one never knows, especially when withholding information about Jews can result in one's execution."

"Why would they even suspect that I'm not a Christian?"

"When a child comes before you and asks something and you respond in Greek, your Salonikan accent gives you away."

Anna said nothing. She thought she was being so careful. She only uttered a few words to such children. But apparently those few words were enough to arouse suspicions.

"And your family in Salonika...I assume there has been no word from them. In all this time, there has been no word from anyone who was taken away."

"I know that."

"Litsa, the andartes told us there has been no word, nothing, because everyone must be dead."

"No!" Anna whispered in horror. "That isn't true."

"The Jews in Athens will be made to register, just like the Jews of Salonika. And then they also will be taken away to certain death."

"I don't believe you," Anna protested.

"All of your family was in Salonika? No one besides you left the city?"

"One of my brothers had joined the partisans, but he returned when he learned our family was being sent away. They thought it was important for everyone to be together."

"Tell your husband that you should leave Athens and go up to the mountains."

Anna began to feel ill.

"Good-bye. I shall miss you." The woman gave her a quick hug, unlocked the door, and was gone.

Anna felt wooden as she took her place in front of the children with outstretched bowls. Her family dead?

Alexander appeared early today to escort her home. She untied her apron, excused herself, and hurried off to her waiting husband.

She took his arm as they walked through the street. "The rabbi's wife told me they are fleeing into the mountains tonight with the andartes. She said that some of the women at the soup kitchen suspect I am a Jew because the few words I say in Greek to the children identifies my accent from Salonika. She said I should flee to the mountains as well," her words came out in a rush.

Alexander stopped walking and looked down at her. "Take a breath, Litsa."

"And she said that all the Jews from Salonika must be dead, because no one has heard from them. She isn't right, is she? She can't be right. Everyone can't be dead. They just can't be. It makes no sense."

"Of course, no one really knows what happened to everyone from Salonika."

"Then you agree, don't you? I think the rabbi and his family have good reason to flee. After all, he could be forced to give up the names of the Jews."

"His disappearance will be a sign to the rest of the Jews that they should flee to the mountains. The ELAS andartes seem very capable of helping them to safety. Life in the mountains is harsh, but it's preferable to death at the hands of the Nazis."

"I'm telling you, my family isn't dead! Just because there's been no communication doesn't mean they are dead!"

"Yes, Litsa. You must have hope that they are well. But what the rabbi's wife said about your accent worries me. We can assume most of the women who work at the soup kitchen do so because they are good people. But who knows...My father and I have already begun to make plans for leaving Athens. Since the Germans have taken over all of Greece, we think it prudent to consider a plan of escape. And I worry about you, Litsa. All this pretense, this fear of speaking the wrong language, forgetting to make the sign of the cross. In a smaller place, where we didn't have to live with a Nazi, it would be better. Hiding who you are is exacting a toll on you. That lively spirit of yours...I don't see it very often anymore. That would be one of the many advantages of leaving Athens, not to be living with Von Hoffberg."

"Where would we go? To that island, Zakynthos?"

"It's an option. Patéra and I are working on this. Zakynthos, of course, is no longer under Italian control, since the Italian surrender. It isn't easy to find a place where we can be safe, save for the mountains, and life there is very harsh. I would go there if it were just me. But I don't want to take you there, especially with a baby on the way. You still have extra photos of yourself, don't you? We can use them for new identity papers."

"Yes, they are in my drawer at the house."

"You need to give them to me, so I can have false papers created for us. We shall have them ready when we need them. We won't be in Athens for much longer. But for now we need to hurry back to the hospital. I came early to get you because there has been a train explosion, and you and I are needed at the hospital now. There are many wounded. A train was coming from Salonika. It was filled with Nazi soldiers, and our Greek saboteurs blew it up. The operating theater is being prepared."

Anna was glad to be working in the operating theater, her attention focused on the mangled body draped before her. She watched Alexander deftly try to repair the muscles and arteries of the damaged body. She forced herself to concentrate on the operating procedures. She wouldn't permit herself to think about her family or the possibility that someone in the soup kitchen would inform on her. Today for the first time in many months, she thought of the man lying before her, a Nazi, a man who wanted to find Jews and have them thrown out of their homes. He was a man such as those who had loaded her family into train wagons, where there was only enough room to stand, with no food or water. Anna heard the sound of the train cars being locked. She felt the panic of her family, of children and old people.

"Litsa?" Alexander was addressing her, as he waited for her to close the incision he had made. "Litsa?" When she stood immobile, he proceeded to thread the sutures himself.

Anna took a step backward. She couldn't stop thinking about the young Nazi on the table. I want him to die, she thought. I don't want to help save his life. I want him to die!

"Kiría Litsa." A nurse at her side bent close to her. "Are you not well?"

"Please excuse me." Anna turned and left the operating theater.

She stood in the changing room, taking deep breaths. She'd taken a vow to save lives. What was she becoming? Was living in the midst of so much evil corrupting her soul, permeating the essence of who she was?

She was glad Alexander couldn't enter the women's changing area. She didn't want to see him just now, to admit to him these thoughts of retribution and revenge. What would he think of her?

The operation was almost over, and Anna was changing into her street clothes. She inwardly sighed as she saw Antoinette approaching her. "Your husband is finishing up. It's so sad about those poor soldiers who were wounded and killed on that train. But Herr Bachmeier, the man who checks the papers at the hospital's front door, told me this will never happen again."

"How can it be prevented?"

"The Germans are going to put Greeks in cages and fasten them to the front of the train. Aren't the Germans so clever? No wonder they will soon conquer the entire world. The Greek saboteurs won't blow up trains when

Greeks are in front of engine cars. Isn't that a great plan? The Germans lost so many soldiers on that train. To teach the Greeks a lesson, they'll go to the nearest village and kill everyone. They call it collective punishment. They have been doing this collective punishment since they arrived in Greece, and they hoped it would be very effective. It seemed to have worked well at first, Rupert told me. At first the villagers told the partisans to stay away. They hoped the Germans would leave them alone if they weren't harboring the partisans. But these Greeks peasants are illiterate you know and therefore quite stupid. Even collective punishment administered to the villages has not dissuaded them from harboring the andartes in their midst."

Collective punishment...women and children massacred, thought Anna. She had heard such stories over and over again. Were these Germans totally devoid of any shred of humanity and compassion?

Anna managed a tight smile. "I need to go. Good-bye." She left the room and walked out to face Alexander, whom she knew would have grown impatient waiting for her.

"Are you all right?" he asked with concern.

"I'm fine. Let's talk on the way home."

His dark eyes narrowed with what Anna knew was annoyance. He didn't like being told that she wouldn't talk to him now. "I still need to check on a few patients," he told her.

"I'll sit in the downstairs lobby and wait for you."

"I want you to talk to me now. It isn't the baby, is it?"

Anna motioned for him to follow her into a quiet unoccupied hallway. "It's not the baby," she reassured him in a quiet voice. "It's me. I don't want to save the life of a Nazi who may have shipped my parents away from their home. I wanted him to die, Alexander. I wanted him to die. I'm a doctor. I've sworn to save life, anyone's life. I'm ashamed of my feelings."

"You are a doctor, but you're also a human being." He looked down at her. "When my hands are inside one of these evil pigs," he whispered, "do you imagine I never consider cutting an artery by mistake?"

That Sunday during the church services, Anna observed many people she'd never seen before. She noted their nervousness, their hesitancy during the service. They are Jews, she thought, given false baptismal papers, false identity papers, new Christian names, just as she had been given two years ago. She wanted to reach out to them, to offer them reassurance and comfort, but she knew Alexander would disapprove. And in her heart, she knew how important it was to keep her own identity uncompromised. With the Germans now fully in charge, with many people following the rabbi to the mountains, others were hiding out in the open in Athens as she was. And some were in an attic or a cellar, hoping to never be discovered. Anna understood how difficult it was for a family to be hidden by the Christians, for obtaining food when food was so scarce was extremely difficult. But so many Orthodox Christians were good people, and in addition, they listened to the priests who told them to hide their Jewish neighbors. Of course, there were others who hid Jews for the money the Jewish families could pay them.

November 1943: Athens

Herr Von Hoffberg had finished his breakfast and had departed for the Gestapo headquarters on Merten Street.

After Ariadne cleared the table, Kìrios Antonios began speaking. "The plans for our escape are in place. We are all at risk. I have been helping to transport Jews out of the country and, Litsa, we thought you were safe, but there have been rumors. Anyone whom we might not expect may turn against us. There may be someone whom we trust who is a collaborator, or perhaps there is someone who wants to earn drachmas by turning us in to the Nazis. Hiding or helping Jews to escape is a capital offense. So many good Orthodox Christians are helping Jews, but the penalty for helping a Jew is death. And so some Christians are not willing to put their families in danger and are informing about a Jewish family's whereabouts. It is no longer prudent for us to remain here in Athens. Delaying our departure much longer isn't wise. Make sure you gather together clothing and whatever else you think necessary for the journey. Everything will be stored at

Karatasos' house. He is a tailor for the Nazis but also a Greek patriot. By December first, we must be ready to leave. Make sure you know where to go and how to get there as quickly as possible, in case we need to flee before the appointed day and time. When you get to Karatasos, he will hide you until the caïque arrives for your transport."

"I want to take medical supplies with me," Alexander proposed. "Who knows what we will find where we are going."

"You can't take very much, Alexander. But do what you must. I think it's better if we separate. You two go to the island. I will go elsewhere."

"We're going to Zakynthos?" Anna asked.

"Yes, Zakynthos," said Alexander. "That island I mentioned to you is now under German control of course, as is all of Greece. But my father and I heard the most incredible story from there. The Nazis on the island went to the Metropolitan Bishop Chrysostomos and to Mayor Carrier asking for a list of the Jews."

"Is nowhere safe?" Anna said almost to herself. Greece had so many small towns and villages on the mainland and on the islands where the Jews had lived for countless centuries, causing no trouble living beside their Christian neighbors. It's true. The Germans intended for not one Jew to survive inside Greece. All the Jews would be taken away.

"Litsa," Patéra continued, "the bishop and the mayor were given a few days to compile the list."

"This is the same story. I've heard it over and over again," Anna commented sadly.

"No, this story is different. While the authorities were supposedly putting the list together, they told the Jews to flee up into the mountains. All the Jews vacated the town and are being hidden by the Christians in the mountains and the surrounding villages. When the authorities appeared in front of the Nazis and handed them the list, there were only two names on the paper. The names of the mayor and the bishop. We are the Jews, they told them."

"What an incredible story." Anna smiled and shook her head in disbelief.

"That is why we're going there," said Alexander. "I have smuggled a letter to my friend Adamos on Zakynthos. We will have false papers drawn up for both of us. I will be a doctor of course, and you will be my wife, the nurse. Your papers will identify you as French, and that means whenever you have to speak Greek, your accent will be acknowledged as merely foreign. Father is going elsewhere. It is best you don't know where."

In case I'm caught and tortured, thought Anna. "We will be safe there on the island?"

"I hope so. It seems like the best option. Von Hoffberg continues to say things to my father about the Haidari Prison. I fear our days of safety in Athens are numbered. By the end of the month, we must be ready to escape."

Late November 1943

It was cold that night and Anna had placed an additional quilt on their bed. She was lying beside her husband, as he read a chart under the dim light of the lamp next to their bed. Months into her pregnancy, her only symptom was growing tired much more easily. Her waist was just beginning to swell, and no one could discern the child growing inside of her. Next week, they planned to leave. First they would seek refuge at the house of Karatasos, and then they would sail on the caique to Zakynthos. Another identity, this time as a French woman, Angelique, and Alexander would become Stephano Christakis. There could be no trail leading the Germans back to their former identities. Alexander had assured her his friend on the island promised them a home of their own, without a resident Nazi.

A home of their own and a child…Could that really be possible? She never expected to feel so happy about this pregnancy. The last few years had been filled with so much sorrow and death and suffering. The starving children, the corpses in the street, the gunshots echoing through the night. And now to be creating a new life with the man she loved was the one good thing in her world turned upside down. She had passed the time in her previous pregnancy when she had miscarried, and she prayed for the health and well-being of this baby.

Alexander placed the chart on the bedside table and tenderly placed his hands on the nightgown over her belly.

"It's too soon for any movement." She smiled at him.

"I know that. I just like to put my hands on your belly and think about the child. You aren't the only one who's looking forward to a child of our own." He kissed the top of her head.

Anna closed her eyes waiting for sleep. She was confident this escape plan would work, and the Nazis wouldn't find them before they could board the caique. And she hoped their false papers wouldn't arouse any suspicion when they landed on the island.

As Alexander leaned over to turn off the lamp, there was a soft tapping on their bedroom door. Anna opened her eyes as Alexander threw off the covers and hurried to the door.

He opened the door to find his father, his face pale, clutching a piece of paper in his fist. "Come in, come in." Alexander stepped aside and closed the door.

"My son, we are being blackmailed. We must flee tonight. Hurry and get dressed. We'll leave out the kitchen door."

"Blackmailed? By whom?" Alexander asked.

"Just now, a pebble was thrown against my window, and this letter was delivered to me. There is no signature from the coward who sent it. I'm accused of transporting Jews out of the country. Alexander, it says you have been deliberately murdering wounded soldiers on the operating table. And it says my daughter-in-law is a Jew. I must bring one thousand pieces of gold bullion to a bench in the botanical gardens tomorrow at eight o'clock, or we will be reported to the Gestapo."

CHAPTER 17

"CAN YOU IMAGINE accusing me of killing my patients on the operating table? I only wish…" he said in exasperation.

"I know, Alexander," she told him. "Of course more of your patients died. They only gave you the most seriously wounded."

Alexander patted the two lugers and the knife concealed beneath his coat. He silently cursed himself for not having silencers for the revolvers. If he had to use the weapons tonight, he couldn't risk the sound of gunshots. The knife, he thought, if I need to protect us, I must be close enough to use a knife. He looked over at Anna, watching him hide the weapons under his coat. But she said nothing as she buttoned her coat. "We will be at Karatasos by dawn. Everything will work out just as we planned," he tried to reassure her. He knew she wanted to question him about the need for weapons. But he also knew she trusted him. And tonight there was no time for discussion of such things.

The three of them soundlessly walked out the backdoor into the desolate early-winter garden. They embraced Patéra and said their farewells. "*Theós mazí sou,*" Kìrios Antonios blessed them to keep them safe from harm. For a brief moment, they held each other close again, and then Patéra hurried away down the street, turning the corner and vanishing from view.

They were confident Von Hoffberg wouldn't notice they were missing until morning, when they didn't appear at the breakfast table. Alexander was certain whoever was attempting to blackmail them would be furious he wasn't getting his gold, and he would definitely make good on his threats to go to the Gestapo. And the Gestapo would waste no time knocking on the door of the Giannopolous villa. Von Hoffberg, of course, would be furious to learn he had been living with Anna, a secret Jew. Alexander felt certain that Von Hoffberg suspected his father's activities and was just biding his time, until the Nazi decided to give the order to have Patéra taken away in the middle of the night. But to be living with a Jew? The Nazi would spare no effort to find them. And this trumped-up charge about Alexander killing his patients was laughable, if one could laugh about such things.

"*Anàthema*, damn," Alexander swore under his breath as he looked up at the huge full moon that shone a brilliant light on the streets of the city. Was it possible to escape without being discovered when the streets were so bright? What was the point of such worries and concerns? he asked himself, when they had no choice but to leave tonight.

The course the andartes had charted for them, with meticulous detail, took them down quiet, deserted thoroughfares and back alleyways for most of their journey to Karatasos' house. The tailor lived in a modest neighborhood outside of Athens, and it would take them several hours on foot to reach him.

Anna and Alexander had memorized every twist and turn that had been plotted for their escape. The andartes had made certain that their route would not have any German checkpoints. But as they hurried down a small street, they could hear the sounds of a party, German drinking songs echoing through the night. Alexander motioned for her to stop. He turned around, thinking they would have to retrace their steps back from where they had just come. But at the top of the street were several Germans soldiers with Greek women of the night, obviously on their way to the gathering.

Alexander drew Anna into the shadows between two nearby houses. He shielded her behind himself and reached inside his coat for the pistol and knife. If they were discovered like this in the middle of the night, it would mean certain death. There was no legitimate excuse for Greeks to be out after curfew. About that he had no illusions. It would be assumed they were up to no good, perhaps working for the resistance.

They waited as the group, laughing and singing, sauntered down the street, passing them without any notice. Anna and Alexander were about to emerge from the shadows when they heard the sound of another man proceeding down the street, his voice loud with drink. Alexander grabbed his knife and held his breath, as the soldier neared the place where they were hiding. The Nazi slowed his pace and turned in their direction. He looked down as he struggled with the buttons on his trousers, obviously in an attempt to relieve himself. Then he looked up, and he was staring into Alexander's eyes. "Damn! *Gott verdammt!*" swore the solider, as his hands clumsily reached for his pistol.

"Nazi pig!" uttered Alexander as he stabbed the knife into the soldier, who staggered backward. Alexander grabbed the man, dragged him between the houses and threw him on the ground. Red blood bubbled on the German's lips as he looked up at Alexander, and then he groaned, shuddered, and closed his eyes. Alexander quickly stacked nearby boxes on top of his body to shield him from any passersby.

He glanced at Anna, who was standing mute, her eyes wide. "We must get to Karatasos," Alexander said and grabbed Anna's hand. As they fled back up the street, he tried to slow his stride, for Anna's legs were not as long as his. He heard her labored breathing. They finally came to an area darkened by shadow where they stopped to rest, and Alexander pulled her against himself. "Are you all right? I'm sorry you had to see that, but I had no choice," he whispered.

"I know," Anna replied.

"We need to get to safety before sunrise. Once Von Hoffberg realizes we're gone, there'll be an alert out to find us. They won't notice that soldier until morning, and our disappearance shouldn't be connected to him."

"I'm all right. Let's go." She took a deep breath, and they resumed their flight down the cobblestone streets.

They reached Karatasos' house just as the sun was streaking the sky pink across the horizon. They knocked on the wooden door. There was no answer. Alexander knocked again.

They heard a shuffle and then a tentative voice. "Who is it?"

"Giannopolous," Alexander announced as he tightly gripped Anna's hand.

The door opened, and a husky man in his nightshirt cracked open the door. He ushered them into his modest house.

"I wasn't expecting you tonight." The man closed the door and nodded at his wife, motioning for her to leave them alone. "There must be trouble. It's almost daylight, and you can't be seen. I have a storage room in the back with cots, chairs. You must stay there until darkness. My wife will bring you some food. Come, come." He ushered them into a backroom and closed the shutters, creating total darkness. Karatasos fumbled for a moment and then lit a lantern for them.

Anna collapsed on a chair in exhaustion, while Alexander explained to the man why they had to flee unexpectedly tonight.

"Everything is ready for you here," Karatasos told them. "The possessions you sent ahead these last few weeks are waiting for you. But I don't know when the caïque will arrive to take you away. I'll send a messenger, and we'll be told when we can expect them. In the meantime, you must stay in this room during the daytime hours when I do business with the Nazis. At night, you'll join us in our living quarters. There are blankets stacked in the corner to keep you warm."

"*Epharisto*," Alexander thanked him.

"*Parakaló*," the man acknowledged his thanks. "It is my pleasure to do whatever I can to thwart those evil Nazi beasts and to help save my fellow Greeks. I never refuse a request from the andartes to help in the struggle against the Germans."

The next day, Anna and Alexander sat in the storage room silently playing cards and rereading the newspaper Karatasos had given to them. They listened to the sound of Karatasos measuring Nazis for new clothing and repairs to their uniforms. Anna was thinking of all the Jewish people who were forced to live under such conditions for months and months, perhaps years. She and Alexander were so fortunate that soon the boat would be coming for them, and they would be able to live out in the open on Zakynthos. She thought of her family and was confident that her father with so many business connections must have fashioned an escape plan for her family. Surely they found refuge somewhere. They had evaded the Nazi roundup, she tried to convince herself. Yes, when the war was over, they would all be reunited, and the presence of a grandchild would help to warm the family's feelings toward her Christian husband.

She looked over at Alexander, who was rereading the newspaper again. She thought he would go mad with nothing to do while they waited for the caïque to arrive. Ever since she met him, she had never seen him idle. Anna was stretching her arms over her head, when she heard a voice that made chills run down her spine. It was the voice of Von Hoffberg in the next room, and he was clearly agitated.

"Don't you have any ouzo?" he thundered. It was more a command than a question.

"Yes, of course, Herr Von Hoffberg."

"I needed that. Can you imagine? Can you imagine the audacity of those people! To think they lived with me for so long. Of course, it isn't as if I didn't suspect them. That doctor always so cool, so beyond reproach, while murdering one wounded brave soldier after another. The hospital authorities never should have trusted him. What fools they were. Didn't they realize what he was doing! Karatasos, did you know the Giannopolous family? Antonios, Alexander, and that bitch Litsa?"

"No, I don't believe I know them."

"Of course you wouldn't know them. You're but a simple tailor. But it's just as well that you have no connection to them, or you would be under suspicion. And that bitch of a woman, a Jew under my own roof. I never liked her and her uppity ways. I'm a man of such compassion, and although I knew there was something not right about her, I didn't investigate her background as I should have. She didn't have the proper decorum for a Greek wife, and no wonder... After all, she was a miserable Jew. And Antonios, that Jew lover, transporting those despicable vermin. We will find those Jews no matter where they are, and we shall make the world *Judenfrei*, I promise you. But as for the three of them, there is a bulletin out for their arrest. And there is a generous price on their heads, generous enough to make anyone think twice about helping them. How far could they have gone? It was those damned andartes who must have helped them. I'm certain of it. And when I find the Giannopolous family, they will be tortured until they give up the names of others such as themselves, who are enemies of the Third Reich. We have brutal tortures that will break a man in a very short period of time. And for a woman…" He laughed. "There is a very special torture for a Jew whore, which I will conduct myself. And then they will be hung in Syntagma Square, and their corpses will remain there as a warning to others. It will be my pleasure to watch the birds of prey tear their bodies to pieces."

Alexander soundlessly reached over and took Anna's hand. "It's all right," he mouthed to her. "We are safe."

"When will my repairs be ready?" Von Hoffberg was asking, and then they heard the sound of the door closing.

They finally received word that the caïque had arrived and their possessions were loaded on board. A car arrived at their door shortly after darkness. The andartes who drove the car wore stolen Nazi uniforms, steel helmets, and jackboots. Anna and Alexander bid a heartfelt good-bye and thank you to Karatasos and his wife. The andartes instructed Anna and Alexander to climb inside the trunk of the car. They did as they were told, glad for the blankets to cover themselves against the frigid night air. The car stopped several times at German checkpoints, where they heard the exchange of words in German, and then the car would continue making its way down to the harbor. The car came to an abrupt stop, and the trunk was opened. "Over there." One of the men pointed to a lantern that illuminated a boat bobbing in the dark water. "Hurry."

Anna and Alexander thanked the men who had transported them. Alexander held Anna's hand, as they walked down the gangplank to the boat.

"Hurry," a disembodied voice instructed them, and then the light from the lantern was dimmed. "Over there," the voice told them. After a moment their eyes accommodated to the darkness. They made their way across the deck and stood next to a dark figure who was leaning over and dipping his hands into a bucket. The strong smell of fish was overpowering, as the man appeared to be slathering something over his arms. "This will make me very unattractive." He laughed heartily. "I'll put the bucket here under the tarp with you, in case the Germans want to see what is underneath. You will go under the tarp and sit there on the other side."

Anna and Alexander walked into the shadowed corner, and the tarp was placed over them.

"We'll wait a few more minutes," the commanding voice told them, "and then we will be off. You must stay hidden until we leave the harbor. I'll let you know when you can come out."

The smell of fish was strong in Anna's nose, and she hoped it wasn't going to make her sick to her stomach. This was supposedly a fishing boat, she told herself. She should have realized it would stink of fish. She wasn't on a pleasure boat. She tried to breathe through her mouth, so the stench of fish wasn't so overpowering.

Anna reached for Alexander's hand as she listened to the sound of the waves lapping against the sides of the boat and felt the gentle rocking of the water beneath them. She heard the sound of the rope being untied, and then the boat began to move. Soon they would be safe. They would be on the island where Jews weren't turned over to the Nazis.

"Who goes there!" a loud German voice was shouting. She could see the searchlight leaking through a rip in the tarp. Were they about to be caught? Her heart started to pound. To have gotten this far and to be discovered by the Nazis now when they were so close to escaping...

"It is Musto. I go early. I get fish before others," the fisherman stammered in broken German.

"Your papers!" Anna heard the sound of boots on the deck.

"Papers? Papers?" The voice that had spoken to them with authority when they boarded the boat now was that of a dim-witted peasant.

"Yes, your papers!"

"Here are papers."

"What is under those tarps?"

"Tarps…What is tarps?" He pretended not to understand the word.

"*Mousamades!*" the Nazi screamed at him, the Greek word for tarps.

"Oh, yes, *mousamades*. Under is bait for fishing. You want bait? I give you some."

"No, I don't want bait!"

"You want currants, figs? I have for you. Taste so good."

"Where did you get figs and currants?" The boots stopped thundering across the deck, and the light from the searchlight, which had rested on the tarp, was now focused elsewhere.

"My cousin—he lives on a small island. Good figs and currants."

"We'll take them. But first show me your papers. You own this boat?"

"Yes. Here are figs and currants. Taste. They so good."

"Your papers are in order. But you aren't supposed to be out here at night. You are a fisherman. You stink like a fisherman. So where are your fish?"

"Fish?"

"You're a fisherman, aren't you, you dumb Greek?"

"No fish now. I go get some. Almost morning. Best time for go fishing."

"Be on your way, you stupid Greek! Your boat stinks and so do you. Don't be out again at night, or your boat will be confiscated!" The sound of jackboots thundered across the deck and was gone.

The caïque sailed on for what seemed like an eternity before Musto lifted the tarp and told them to come on deck. Anna sank down on a bench, fighting the bile rising in her throat.

"Your wife doesn't look so good, Doctor. Kiría, you will get used to the smell of fish." The burly man smiled at her. "To me it smells lovely."

Anna smiled weakly and tried to take deep breaths of the sea air.

"Do you think we will encounter more Nazi patrols?" asked Alexander, his arm around Anna's shoulders.

"Not tonight. There are some areas tomorrow where I'll need to be careful. There are lots of German patrol boats in the water. But for tonight, you can rest. Would you like something to eat? Some currants, some ouzo?"

Anna shook her head and peered out into the darkness. Currants? God, no.

"Angelique?" Alexander was talking to her. "Angelique, remember," he whispered, "Angelique."

"Yes, yes, I remember. I'm Angelique. I'm trying not to be sick from that smell."

"I'm sorry."

"It isn't your fault. The pregnancy makes me more sensitive to odors. Don't you think this boat smells awful?"

"It smells like fish." He laughed at her.

Anna did get used to the smell of fish, and soon she no longer noticed the stench. On the days when the sun was shining, she was beguiled by the beautiful turquoise water and the deep blue sky. She could almost forget their peril, save for when a dark dot appeared on the horizon, the dot coming nearer and revealing itself to be a boat. She and Alexander would duck under the tarps again. If it were a Greek boat, words of greeting would be exchanged. If it were a Nazi patrol boat, Musto would coat himself with foul fish guts. They would be boarded; papers would be inspected. The German officers would spend as little time as possible near the foul-smelling fisherman. Avoiding the patrol boats, hiding in safe harbors extended their voyage by many extra days and nights.

Musto rarely spoke to Anna but spent much time conversing with Alexander, talking about his family, how things were before the Germans came. "I had a good life fishing, providing for the tavernas, the restaurants, the markets. My reputation was the best for the freshest fish. And that first night, when they bombed Piraeus and they killed all the fish...For days the smell of dead fish and the sight of them floating in the harbor made us sick;

our livelihood, the food to fill our bellies, all gone in an instant. The Nazis forbid us to go out in our boats for weeks. How were we to make a living? How were we to feed our families and all the others who depended upon us? I have a wife and five children. Eventually the Nazis realized their stupidity, probably when they realized they also wanted to eat our fish, and they let us go out to fish again. My good friend, Haddad, was also a fisherman, and he'd been secretly helping escort his fellow Jews out of Greece. Once the Nazis issued their edicts that all Jews must register, he left with his family for Palestine, but not before he instructed me in how to evade the German patrol boats, so I could continue his work. Am I a righteous man? I don't think of myself in that way. The Jews they are Greeks like me, so why should the Germans be rounding them up as if they were subhumans? It is also true the transport of the Jews has been very profitable for me. Doctor, you're being most generous for my troubles, and for that I am grateful. And I must admit I love to outwit these arrogant Nazi pigs. They march into our country like they own it, believing we would welcome them with open arms. Every time I smuggle those such as you out of Piraeus, it gives me great joy."

While Alexander and Musto talked, Anna's thoughts traveled to the new home awaiting them. She was anxious to reach Zakynthos, to meet the Romaniote Jews who lived there. She would be safe on this island where the bishop and the mayor refused to give up the names of the Jews. She knew the Jews were Romaniote, not Sephardic as she was. They didn't speak Ladino, and many of their customs were different, for their ancestors didn't come from Spain. They had been in Greece for two thousand years. But despite their differences, they were Jews, and the Nazis didn't differentiate between Romaniote and Sephardic. They were rounding up all the Jews of Greece and taking them away.

Zakynthos

Anna and Alexander arrived in the middle of the night. Their clothing was soaked from the cold rain that poured from the skies, as they quietly disembarked from the boat onto the sandy beach of Zakynthos. Adamos, Alexander's friend, was there to greet them. He embraced Alexander and Anna and led them to his home. Finally, thought Anna, as she followed the two men, finally to be away from the threat of discovery by the Nazis. They would be safe here.

While they dined on olives and bread in the kitchen, Alexander asked Adamos about the arrangements for their own house. Adamos seemed to change the subject by saying there would be a visitor early tomorrow morning, who would discuss everything with them.

Adamos and his wife, Lina, gave up their bedroom for the night. Alexander and Anna didn't protest for it was Greek hospitality, and to not accept the offer would be considered unthinkable. It would be so good to lie on a mattress after nights of sleeping on the hard wooden deck of the boat. After washing, Anna hoped she no longer smelled of fish. She began to pull her nightgown down over her head.

"Wait. Don't put it on," Alexander said softly and held out his arms to her. "Come to me, Anna Litsa Angelique."

"Three women for you tonight?" she laughed.

"Come here, my love." He cupped her breasts and kissed her on the mouth. "I love you," he murmured as his body began to move with hers.

Creak! Creak! The springs of the mattress were deafening.

"Alexander, they'll hear us," Anna cautioned between gasps of pleasure.

"I don't care. I am your husband."

Alexander making love to her, giving her pleasure, made her forget the noise of the springs and the knowledge that surely everyone in the house could hear them.

After their lovemaking, Anna, exhausted by their journey, should have quickly fallen asleep in the warm bed. Instead, she lay awake wondering why Adamos didn't tell them about their new home. Had a Nazi taken it over since the last time Adamos corresponded with Alexander? Who was this early-morning visitor? How well did Alexander know Adamos? Was this early-morning visitor a German? Was she going to be denounced as a Jew? If both of them were arrested, would they be together or separated?

"Are you going to stop twisting and turning?" Alexander sighed and kissed the top of her head. "Or shall I sleep on the floor and you can have the bed to yourself?"

"I'm sorry." She laid her head against his chest. "I can't sleep. I'm worried. Will we be safe here? Maybe there is nowhere that's safe from the Germans."

They were having breakfast with Adamos and Lina.

"Thank you for letting us have your bed," Anna told them. "Sleeping on that boat was so uncomfortable."

"We could hear how much the two of you enjoyed our mattress," Adamos laughed.

"Adamos, stop that," his wife admonished him.

Anna felt herself blush with embarrassment.

The sudden knocking on the door put an end to their awkward conversation.

"That must be our guest. Lina, let us go out and leave Alexander and his wife alone." Adamos got to his feet and opened the door.

Standing there was a man clothed in the garb of a church bishop. Anna was puzzled. A bishop was the visitor Adamos had spoken of? Why would he want to see them?

Lina and Adamos bowed to the bishop, kissed his hand, and left the house.

Anna awkwardly got to her feet as Alexander approached the bishop, bowed, and kissed his hand. She looked at the man with the full flowing beard. Was she still to pretend to be a Christian? But you are a Christian, her thoughts spun in confusion, you've been baptized. Yes, yes, she must do as the others had done. She must bow and kiss his hand.

"Come," the bishop entreated her with his outstretched arm. "Do not be afraid, my child. I am Metropolitan Bishop Chrysostomos. And you are?"

"I am Angelique Christakis." She kissed his hand.

"Is that your real name, my dear? We have serious matters to discuss, and I want to know who you really are."

"Anna Carasso, I mean, Anna Giannopolous," she said firmly. This was the man who refused to give up the list of the Jews. Surely he could be trusted.

"And I am Alexander Giannopolous. This is my wife." Alexander indicated a chair for the bishop to seat himself.

"Let us all sit and discuss your future." The bishop sat down.

Your future? wondered Anna. What did this cleric have to do with their future?

"I have all our papers ready," Alexander began. "We have new identities; everything is in order. I can show them to you."

"No, no, that is not necessary. Adamos has told me that you are a doctor and a nurse. Is that correct?"

"I am a doctor as well," Anna spoke up. "I couldn't practice in Athens without drawing attention to myself."

"Because you are a Jewess?"

"Yes, I am," said Anna, glad to admit who she was, glad not to pretend any longer.

"We have brought medical supplies with us. We want to provide medical help to the people of Zakynthos," said Alexander.

"The Germans on the island have been sent an alert to look for a doctor and a nurse who have fled from Athens. The nurse is a Jew masquerading as a Christian, and the doctor has killed his Nazi patients."

"It's true many of my patients died," Alexander said with impatience. "But that's because I was given the most serious cases. I was the surgeon with the most skill. I took an oath to save lives, no matter how despicable the person might be."

"That's good to hear. As a friend of Adamos, I was certain you must be an honorable man."

"We came here to Zakynthos, because we heard that you didn't give up the identity of the Jews on the island. I trusted that my wife would be safe here."

"It's true. I refused to give up the names of the Jews and their assets, as demanded by the Germans. Did you not hear that after my confrontation with the Nazis, I insisted all the Jews flee the town and go to the surrounding villages? The mountainous areas are completely unknown to the Germans. They can't maneuver on the roads. They don't know where they are going, and they are easy targets for the andartes. Our villagers are good people and will not inform on the Jews within their midst. They desperately need medical care. The doctors who have remained in town have been sent to work at the German hospital. That's the only facility where there are any medical supplies."

"What are you telling us?" Alexander cleared his throat.

"As a Jew, your wife must not stay here. I cannot guarantee the safety of anyone in town. Many of our Jewish neighbors didn't want to leave, being too old or too sick. But I found carts and other means of transportation for them. No one could remain, and now every Jew is gone. They also had false papers. When the Germans first arrived, they insisted that Jews place a yellow star on their doors. But no one felt they needed to comply, because they had false papers. But it is not safe. I tell you it's not safe, and I feel it is my duty to protect the Jews, and so I am telling you that your wife must leave. And I'm also saying the villagers need your medical skills and the supplies up in the mountains and the surrounding areas."

"We will go," said Anna.

"Yes, of course, we'll go," Alexander agreed.

And so the next day, Anna and Alexander were led up into the mountain villages, where they lived among the Orthodox Christians who gave the Jews shelter and never informed on their identity to the Nazis.

By March 1944, many of the Jews who went into hiding in Athens felt they could no longer put the Christian families who hid them in jeopardy. They registered with the Nazis, as did the Jewish men who needed identity cards in order to work and support their families. All the while the Nazis proclaimed they had no bad intentions toward the Jews. But it was well known that the Jews of Salonika had been given similar assurances, which turned out to be lies. And no one ever heard from the Jews who had been taken from Salonika. More and more people realized that those taken away must have been murdered. At the time of Passover, the Nazis in Athens let it be known that they were bringing in special flour to the Beth Shalom Synagogue to be used to make Passover matzos. There had been no flour of any kind available for so long, so the promise of this special flour led the men to the synagogue. Once inside the synagogue, where the flour was supposed to be distributed, the men were locked inside. Their families were rounded up, and within a few days everyone was transported out of Athens. It was later learned they were taken to Auschwitz and put to death in the same crematoriums where the Jews of Salonika had been murdered the year before.

In October 1944, Greece was liberated from Nazi occupation. The Germans had ravaged the country; destroyed the railway system, the phone system; one thousand villages, burned to the ground; 87 percent of the Jewish population annihilated; the infrastructure of the country was devastated. The British, blind to the role the andartes had played fighting against the Nazis, saw them as the enemy because of their communist beliefs. The Nazi collaborators weren't punished but enlisted to help fight against the communist andartes. The partisans were sought out, and many of them, executed. Greece was the only country in Europe where the antifascists were vilified. Within months of the liberation, the government was in disarray, and Greece was plunged into a bloody civil war, which would last for several more years. The andartes who fled the country were not able to return to Greece for almost forty years.

CHAPTER 18

1963: Salonika

ANNA SLOWED HER step as she passed where the synagogue had stood. Today there was no trace of the beautiful building. Houses had been erected in its place. She walked past, remembering the times her family had attended, mainly because of her father's standing in the community. Anna hadn't been raised in a religious family, and now God, a merciful God, was not part of her universe. How could there be a God when she had witnessed so much suffering in Athens, children, infants starved to death, innocent men and women executed by Nazis for savage reprisals? Villages burned to the ground with people trapped inside their homes. How could a God exist who stood by while six million Jews were murdered only because they were Jews?

Culturally in her heart she was a Jew, but she was a Sephardic Greek Jew, not an Ashkenazi Jew, like Daniel and his family. It seemed she had spent a lifetime denying who she was. But here in Salonika, Anna Carasso, a Sephardic Greek Jewish woman, could become alive again.

She was nearing the hotel, and she smiled at the turquoise water lapping against the seawall, the puffy white clouds in the brilliant blue sky. She'd swum in that sea with her brothers and sisters when she was a child. And then her thoughts returned to Alexander and their infant daughter playing in the sand on Zakynthos, splashing her in the water, while they waited to hear if it was safe for them to go back into town and sail to Athens. When they heard about the liberation, they started packing, ready to descend down to the town. But their joy was short-lived for they were told by the andartes it was not yet safe to return. The Germans had gone on a rampage, looting, killing, even burning down the church in their rage against losing the war. Until the Germans boarded boats to take them away, it wasn't safe to go back to town. And so Anna and Alexander spent time on a sandy beach, marveling at their wonderful daughter, making her laugh with delight as they played in the waves. How good life had seemed in those days with such a bright future ahead of them. The Germans had lost the war. Greece was free. Jews were no longer being hunted down and murdered.

Anna admonished herself that she should have held Alexander more tightly in her arms. She should have told him she loved him more often. How could she have known they would have so little time together? Be grateful for the time you had, she told herself, as she entered the hotel lobby.

After the hotel clerk told Anna that Suzanne and her friends had not yet returned, Anna took the elevator up to her room. She had left a note for her daughter to join her as soon as possible.

Anna enjoyed a brief shower, changed into a fresh sundress she had recently purchased for the trip, and looked down at her watch. Suzanne should be returning any time now. There was so much to tell her, so much to share with her daughter about her people, her family.

Anna heard the key turn in the lock.

"Hi, Mom." Suzanne walked across the floor with a noticeable limp and her ankle wrapped in a bandage.

"What happened to your foot? Are you all right?" She approached her daughter, trying not to show the worry that took hold of her. All the years when her two children were growing up, she tried so hard not to overreact to every small concern. Anna recognized that even a simple problem often triggered her feelings of powerlessness. She fought against the overwhelming fear something bad would happen to her children, that she would lose them as she had lost everyone else in her life. And so she fought that feeling again and smiled at her daughter. She's all right, Anna told herself. Don't show your alarm. Calm yourself.

"I fell. But it's just a slight sprain."

"Are you sure it's OK? Do you want me to look at it?" Anna bent down and began pressing on her bandaged ankle.

"No, Mom. I'm fine; really I am. My friends brought me to a hospital to have it checked out. Mom, I have so much to tell you. This man…"

"Wait, wait. I'll be glad to hear all about him, but later. First I have much to tell you, Suzanne. Sit down and prop up your foot," Anna told her, relieved it did seem to be a simple sprain.

"Mom!" Suzanne protested. "It's really important." She sat down.

"I'm sure it's very important. I promise you, I'll hear all about it later. But now there's so much I need to tell you. I wanted to meet you here in Salonika because this is where I came from. This was my home before the war. Those Jewish tombstones we saw today; they may belong to my ancestors. So much was taken from me during the war, vanished as if it never existed. I want to tell you all about it. I want you to understand where I came from, who I am.

"*Mi famiya*…I want to talk to you about my family. We had our own special language. Ladino was the language of my childhood." Anna hurriedly wiped away a tear from her eye.

"Oh, Mom, please don't be upset." Suzanne reached out and squeezed her hand. "Tell me about your family." Suzanne sat up straight in her chair with her foot elevated on a stool. "But those words '*mi famiya*'…It kind of sounds like Spanish. You say it's Ladino? I never heard of a language called Ladino. I never heard you speak it."

"Your dad requested that I only speak English to you. After all we lived in America.

"The story of our family begins in Spain hundreds of years ago. My ancestors, your ancestors, came from Spain during the Spanish Inquisition, after they were told to convert, leave, or die. That was in 1492, and many Jews went to Italy, to Turkey, to what is now Greece, and to many other places that were part of the Ottoman Empire. And, Suzanne, many Jews didn't leave Spain but pretended to be Christians. They were called *conversos*. Can you understand that a person would do such a thing?"

"Yes, I can," Suzanne said slowly. "Those are difficult choices to make. Our life in America is so easy. It's hard to imagine what life was like for Jews in the past. It must have been so awful for you during the war before you came to America. How old were you then?"

"Somewhat older than you, but still very young. All these years I've kept my story inside. For so long I never wanted to tell you. I didn't want to burden you and your brother with the horrors of the war. But coming back here to my home, where I grew up…There was so much joy here, so much love in my family. I want to remember it, and I want you to learn about it," Anna said earnestly. "I know you may have plans for later today with your friends, but I was hoping we could go to that new Jewish cemetery we heard about. There may be tombstones of my relatives, of our relatives. Will you go with me?"

"Of course, Mom. I already stopped by my room and told my friends I was spending the rest of the day and the evening with you."

"There's so much to tell you. Before the war, Salonika had a huge, vibrant Jewish community. This was my home. But, Suzanne, is there something wrong besides your ankle?" Anna had the sense that something else was not right. "You're sure you only hurt your ankle?"

"I'm just a little sore, and there is something else we need to talk about. But I want you to tell me about our family. When I was little, I wanted to know about your family, but Bubbie told me not to ask, and when you did speak about Greece, you always seemed so sad."

"It did make me sad; but my family was wonderful. Three brothers, three sisters, all of them married, except for my brother Zaco. Lots of nieces and nephews, cousins, my parents, my Nona. For so long, I tried not to think about them and what happened to them. They were all killed at the death camp called Auschwitz in Poland. Later I learned that many Jews from Greece died on the transport trains. Jews who came from Poland and France didn't have such a long journey as the Greeks. Many of the Greek Jews were already dead when they opened the cars to begin the 'Final Selection.' In Athens, after the war, I met men and women survivors who could never have children because they were sterilized in the camps. Suzanne, I tried so hard to never think about my family and what happened to them, what they might have endured before their deaths, how they died, how much they must have suffered." For a brief moment, Anna closed her eyes, willing those terrible images of death and crematoriums to leave her mind.

"Mom, you always told me you didn't go to one of those horrible camps. Our neighbor Ruthie's mother went to one of those camps. Mrs. Bloom said all the Jews were sent to those camps. She said she didn't think you were really Jewish, because you didn't speak Yiddish, and why hadn't you been sent to a concentration camp? I didn't like going over to their house anymore, after she said you tricked Dad into marrying you by pretending to be Jewish."

"You should have told me. I would have talked to her. She shouldn't have said such things to you."

"She was just a nasty lady, Mom. But now that you're going to tell me about Greece and your family…You are going to tell me the truth about everything, aren't you?"

"Of course. Suzanne, I didn't talk much about my past, but I never ever lied to you or to your brother or, of course, to Dad."

"You didn't go to a concentration camp? Please, I want to know the truth."

"I was never sent to the camps."

"Why weren't you sent there with your family?" Suzanne looked puzzled. "Mom, what happened to you?" Her daughter's voice trembled, as if she was afraid of her mother's answer.

Anna took her daughter's hand in her own. "My father sent me to Athens to the home of a close friend, a Christian Greek Orthodox friend. It was in late 1940, before the Germans had entered Greece. No one knew of the death camps until years later. My father seemed to have a sixth sense that bad things lay ahead for the Jews. His friend Antonios Giannopolous agreed with him that bad times were coming for us. It was assumed that

Jews would be safer in Athens, where they didn't all live together in neighborhoods but were interspersed all over the city. My family was too large for all of us to leave Salonika. My father and my brothers were involved in profitable businesses. I was the youngest, the only girl not married. Within our large family, I was the only one who could easily leave. I had a medical degree from America, and my father feared if or when the Nazis came, they wouldn't allow me to practice medicine. So he sent me to the Giannopolous family. That's where I met their son, your father, Alexander. I spent the war hiding who I was and that I was a Jew. That is how I survived. I pretended to be a Greek Orthodox Christian and married your father in a church. It…"

"Mom," Suzanne interrupted her. "You always said what a good man my father was. Did you love him? Did you love him even a little? Did you only marry him so people would believe you were a Christian? You can tell me. I want to know."

"Did I love your father?" Anna repeated her question. She didn't want to talk about Alexander. She only wanted to talk about her family.

"Did you love him?" Suzanne asked again.

"Yes, I loved him," Anna sighed and took a few moments to regain her composure. Why had Suzanne asked her such a question?

"Let me tell you about our family," Anna continued. "I was the only one in my family who survived, because of your grandfather's foresight and the protection of the Giannopolous family. There is also one cousin who survived, but he was angry and wanted nothing to do with me."

"Why was he angry?"

"Because I survived, because I hid my Jewish identity. I worked with survivors after the war, and many from the camps thought the same way. They felt that those of us who hid, and especially those who pretended to be Christians, had forsaken our people and didn't deserve to be treated with respect.

"They were bitter. They were angry. They came back to Salonika to find their shops, their homes, all their possessions were gone. They were hoping to be reunited with family, only to learn everyone else had been murdered. What right did I have to judge their bitterness? And to make matters even worse for them, the men who survived the camps were being drafted, pulled off the streets, put into the Greek army to fight in the Civil War. Because of that, many men immigrated to Palestine or what is now Israel.

"I didn't tell you and your brother about the war years because your dad's family thought much like Mrs. Bloom, that being a Sephardic Jew meant I wasn't actually Jewish. At first when I came to America, I wanted to tell everyone. I wanted everyone to know what had happened. But I was told there were no Jews in Greece. There was no holocaust in Greece. It was as if my people didn't exist, what happened to them had never happened. Dad and his family requested I not talk about my life in Greece. I could have protested, but it was easier to push it all away and try to forget. Though, of course, how can one forget one's family, one's culture? Your dad advised me to forget everything. There was a new future in America. Forget the past. Forget who I was," Anna murmured sadly.

"I'm sorry about your family," Suzanne seemed to struggle for the right words. "No wonder talking about Greece made you sad."

"Oh, Suzanne. Let's not be sad. We're here today in Greece, in my home, and I want us to embrace the memory of my family and move forward," Anna said to both her daughter and herself. "Let's go to the cemetery to look for some evidence of our family. I'll get us a taxi. The cemetery isn't very far from here. And tomorrow I will take you to where I grew up, to my favorite places, if you have the time before you leave with your friends."

"I'll tell them to go on without me, Mom. This is all too important. I want to know about your family, about my family. I want to see where you lived, the streets where you played as a little girl. Your parents, your brothers and sisters—all gone. How horrible for you. They are my family, too." Suzanne's eyes brimmed with tears. "Did my father's family come from here?"

"No, no, they were from Athens."

Suzanne got to her feet and wiped away her tears. "Mom, today I met…"

"Suzanne, now is not the time to talk about that. I'm sure he is quite charming. But beware; a Greek man could never be really serious about a relationship with you. There is no marriage allowed in this country between Orthodox Christians and Jews."

Suzanne had reached for the doorknob and then turned around to face her mother. "Really?"

"Just have a good time," Anna advised her.

Anna and Suzanne stood outside the stone walls of the cemetery. Even from this distance, Anna could see the tops of the cypress trees. They reached up to heaven, the Greek people believed. She looked over at her pretty daughter, who so resembled the photograph of Alexander's mother. Suzanne was the girl who liked boys and party dresses, and who didn't take her college studies seriously. Her child who was born in the mountains of Zakynthos. Anna wanted her daughter to be carefree, not shouldering the burdens of the past. She wanted Suzanne to be what she was not. But this afternoon, Suzanne seemed to show a maturity that Anna had never seen in her daughter. She did understand. She wanted to know. Anna felt closer to her than ever before. She'd made the right decision to bring her here. It was the right decision for both of them.

As they entered the cemetery gate, a young man approached them. "May I help you?" he asked.

"We've come to look for tombstones from the old desecrated cemetery that may have belonged to my family," Anna told him. Please, she thought, please let there be something remaining of those tombstones. Something I can touch with my hand, somewhere that I can say Kaddish, the prayer for the dead. My family became chimney smoke….no bodies to bury. Anna took a deep breath. You cannot dwell on the horrors of the past. You need to look forward, to help Suzanne and eventually Joey connect to their Greek Jewish roots.

"I shall look it up in my book," he told them. "The names?"

"Carasso and Faren," she said, giving him the surnames of her father and mother.

"Carasso?" He smiled. "I don't have to look up that name. See over there." He pointed across the cemetery grounds. "Where that tall man is standing. He comes every week. I'm new here. But the old caretaker told me about this Greek Christian who comes and stands before the monument erected to the Carasso family who died in the camps. He's a Christian, but he puts on a head covering, and according to the old caretaker, this man knows how to say Kaddish. It's getting late, and soon I must close the cemetery to visitors. If you still want me to look up Faren, come back to my station at the front gate, and I'll look them up."

Anna's gaze had followed the man's outstretched arm, and she felt herself stiffen with shock.

"Mom, Mom," Suzanne was saying to her. "That's what I wanted to tell you. That's the man I met today."

It can't be. It can't be, Anna told herself. It was only the back of a man, who possibly resembled Alexander.

"I met him this afternoon at the hospital." Anna heard her daughter's voice. "He's my father. He thought we went down on the boat. He wasn't killed like you thought. He was only wounded."

Anna was frozen. She couldn't move. It wasn't Alexander. It wasn't possible. She felt like she couldn't breathe.

"Come on, Mom. Let's go say hello. I was going to tell you all about meeting him. We arranged to get together at a taverna tonight. I know he'll be glad to see you now."

"Mom," her voice showed her impatience, "you can't just stand there."

"Alexander Giannopolous? You met him today at the hospital?" Anna's brain was trying to make sense of what she was seeing, of what her daughter was saying.

"Yes, he was the doctor who took care of my ankle. He knew who I was, Mom. Look, he's turning around. He sees us." Suzanne waved at him.

The man had turned around. It couldn't be Alexander. This was a cruel joke being played on her and her daughter. He looked like Alexander. But it wasn't her Alexander. It wasn't.

"We need to leave." Anna started to turn around, to flee from this place of death and strange apparitions.

Suzanne grabbed her arm.

"That is not your father." Anna tried to pull away from her. "Your father is dead. Someone is playing a cruel trick. We need to leave right now!"

"Mom, come on. It's him. He knew all these things about you. He showed me your wedding photograph. Come on." Suzanne took her hand and started pulling her along the path toward where the man stood, the man who was staring at them.

"Let go of my hand!" Anna pulled away from her daughter. She forced herself to slowly walk toward this apparition from her past. The crunch of gravel under her feet was loud in her ears. The sound of the birds chirping in the trees was too shrill. Her senses seemed to magnify everything in her world, the blue of the sky, the white of the clouds, the green of the cypress trees; every color had grown so intense, too bright. Her daughter was chattering about something, but Anna couldn't process what she was saying. Every step Anna took was leaden. It can't be. It can't be him. And then she was standing before him, looking up at him—Alexander, older, Alexander. He was real. He was alive.

His face was distraught with emotion. "Anna," he said softly. "It's me, Anna. It's me."

"I didn't have a chance to tell Mom about you," Suzanne was saying to him. "She wanted to come here to look at tombstones. I was going to tell her..."

Her daughter's words swirled around her, making no sense, as she stared at this man's face, his eyes, his mouth. Alexander, Alexander...Her heart pounded in her chest. Anna reached out to his mouth with trembling fingers. "Where is your mustache?"

"I was told it's too old fashioned." He smiled warmly at her, the smile she remembered, the smile that lit up his dark brown eyes. "I will grow it back if you want me to."

Anna let her hand drop to her side. Why had she said such an inane thing to him? Because, she thought, because I don't know what else to say. A cold wave washed over her. "I came here to see if there were any tombstones left from the old cemetery." I don't know what to say. I don't know what to feel.

"Anna, here's the monument erected to all those in your family who perished. I come here each week and say Kaddish for them. They aren't forgotten." He indicated a tall marble slab, but his gaze never left her face.

"You come here to say Kaddish for my family?" The tears began to well in her eyes.

"I needed to feel close to you. I moved to Salonika to practice medicine, to help your people, the survivors of the camps. I didn't know what else to do after I lost you and our daughter. Here." He retrieved a handkerchief from his pocket and handed it to her.

They looked at each other, no words between them.

"Suzanne." He turned to their daughter. "Come here and I will tell you about your mother's family." He extended a hand to his daughter, who took it and smiled at him. "Now, this is Victoria," he began as they stood before the monument. Anna listened as he recited one by one the names of her family, and he told their daughter about each of them, relating the stories she had shared with him so long ago.

The tears slipped down Anna's cheeks, as she walked closer to the monument.

"Suzanne," Alexander said, "go to your mother. This is a very sad time for her."

"Mommy," Suzanne called her by her childhood name, as she put her arm around Anna's waist. "I'm so sorry, Mommy. So many names…"

With a trembling voice, Anna read each name out loud that had been carved into the marble. She wiped her eyes with the handkerchief. "Yes, Suzanne, so many names. So many wonderful people all gone because of the madness."

"I always wished for cousins, aunts, and uncles. With Dad as an only child..."

"In Salonika there were so many aunts and uncles and cousins, Suzanne. The house would be bursting with noise, with laughter, when we all came together."

"My Greek father told me he has a sister in Greece, and she has children. They'd be my cousins. I want to go to see them. Can we all go together?"

"But your plans with your friends..." Anna searched for any excuse to tell her daughter, No, you can't do this. And certainly she couldn't do this.

"This is so much more important, Mom. My friends can go on without me. Alexander, I mean, Patéra told me that Greece is so beautiful and that he'd take me to see the islands."

Anna said nothing. Patéra...Their daughter has learned to call him Patéra. Of course, she deserves to know her father. He'll want to spend time with his daughter. Anna felt as if she weren't standing here but was somewhere outside of herself. She wasn't going anywhere with Alexander and their daughter. She needed to go home to America to her life as a doctor. How could Alexander be alive? How could he be standing here beside their grown daughter? She desperately wanted to turn around and run away. She couldn't do this, for the numbness in which she had wrapped herself was beginning to ebb, and in its place was pain, terrible pain, etching through the wall she had erected around herself for protection, so many years ago.

Anna wiped her tears again with his handkerchief and straightened her shoulders. Suzanne could go away with Alexander, but she would be on the first flight home to America. "Yes, of course, you should meet your family in Leonidion," she told her daughter, avoiding eye contact with Alexander.

"He said he also has a brother in California. Can we go to see him?"

"Perhaps." Anna turned to the names carved into the marble monument. She couldn't look at Alexander. She didn't want to look at him. Yes, focus on your family, your family that was lost. My family, she thought. I came here this afternoon to reconnect with my family, to teach my daughter about all those who were lost. "I wonder who erected this?" she asked Suzanne.

"I did." His voice cut through her. "Your cousin Moises told me the names to inscribe in Ladino."

"How long ago did you leave Athens?" She forced herself to turn back to him.

"As soon as I returned and was told by Ariadne that you and our baby had drowned, I realized there was nothing left for me there. My father had died. I needed to be close to you, to help your people."

Anna swallowed hard. Her words failed her as her heart pounded. She didn't want this. She'd tried so hard these many years to shield herself from any emotion, to forget all that had been between them. She didn't want to look at him, this man who had been her husband. But she couldn't take her eyes away from the pain she saw on his face.

"Mom, we're supposed to go to a taverna tonight." Suzanne seemed to sense the unease between them. "Why don't we take a taxi back to the hotel, and we'll meet up with him later as we planned?"

"No," Alexander said firmly. "My car is here. Suzanne, I will drive you back to the hotel. Anna, please come with me to my apartment. I need to have some time with you, just the two of us. Please, Anna, come home with me for just a little while, for us to talk before we go to the taverna tonight."

I can't, she thought. I can't. But the pain she saw in his eyes made it impossible to refuse him. "Just for a few minutes. I will go with you but only for a few minutes."

"A few minutes?" He breathed. "After eighteen years…I can have only a few minutes of your time?"

"I'm sorry, Alexander. I'm sorry."

During the drive in his car, Anna sat in the front seat, looking out the window, desperately trying to gain control of her emotions. Suzanne was talking to Alexander about her studies in college. After she was dropped off at the hotel, there were no words, only an uncomfortable silence between them.

Anna knew as soon as she walked inside the door. A man lived here alone. There was no touch of a woman.

"Please, come inside," he said politely.

"You live here alone?"

"Yes, I do. Can I get you a drink, something to eat?" he offered, walking over to the refrigerator.

"I'm not hungry, thank you."

"Well, just in case." He brought out a dish of olives and a bowl of *taramosalata*. He turned his back to her to slice a loaf of bread.

I can't do this, her thoughts spun in confusion. Polite conversation? I need to go back to the hotel. She was breathing too fast. She felt light-headed.

"Sit down." He indicated a comfortable chair, as he poured two glasses of wine.

He sat down across from her and pulled out a package of cigarettes from his shirt pocket. He tapped down the cigarette and withdrew his lighter. "You still don't smoke?"

"No," she paused. "Haven't you seen the growing evidence that smoking is harmful?"

"We in Greece are not totally backward, Dr. Caplan. We also read the medical literature. I choose to smoke. But thank you for sharing your medical expertise." His voice bristled with sarcasm.

"I'm sorry." Why did she say something so patronizing? She reached for the glass of wine and took a swallow. "Alexander, we must talk."

"That's why I brought you here."

"It's been eighteen years," she began.

"You think I don't know how long it's been?"

"Please let me finish. We are different people, you and I. We've both lived separate lives." She wanted him to understand, and he didn't. Eighteen years had gone by. Too many years.

"Are we really so different than we used to be?"

"I've been married. I have a son with another man. I have my career." She paused. "Alexander, I've changed from that person you knew so long ago. I'm empty inside. I have nothing to give you or any other man. I'm hollow. There's nothing inside of me."

"I know what it means to let a wall grow around one's heart, not allowing anyone to get close. But is not Anna Carasso Giannopolous still inside that barrier you have erected that keeps you safe from any feeling?"

"I work hard. I try to give love to my children, but even that isn't easy for me. I'm glad you are alive. Of course, I'm glad. Get to know Suzanne. You'll see she is a wonderful girl."

"Can't we try again, Anna?"

"I can't try again. I can't," she said in a soft voice.

"You can't or you won't?"

"I won't be hurt again. Don't you understand? I don't want any more pain. I'm happy the way I am."

"Happy? Really? Shielding yourself from pain and shielding yourself from joy.... Is this how you wish to live the rest of your life?"

"You don't understand the hurt I had, the pain I felt. Finally I have none, and if I must be numb, so be it."

"I don't understand? What gives you the right to talk to me like that?" His voice was filled with anguish. "Was it only you that had pain and hurt? Why do you think I live alone? Why do you think I never married, never had children? Because every day, Anna, every day, I cursed myself for leaving you and the baby. It was my fault you were gone. I blamed myself, as I should, for leaving you to go off and fight in that senseless Greek Civil War. I didn't deserve to be happy. I didn't deserve to have a family."

"It wasn't your fault," she murmured. "Please, Alexander," she started to cry. "I can't do this. I can't." She got to her feet. "Where's your bathroom?"

"Over there." He pointed to a door across the room.

Anna put down her glass and fled across the room. She closed the door behind her, found the lock, and fastened it. She bent over the sink, turning on the faucet full force. She didn't want him to hear her, as she burst into uncontrollable sobs. She slid down to the floor and cried. Her heart felt as if it would break. The pain engulfed her, pulling her down, until she was nothing but pain and hurt. All the hurt that she had tried to block out for so many years came flooding back. And she was there again that day when the andartes came inside her house and told her Alexander was dead. She didn't want to be there, but it washed over her again, that horrible grief, the feeling that life was over.

"Alexander," the andarte was saying, "was executed by firing squad last week. We witnessed his execution and saw his body in a pit with the others. I came as soon as I could."

"No, you're wrong! My husband is a doctor. He was not executed!" she had screamed. And then she remembered the room was growing dark, as she felt blood rushing in her ears, and a terrible coldness took hold of her as she crumpled to the floor.

That terrible memory she had kept buried began replaying in her mind again and again.

She knew she couldn't stay here on his bathroom floor. However, when she tried to get to her feet, she failed, and again she dissolved into sobs that wracked her body. "Alexander," she whispered. "Alexander, I can't. Please I can't."

"Anna." It was his voice, and he was twisting the doorknob. "Open the door."

The sound of his anguish made the tears flow harder. He was hurting, and she was making his pain even worse. She couldn't do that to him, but she felt powerless to do more than cry on the floor in a state of helplessness.

"Go away. Leave me alone," she pleaded tearfully.

"Anna, I'm not going anywhere. This is my home. I live here. Please unlock the door. You can't stay inside the bathroom forever. Let me help you, my Anna Litsa." His voice broke. "*Agape mou*, my love, I know you are hurting. Please let me help you. We can help each other."

He couldn't help her. No one could help her. She needed to make him understand. She couldn't ease his pain when she lacked the capacity to ease her own. He wanted what she couldn't give him.

Pull yourself together, she told herself. She took a deep breath. She got up off the floor and splashed water on her face, glancing in the mirror at her ghastly reflection of swollen, red-rimmed eyes and puffy cheeks.

"Anna, please." Alexander was twisting the doorknob again. "Unlock the door."

She wiped her face with a towel hanging on the wall. She turned off the faucet. She needed to tell him. "It was all my fault," Anna said through the door.

"What was your fault?" he asked.

"I shouldn't have left Greece. If I went up to Salonika to help my people as you did, we would have found each other. I never should have gone to America."

"Anna, you had our child to think of. The civil war was still raging. It was dangerous to stay here. There was so much bloodshed everywhere, all over Greece. Going to America was a wise decision."

"Do you really believe that?" she asked, wiping the tears from her face.

"Of course I do. You did what was best for yourself and for our daughter. Now come out of the bathroom."

She unlocked the door. He was standing there, his face filled with pain. She knew he ached to reach out to her. He shoved his hands in his pants' pockets, and she knew he understood she didn't want him to touch her.

For a long time, they stood there just looking at each other. So much time had gone by. They weren't the same. How could a future for them together be possible? But standing before her was the man she had once loved so very much.

It was Anna who broke the silence. "I have a wonderful position in the emergency room. Over all these years, it's the only place I've felt alive, when I experience the rush of life and death."

"Come, let's sit while we talk." He had gained control of his emotions.

"All right." Anna followed him to the couch, and it felt natural to sit beside him. It felt good in a way she hadn't expected, and it surprised her. She watched him light another cigarette.

"I still have so much hurt inside me, Alexander," she tried to put into words what she was feeling. She wanted him to understand.

"I know, I know. But I'll be here for you, to help you, if you'll let me. Can't we be there for each other?" He was waiting for an answer, but she couldn't speak. Could anyone relieve all the pain she had, and could she ease the suffering he'd inflicted on himself believing he had caused her death? Those terrible wounds they had both suffered could never be healed, could they?

"I could come to America." He inhaled on his cigarette. "I have nothing to keep me here. We could try again, Anna. Please. God has given us another chance."

"I don't believe in God," she said in a voice that challenged him. "What kind of God allows six million innocent souls to perish?"

"That is a question many theologians are still struggling to answer. Ah, my Anna, I now have proof you haven't changed so much, in spite of what you say. Remember how we used to lie in bed and argue about philosophical questions until long into the night? You want to argue with me about the existence of a merciful God?" He smiled at her as he blew out the smoke from his cigarette.

"Yes, I do remember those nights." She smiled back at him, her body starting to relax against the seat cushions. "I always enjoyed our arguments, especially when I won them."

"Anna, Anna, whether God or some unknown force in the universe gave us this second chance, please don't throw it away. I know you have changed, as have I. We're both older and perhaps a bit wiser. Let me get to know who you are. Perhaps you could help me find a position in an American hospital. When you and our daughter go back to America, I want to go with you. The thought of ever letting you out of my sight is unbearable, Anna."

Anna placed her hand over his, and that familiar feeling of connection between them enveloped her like a warm cocoon, a place of safety.

He looked at her, his eyes filled with emotion. He cleared his throat. "Do you think it will be difficult for me to gain permanent entrance into the United States?" he asked.

"It shouldn't be difficult. I'm a US citizen now. You are my husband, aren't you?"

"Yes, I am your husband. Anna," he whispered and put his arm around her, pulling her close. "We will try, you and I?"

"Yes, we will try. I want to try." She paused and looked up into his eyes. "But I have one request of you, Alexander."

"Only one?" He kissed the top of her head.

"I was always fond of your moustache." She raised her fingertips to his lips.

"Then I shall grow it back for you." He kissed her fingers.

THE END

Author's Note

HIDDEN IN PLAIN *Sight* is a work of historical fiction. The main characters—the Giannopolous family, the Carasso family, and Von Hoffberg—are entirely products of my imagination.

The conditions described in Athens and Salonika are factual depictions of what happened during those dark days of the Nazi occupation. 80% of Greek industry, 90% of ports, roads, railways and bridges were destroyed. 25% of the forests were also destroyed. Over 1000 villages were burned to the ground. 40,000 people died of starvation in Athens. Greece has the sad distinction of being home to the largest percentage of Jews annihilated in Europe. 87% of Greek Jews were murdered. Salonika lost 97% of the Greek Jews who lived there at the beginning of World War II.

Metropolitan Bishop Chrysostomos, Archbishop Damaskinos, and Mayor Lucas Carrer are actual heroes who lived in Greece. Their brave deeds are recognized by Yad Vashem in Israel in the Garden of the Righteous Among the Nations. The letter from Archbishop Damaskinos to the Nazis was the only such document written by a Christian clergyman during the war. On Zakynthos, Metropolitan Bishop Chrysostomos and Mayor Carrer were responsible for saving every Jew on the island. Also honored at Yad Vashem is Princess Alice, the mother of Prince Phillip of England. She hid a Jewish family in her home and saved them from the Nazis.

Rabbi Barzilai of Athens fled with his family to the mountains. Rabbi Zvi Koretz of Salonika remains a figure of controversy because of his actions during the war.

The following are some of the many sources I used. Some of the information is conflicting, but I did my best to recount an accurate portrait of the terrible toll inflicted on the Greek people.

Bowman, Steven, *The Agony of Greek Jews* (Stanford, California, Stanford University Press, 2009).

Hionidou, Violetta, *Famine and Death in Occupied Greece, 1941–1944* (Cambridge, England, Cambridge University Press, 2006).

Fleming, K. E., *Greece A Jewish History* Princeton, (New Jersey, Princeton University Press, 2008).

Seder, Deno, *Miracle at Zakynthos* (Olympia, Washington, Philos Press, 2014).

Wason, Betty, *Miracle in Hellas* (New York, MacMillan Co, 1943).

I tried to read every source written in English about this terrible period in history.

My main source was Mark Mazower's *Inside Hitler's Greece* (New Haven, Connecticut, Yale University Press, 2001). I encourage anyone who wants to learn more about this time in Greece to begin with this book.

—Karen Batshaw

Back cover

THE TOMBSTONE DEPICTED on the back cover is one of many tombstones that can be found in the courtyard of the St George Rotunda Church, which is located across the street from Aristotle University in Thessaloniki (Salonika), Greece. The University's expansion was built over the grounds of the Jewish Cemetery, which dates from the fifteenth century. At that time, the Jews fleeing the Spanish Inquisition were welcomed in Greece, which was part of the Ottoman Empire.

About the Author

KAREN BATSHAW IS an author living in Washington, DC and Williamsburg, Va. Her previous novels include **Love's Journey, Kate's Journey** and **Echoes in the Mist**. It was her immersion in Greek culture as part of her research for **Echoes in the Mist** that led her to the tragic story of Greece during World War II. Karen has a master's degree in social work and developed an international program for adoption in Cambodia.

Made in the USA
Middletown, DE
09 October 2016